FULL OF PROMISE

Before Sheldon realized it, he was pulling Daryl closer. His hands wandered of their own accord, discovering the titillating curves and swells of her body. She moaned softly as Sheldon tenderly kissed her throat and moved upward to her mouth. His lips moved slowly, but thoroughly, against hers.

Somewhere in this fog of pleasure, Daryl felt Sheldon's hand travel down to her thighs.

"Sheldon," she whispered against the curve of his shoulder. Her voice caressed him, touching him all over.

"Yes, Baby?"

"I . . . I think we should slow down some."

Sheldon gave no argument. He merely smiled and nodded his understanding.

"You're not upset, are you?"

He shook his head. "I don't have a problem waiting. I know when the time is right, there won't be any stopping us." Kissing her once more on her full lips, he announced, "I guess it's time for me to head back to L.A. I really had a nice time tonight."

"I did, too. We're going to have to do it again sometime."

Nodding, he said, "Sometime real soon."

His gaze heated Daryl's already flushed body. She placed trembling fingers to her lips as she watched Sheldon leave. She needed to be as far away from him as possible right now. He was too intoxicating.

A
RESOLUTION
OF LOVE

Jacquelin Thomas

Pinnacle Books
Kensington Publishing Corp.
http://www.arabesquebooks.com

PINNACLE BOOKS are published by

Kensington Publishing Corp.
850 Third Avenue
New York, NY 10022

First Printing: December, 1998
10 9 8 7 6 5 4 3 2 1

Printed in the United States of America

ACKNOWLEDGMENTS

To my editor, Karen Thomas

Thank you for giving me the opportunity to write this story. It's one that I've always dreamed of telling.

To Lynne Williamson

Thanks for your words of encouragement and helping me come up with a title.

To the Orange County Chapter of Romance Writers of America

Thanks for the roses, and the many kind words of wisdom and support.

DEDICATION

This book is dedicated to my husband, Bernard.

For all of your unwavering support and your love. I'm so thankful I stood in faith for you. You were truly sent from heaven above.

Chapter 1

"Daryl, what's your New Year's resolution? Don't tell me you're still hoping to find a husband . . ."

"She is, Margo," Audrey conveyed while combing her fingers through short jet-black curls. "Nothing's changed since you've been away. Daryl's still setting the table for two. Girlie, she's even got space cleared out in her closet for this husband she's waiting for."

Zipping up her dress, Margo looked from one woman to the other. "You're kidding, right?" Looking at Daryl, she asked, "Audrey's kidding, isn't she? When I moved to San Francisco five years ago, you'd cleared out half your house for this anticipated husband."

Standing in the middle of her bedroom, with its rich burgundy and gold color scheme, Daryl shook her head. "I'm still standing in faith for my husband." Retrieving her lipstick from a black and red floral cosmetic bag, she turned toward the gilded Baroque-accent mirror that hung above her mahogany dresser. "And anyway, you two have it all wrong. I'm not planning or hoping. I'm going to meet him. Soon." Having said that, Daryl applied the creamy scarlet color to her lips.

Margo and Audrey both doubled over in loud peals of laughter.

Daryl turned away from the mirror. In a defensive gesture, she folded her arms across her full bosom. "We'll see who has the last laugh when I meet my Mr. Right. I've got a feeling it's going to be very soon."

Margo sank down into a Louis XV style leather chair. "But, girl, you've said that same thing for the last five years."

Waving her freshly manicured hands in a gesture of dismissal, Daryl appraised herself in the mirror once more. She made sure every strand of her reddish-brown hair was in place. Hanging just below her chin, the shining straight hair was cut to perfection in a bob. The glimmers of golden-red highlights complimented her bronze complexion. The slim empire-waist column dress, accented with princess seams and bow-back styling, emphasized her regal bearing. Pleased with what she saw, Daryl turned away from the mirror and stood, leaning against her dresser for support. "It's going to happen—just you wait and see. Who knows, I may even meet him tonight."

"Where? At Tyrell's party?" Raising fine, arched eyebrows, Margo protested. "Honey, I doubt that. My cousin will most likely have those same old tired friends of his."

Audrey sat down on Daryl's queen-size bed, bending over to adjust the gold straps on her shoes. "Well, I've never been to any of Tyrell's parties because I've usually had to work. I'm looking forward to having a good time."

Walking into the bathroom, Daryl nodded in agreement. "You will. Margo's just saying that because most of Tyrell's friends are her ex-boyfriends."

From the full-length mirror standing over in a corner of the room, Margo glanced briefly over her shoulder. "You know you need to stop, Daryl." There was a faint glint of humor in her greenish eyes.

"Girl, you know it's true. I'm surprised you didn't have a date for tonight. You've been dating like crazy since you and Rob split up. We've only seen you three or four times in the three months you've been back."

"As a matter of fact, somebody did ask me out, but I'd already invited you and Audrey . . ." Margo ran her hands down the front of her emerald green, floor-length gown. "Y'all being my good friends and all."

Daryl gave an exaggerated wink to Audrey. "Yeah, right. You know you didn't want to be with anybody but Rob tonight. When was the last time you saw him, anyway? I heard he moved back right before Christmas. But I bet you saw him last night."

"I'm not seeing Rob," Margo said defensively. "And it was . . . oh, hell, it was a couple of days ago."

"Uh huh. And I bet he spent the night, didn't he?" Daryl grinned knowingly.

Margo put her hands to her mouth, stifling her laughter. "Hey, I still love the man. I was in the mood for sex, so I invited him over. Call me stupid, okay?"

Daryl and Audrey joined in the laughter.

Audrey was the first to recover. Waving her hand sympathetically, she said, "Margo, don't feel bad. None of us has had any luck lately in the men department. That last guy I went out with thought I had fool written all over my face. He was seriously tripping."

"I guess each one of us has sucker written somewhere, cause we seem to attract men who want something for nothing," Margo agreed as she sat down beside Audrey on the bed.

"Not me," Daryl denied, coming out of the bathroom. "I'm not dating because I'm waiting for my husband. That perfect man is out there somewhere."

Margo snorted. "Huh! Perfect man, my eye. If he's perfect, he's definitely not living in Los Angeles, or anywhere else in this world. Maybe on Mars . . ."

"Wait and see," Daryl murmured, pushing strands of hair away from her face.

"While Daryl's finding Mr. Right, I'm going on a diet.

This new year will be the year I finally get into my size eights," Margo announced.

Daryl glanced down at Audrey and chuckled. "And she thinks I'm the one being unrealistic." Looking at Margo, she said, "Girl, ever since I've known you, you've never worn a size eight."

"Maybe when we were in junior high," Audrey added as she stood up, straightening her gold sequined gown. "You might as well give me all those dresses, instead of letting them go out of style just sitting in that closet of yours."

Daryl raised an eyebrow. "You mean she finally moved them out of her hope chest?"

Margo's full-figured body shook with her laughter. "Y'all are cold. Neither one of you are right."

"Now, Margo, you know we're telling the truth," Daryl said as she walked over to her closet. She reached in to retrieve a black velvet full-length swing coat. "I've never been a size eight either. That's for sure. I'm happy being a twelve."

"I could be a size eight, if I go on a diet. I'm only a twelve myself—"

"Sixteen," Audrey interjected. "Remember, I went shopping with you for that dress you have on now."

"Humph!" She shot Audrey a withering glance. "It runs small—that's all."

Daryl tapped Margo on the shoulder. "That's all right, girlfriend. Audrey's just jealous of your shape. Something she don't have. She's just tall and skinny. Just look at her. All skin and bones."

The dark-skinned woman threw her hands up in resignation. "Oh, so now it's pick on Audrey time. That's okay. I may not have big breasts like you, Daryl, or Margo's big butt, but that's okay. I still get mine."

"Mmmmmm," Daryl and Margo both chorused.

Audrey strutted across the polished hardwood floor, a slender leg peeking out now and then from the thigh-high split on one side of her gown. "That's right."

"Well, Miss Thang, what's your resolution for the new year?" Daryl asked.

"To live my life to the fullest. And take those size eights out of Margo's closet, cause she's not gonna use them. Did you see the black and red suit she just bought? Let me tell you. It's sharp, and it would look so good on me—"

"I don't think so," Margo interjected. "I'm going to wear my eights. After tomorrow, I'll start my diet."

"What about exercising? You planning to go to the gym with Audrey and me?"

She considered that for a moment, then shook her head. "No, I think I'll have to slowly work up to that. Exercise is really not my thing."

Daryl threw back her head, laughing. "I don't know why you're talking about dieting in the first place. You look good. By the way, I just love that gown you're wearing." She admired the way the beaded and embroidered jacket brought out the green in Margo's eyes, while the full chiffon skirt minimized the fullness of her hips. "Emerald green looks good on you."

"You know I gained most of this weight after having Kiana."

"Seriously, Margo. You look really good," Audrey agreed. "I think the weight looks good on you. You're big boned and being a size eight—I don't know about that. I think you'd look kind of anorexic myself."

Margo laughed and waved her off. "You're just saying that because you want my clothes."

"No, I really mean it," Audrey insisted.

Daryl glanced over at the crystal clock sitting on the night stand beside her bed. "If we don't hurry up, we're going to be late. Traffic's going to be heavy going into L.A. tonight. I expect the ten freeway to be crowded."

"Before we go, I need to call Mrs. Benedict and check on Kiana."

Raising her camel-colored eyes in surprise, Daryl asked, "Ursula Benedict has Kiana?"

Margo nodded. "She called and asked if she could keep Kiana for the next couple of days."

"I guess things are getting much better between you and Rob's mother then?" Audrey inquired.

Margo shrugged. "We're pretending to like each other for my daughter's sake. She's being very nice. We want Kiana to be happy and feel loved. That's the one thing we all agree on."

"That's good," Audrey said, running her fingers through her hair once more.

"While you make your call, I'll finish my make-up. You can call her from the kitchen, so that you'll have some privacy."

"Thanks, Daryl." Margo stood up and left the room.

"Daryl, you look real nice tonight," Audrey complimented her. "Where did you find those black and gold earrings?"

"My mother gave them to me for Christmas. I think they really look good with this dress," she said, pointing to the black gown she wore.

"They do." Getting up to stand beside Daryl, Audrey pulled a tissue out of her purse. Wiping a lipstick smudge off Daryl's cheek, she asked, "So, you really think you might meet that special someone tonight?"

"Yes, but if not tonight, eventually."

"We'll all meet someone eventually, Daryl, but we don't go around setting up for him in advance." Audrey screwed her face into a frown. "Don't you think that's going a little bit too far?"

Shaking her head, Daryl responded, "Remember when I went to that singles retreat with my church five years ago? Well, one of the things they talked about was finding your mate. My pastor's wife said when you pray for something, you thank God in advance and then you act as if you've already received it. She said that's how she got her husband."

"But didn't she mean to just have faith?"

"That's why I've done all this, Audrey," Daryl explained patiently. "Because I do have faith."

"You haven't bought your wedding dress yet, have you?" Daryl laughed. "No."

"Whew! You almost had me worried."

Margo strolled back into Daryl's bedroom. "My baby's fast asleep. So, are we ready to go?"

Daryl grabbed her purse and her coat. "Let's go. My future husband may be waiting."

Audrey and Margo exchanged quick glances.

"Come on you doubting Thomases. I'll see what you both have to say when I finally meet my man."

Standing alone near the door, tuxedo-clad, Sheldon Turner discreetly surveyed the crowded room at the popular Precision Club. Neoclassical lamps cast a glow throughout the room as their faceted crystal teardrops caught and refracted the light in a soft, prismatic display. He noticed that there were lots of people here tonight—people who believed whatever they read or heard about him. Almost everyone he'd spoken with tonight had mentioned some juicy tidbit they'd heard or read about in the media. They all wanted to know if what they'd read or heard was true.

Several women walked past him, smiling and pointing. Nodding politely, he was well aware of all the appreciative glances thrown his way. It was a constant reminder that he was the sort of person people liked to read about. Thirty-eight and still bashful, Sheldon hated that part of his success as a professional basketball player. His relaxed manner belied his inner tension—he wondered if he'd made the right decision by coming tonight.

Tyrell walked briskly toward him, holding his hand out. "Hey, man, glad you could make it."

Accepting the offered hand of his long-time friend, Sheldon acknowledged, "Me, too. I wasn't sure I was going to make it—my plane finally left New York after a two-hour delay. I couldn't rest throughout the bumpy ride. Man,

I'm tired, but I wanted to get out of the house. My mom had all of her grandkids over."

"Well, I'm glad you came. Get yourself something to drink and mingle." Leaning closer, Tyrell whispered, "I'm sure all the ladies are glad you're here."

Sheldon felt very relaxed around Tyrell, his childhood friend and the only person outside his family who really knew him. He shook his head and chuckled.

At the bar, he ordered a cognac and stood sipping it slowly, savoring the liquid warmth. As he enjoyed his drink, Sheldon glanced up to find a reed-thin young woman with long, dark flowing hair sauntering toward him. Finding her vaguely familiar, he searched his memory trying to remember who she was.

"Hi, Sheldon. Long time no see."

The black velvet of her dress heightened the translucence of her ivory face and neck. "Hello . . ." For the life of him, he couldn't remember her name. "It's good to see you again. How's everything?"

"Good." She wagged a finger at him. "You know I should be mad at you. You never called me like you promised."

"I was . . ." Sheldon struggled for an excuse.

"I'm sure you were," she said, cutting him off. "I heard from Tyrell that you've come back to stay. Maybe we can get together sometime . . ."

"That sounds fine."

"Do you still have my number?"

"I'm sure I do. I just—with moving I may have misplaced it."

"I'll give it to you again." She pulled a pen from her purse, hastily wrote it on a napkin, and handed to him.

Sheldon was relieved to see she'd written her name on it.

"I'll give you a call, Linda."

She smiled. "Save me a dance, okay?"

He returned her smile.

"Back in town just a few hours and already picking up the ladies," Tyrell's voice came from beside him.

Sheldon turned around. Chuckling, he said, "No, it's not like that, Ty, man. I couldn't even remember her name.

"I'm sure she reminded you. Linda's something else."

"I must have met her at one of your parties."

"My birthday party. About two years ago. You had me introduce you to her."

He looked at Tyrell in surprise. "I did?"

"You were pretty plastered then, but the two of you left together."

Sheldon clasped a hand to his mouth. "That's right. Man, I was really out of it back then. I couldn't hang with that wild life. It will kill you if you don't slow down."

"True that." Inclining his head, Tyrell commented, "You never told me what brought you back to the hometown. I thought you were going to make New York your home."

"I changed my mind, man. Since Pops is gone, my mom is all alone. My brother's not doing right by her, so I thought I'd come home and help her."

"That's cool. I'd heard she was really sick for a while."

Sheldon nodded. "She's doing much better now, but I want to be close by if she needs me."

"That's all right there. Gotta take care of our mothers." Tyrell leaned in closer. "Now see, I figured you must be running from some honey back in New York. I've been seeing pictures of you escorting some model all over New York."

Throwing back his head, Sheldon roared with laughter. "That too."

Tyrell took a step back. "You serious?"

"Hell, yeah. Man, this girl won't leave me alone." He shook his head for emphasis.

"You got yourself a real live fatal attraction, huh?"

"Hope not. Hopefully, she'll find someone else and forget about me. I know one thing though. The last thing I want is a serious relationship. With her or anybody."

* * *

"Hey, cousin, how're you doing?" Margo leaned over, placing a kiss on Tyrell's cheek. "Everything looks great."

"Hello, ladies, how y'all doing? Come on in—the party's just starting."

"Tyrell, you're looking good in that tux. Whenever I see you, you're usually in sweats or jeans," Audrey announced.

"I do dress up occasionally." He assessed her thoroughly. "You're looking good yourself."

Margo grabbed Daryl by the arm. "If you two will excuse us . . . Come on, girlfriend. I think those two want to be alone."

"I'll catch up with you later," Audrey murmured, not taking her eyes off Tyrell for a minute.

Standing at the bar, they each ordered a glass of wine. As they waited, Margo asked, "Did you see the way those two were checking each other out?"

Daryl nodded. "I sure did. I guess Audrey's found herself a date for the evening."

"Well, my cousin is a really nice guy. I hope they do get together. He's been asking me a lot of questions about her lately, so I had a feeling this was coming."

"Really?" Daryl's eyes slid over the attractive couple once more. "That's nice. They do look good together."

"I think so."

Checking out the other guests in attendance, Daryl's eyes fixed on a tall man standing by himself near the other end of the bar. Focusing her full attention on him, her emotions swirled. She was completely awestruck by his good looks. He stood a sturdy six-five, and his good-looking features were chiseled in a toasty almond tone. "Humph, humph, humph! Now, he's the kind of man that could be in my future."

"Who?" Margo asked, looking around the room. "Who are you talking about?"

"That tall gorgeous man over there. The one at the end of the bar."

"Where?" Margo scanned the crowd of partygoers. "There are about four extremely tall men standing at the bar."

She pointed in his direction. "Over there. See the one in the black tux with the red bow tie and cummerbund? The one with the bald head." There was something about him that struck a familiar chord with her. Had they met before? No, it wasn't possible. She would never forget someone so good-looking.

Margo shook her head. "I don't think so, Daryl. You don't want to have anything to do with him."

"You know him? He looks familiar, but I can't place him."

Margo seemed momentarily caught off guard. "Then you're probably the only woman here that doesn't recognize him. But then again, you won't have anything to do with sports."

"Well, who is he? Come on and introduce me." She headed off in his direction.

Margo pulled her back. "No, Daryl, he's not the type of man that you need or want. He's not about to get married. He's too busy being a player. And I don't mean just playing ball."

Daryl halted, shocked. "Now I know who he is. Sheldon Turner. He plays for New York or somewhere, right?"

"Yeah, that's Mr. Turner. He used to play with the New York Rockets. He retired last season."

Staring at Margo, she stated, "You sound kind of bitter. Were you involved with him or something?"

"No . . . he used to date a friend of mine. He hurt her badly."

"It won't happen to me," she declared.

"How can you be so sure, Daryl? He has a terrible reputation."

"I've heard some things about him, but then most of it has been from the tabloids. You know you can't always believe what you read in them."

"Humph!"

"I've heard some good things about him, too. He's done a lot for the community, hasn't he? I heard something about him donating a large sum of money to AIDS research and some children's charities."

"I'm sure you've also heard about his womanizing ways."

Daryl nodded. "Yes, I've heard."

Margo regarded her quizzically for a moment. "And you still want to get involved with him?"

"I can't explain it, Margo, but I know he's the one for me. I can feel it in my heart."

"Be careful. I don't want to see you get hurt. Sheldon thinks he's God's gift to women."

"I'm not a fool, Margo. Now would you please introduce me?"

She sighed heavily. "Come on, but don't say I didn't warn you."

Together they made their way across the room to stand before the man of Daryl's dreams.

"Hi, Sheldon," Margo said stiffly.

He looked down and seemed to peer closely at them. A surprised expression flew across his face and then disappeared in a flash. Brandishing a smile, he said, "Margo, how are you?"

"I'm fine. Sheldon, this is a good friend of mine. Daryl Larsen. Daryl, this is Sheldon Turner."

She raised her eyes to meet his. "It's a pleasure to meet you, Sheldon."

A small wry smile touched his lips. "You, too."

"How long are you going to be in town?" Margo asked.

He seemed amused by her question, leaving Daryl to wonder why.

"Actually, I moved back today. I'll be living in Los Angeles."

"Oh really? What brings you back?"

"My mother. I want to be closer to her."

Daryl smiled. "I think that's very—"

A slender woman, who she'd seen a few times in passing, walked up and stood between her and Sheldon, effectively cutting off their conversation. Ignoring the two women, she spoke to Sheldon. "Sheldon, you promised me a dance. This is my favorite song."

With a blank expression on his face, Sheldon turned to Daryl and asked, "Would you hold my drink for me?" Before she could respond, he'd already placed it in her hand and walked toward the dance floor with the woman.

Margo placed her hands on her hips and tapped her foot. "See, what did I tell you?" Shaking her head, she said, "He's gorgeous, but no good."

"He does have some nerve," she agreed.

"That's all you have to say?" Margo gestured with her hand. I can't believe you're standing here holding his drink. I would've put it down a long time ago. Give a person a little money and he . . ."

While Margo droned on and on, Daryl concluded that Sheldon had his reasons for leaving his drink with her. She didn't believe he would be so arrogant. Returning her attention to her friend, who was still ranting she said, "Margo, just give it rest. I'll just hold onto it for right now. And when Sheldon comes back, I have some words for him."

As soon as Sheldon rejoined them, Margo lit into him. "You've really got some nerve, Sheldon."

His luminous eyes widened in astonishment. "What's wrong with you?"

"How dare you treat her—"

"It's okay, Margo," Daryl interrupted. "I'll take it from here."

Sheldon glanced from one woman to the other. "Is there a problem?"

He seemed totally oblivious to what he'd done. Daryl glared at him with burning, reproachful eyes. "Margo, could you excuse us please?"

"Are you sure?"

Daryl nodded. "I'd like to talk to Sheldon alone."

Margo gestured behind her as she backed away. "I'll be right over there if you need me."

"What's going on, Daryl?" he asked. "Why's Margo so upset?"

"She's just being very protective of me, that's all."

"Why?"

"She thinks—I mean, we both think, that it was rude the way you gave me your drink to hold while you left to dance with another woman. You don't know me well enough to do that." She breathed in deeply to control her growing irritation.

"I asked—"

"But you didn't wait for my answer."

He grinned charmingly. "That's because I didn't want to give you the chance to say no."

Even though his smile warmed her body, Daryl did not return it. "And why is that?" she asked coldly.

"I wanted you to stay right here until I returned."

Nodding, she said, "I see. I'm supposed to just stand here like an idiot. I don't think so."

"No. Right now, I'm hoping we can dance to this song. It's one of my favorites."

Daryl looked up and stared into his eyes, losing herself in their burnt-walnut-colored depths. "I'm a little ticked at you right now. And dancing with you is the last thing I want to do. Nice meeting you." She turned to walk away.

Sheldon reached out to grab her by the elbow. "Daryl, wait. I'm sorry about the way I handled the drink situation. I wanted you to hold it because I have a phobia about leaving my drinks unattended."

"Really?" She raised her eyes to meet his. "And why is that?"

"Because three years ago, someone put a drug in my drink during a party. I almost died."

"I'm sorry. I didn't know. Why didn't you say that in the first place?"

"Can we start over please? I didn't mean to disrespect

you. I danced with Linda only because I'd promised to. I wanted to get that out of the way. So, can we start over?"

A faint smile touched her lips. "Sure."

"Can we dance?"

Daryl nodded. She and Sheldon, hand in hand, waded through the sea of people toward the crowded dance floor.

Chapter 2

Putting a large hand to her waist, Sheldon drew her full-figured form to him. The warmth of his muscled arms as they danced was so bracing; Daryl felt like she was dreaming. Being this close to him made her weak in the knees. She couldn't remember when she'd felt this way about a man, or if, in her thirty-four years, she'd never experienced these emotions. She was more inclined to believe the latter.

When the music stopped, they reluctantly parted a few inches. Leaving the dance floor, Sheldon asked, "Would you like something to drink?"

"Yes, I'll take a glass of white wine, please." She answered quickly over her noisily beating heart.

"Sure."

She pointed toward Audrey and Margo. "I'm going to the ladies' room with my friends. I'll be right back."

He smiled and nodded. "Okay. I need to talk to Ty anyway."

Grinning, Daryl rushed over to Margo and Audrey. She could barely control her eagerness. "That man is so fine. Did you see the way he danced? Boy, for someone so tall, he can really move."

Margo groaned aloud, rolling her eyes. "I guess you still think he could be the one?" she muttered, as they headed to the ladies' room. "Even though he sort of disrespected you earlier with that girl."

Daryl closed her eyes and prayed for patience. "I sure do, and for your information, he didn't disrespect me. He explained why he didn't want to leave his drink unattended. You read the newspapers—and even we don't leave our drinks unless one of us is watching them."

"I've heard that he's nothing but a womanizer," Audrey said in a low whisper, as they stood in the relatively short line of women waiting to use the ladies' room.

Margo turned to face Daryl and Audrey, who stood behind her. "I tried to tell her that." Gesturing toward Daryl, she added, "But, she doesn't want to hear that."

"I've heard those same things, Margo," Daryl whispered back, "but you know that rumors usually consist of just a grain of truth." She made a conscious effort to keep from raising her voice, but Margo was getting on her nerves. "Why does it bother you so much? It's not as if I'm planning my whole life around him. I'd simply like to get to know him better." Relieved that it was now her turn, Daryl walked briskly into a stall.

When she came out, Margo was standing before a porcelain basin, washing her hands. Audrey was apparently still in a stall. Margo was the type of person who was fiercely protective of the people she loved. Daryl supposed that that was why she seemed bothered by her growing interest in Sheldon—a man with a reputation as a womanizer. Fleetingly, she wondered how much of what she'd heard about him was true.

Audrey came out adjusting her sequined gown. Looking from one to the other, she said, "You guys aren't mad at each other, are you? We came here to have a good time. Let's not fight."

Daryl was about to reply, but halted when a woman walked out of a corner stall. Nodding a brief hello, she moved to stand beside Audrey.

When it was just the three of them in the bathroom, Margo smiled. "No, Audrey. We're not mad at each other. We just disagree on a certain person."

"Margo's still my girl. I know she's just looking out for me."

Audrey placed a gentle hand on Margo's shoulder. "It's her life, Margo. Let Daryl handle this situation. You know she's not going to jump into something with blinders on. Now come on. We came here to party and bring in the new year together."

As she touched up her lipstick, Margo said, "Just let me go on the record saying that if he hurts you, I'm going to string him up and castrate him."

"Ouch," Audrey murmured.

Laughing, Daryl placed her arms around Margo, hugging her. "I don't know what I'd do without you. It's almost midnight, and we don't want to bring in the new year in the bathroom—cause if we do, that's the way we're going to end it," she warned.

Audrey laughed. "You and your old wives' tales. Girl, you're something else. I'm surprised you don't wear garlic around your neck and constantly throw salt over your shoulder."

"Well, I don't know about a garlic necklace or the throwing of salt, but Daryl's right about the new year," Margo agreed. "Come on, lets get out of here."

Standing near the bar, Sheldon and Tyrell were engaged in conversation when the three women approached them. Daryl didn't miss the way Sheldon's eyes slid over her body seductively. His gaze, soft and caressing, caused her heart to dance with excitement.

"We were wondering if you three were going to miss the countdown," Tyrell said as they approached. He handed a glass to Audrey. "Here's your champagne, Sweetness."

Sheldon held out a glass to Daryl. "I thought champagne would be a better choice to bring in the new year. I'll get your wine later, if you still want it."

She shook her head. "Oh, no, champagne's good. Champagne is very good."

About to walk away, Margo was grabbed from behind by a muscular man in a black tux with an emerald green cummerbund and bow tie. "Where do you think you're going, baby?"

Complete surprise registered on her face. "Rob? What are you doing here?"

He winked at Tyrell. "I was invited." He pointed to his cummerbund. "I saw your gown hanging in the closet the other night, so I thought I'd match it. We make a great-looking couple, don't you think?"

Before she could respond, she heard one of the band members announce that it was time to begin the count-down to the future.

"Nine, eight ...," the chanting began. "... Six, five ..."

A few seconds later, shouts of "Happy New Year!" erupted throughout the club. Amidst the loud blasts of horns, kisses, and cheers, gold and silver helium-filled balloons rained down on the crowd of fashionably dressed men and women—some wearing colorful party hats.

Daryl was momentarily caught off guard when Sheldon pulled her into his arms. "Happy New Year, Daryl." He leaned over, covering her mouth with his.

Her calm was shattered by the hunger of his kiss. Raising his mouth from hers, he gazed into her eyes. She breathed lightly between parted lips, "Happy New Year, Sheldon." Glancing around, she found Margo and Rob in a tight lip lock, while Tyrell and Audrey looked as if their kiss would never end. Clearing her throat loudly, she announced, "Okay, you guys, quit it." Fanning herself, she teased, "It's really starting to heat up in here."

Margo and Rob were the first to pull themselves away from each other. She reached over to hug Daryl and whispered, "Happy New Year; I really hope all your dreams come true."

Daryl nodded. "I know." Stealing a glance at Rob, she whispered, "I wish the same for you."

Audrey wrapped her arms around Margo. "Hey, what about me?"

Laughing, Daryl placed an arm around her tall, lean friend. "Miss Thang, we already know you got it goin' on. We're not worried about you."

"You're wrong, Daryl. But you know what? This is our year, ladies. I can feel it," Audrey announced.

Peering over at Sheldon, Daryl murmured, "I agree."

"Baby, let's dance," Rob said, as he took Margo by the hand. "Happy New Year, ladies."

"Happy New Year, Rob," they both chorused.

Audrey grabbed Tyrell. "I'm going to dance with Tyrell; see you later."

Daryl was left standing alone with Sheldon. She found herself totally entranced by his compelling personage. She swallowed tightly as he wrapped his hand around hers, causing her to delight in the electricity of his touch.

"So, ready to give it another whirl?" Sheldon asked, gesturing toward the dance floor.

Just then a woman, wearing a dress one could only describe as barely there, walked by and brazenly handed him a piece of paper that Daryl knew contained her phone number. Sheldon glanced over at her and shrugged. "I—"

She shook her head and laughed. "I think we'd better go have that dance."

They danced to the next five songs. Daryl couldn't remember when she'd had such a good time. She loved to dance and Sheldon was good at it.

Two hours later, Daryl was tired and not thrilled about the drive back to Pomona. "Although I'm having a wonderful time, I think I'm going to call it a night. It was really nice meeting you, Sheldon."

He seemed disappointed. "Leaving so soon?"

She nodded. "I live in the Phillips Ranch area."

"Why don't you stay here in L.A. instead of driving back to Pomona tonight?"

"I thought about that, but I have a lot of things I want to do tomorrow. I need to get an early start."

Sheldon found her to be an intriguing young woman. He was suddenly interested in seeing her again. "I hate to see you go. I was hoping to get to know you a little better. You're not going to leave without giving me your number, are you?" he asked confidently.

Daryl nodded her head regretfully. Patting the pocket of his tuxedo jacket, she said, "I think you've collected enough numbers for tonight. Bye." She turned and walked away as casually as she could toward her friends. She could feel the sensual heat radiating from his walnut gaze, and it thrilled her.

"Did I just hear you correctly back there? Did Sheldon just ask for your phone number? And you refused to give it to him?" Audrey asked.

She nodded, a big grin plastered on her face. "Yeah, you heard right. He's going to have to work to get me."

"Oh," Margo teased. "I thought that maybe you'd come to your senses."

"Margo, I know you're not talking. We saw you over there with Rob. Looks like you two might be getting back together," Daryl stated, her hands on her hips.

"No, we're not. We're just trying to get along."

"Honey, Rob was trying to get something else, and it looked like you wanted to give it to him."

"You need to stop it, Audrey." In spite of herself, Margo giggled. "He did say that he misses me. He wants to move back in."

"Well, if you want him to marry you—keep it up. You two have a little baby, and he wants all of the conveniences of marriage without being married," Audrey advised. "Don't settle for that if you want more."

Margo nodded. "It was hard leaving him, but I know I had to do it. As long as we were living together, he wasn't going to marry me. He just kept making excuses."

As they neared Daryl's car, she pulled out her keys, saying, "It's going to work out. Just wait and see."

Margo opened the car door on the passenger side and slid inside. "You know, Daryl, that's your answer to everything. Why is that?"

She waited until Audrey settled into the car before responding. "Because, Margo, I have faith. I have to believe that life will get better. If I don't believe that, then I'll be like a lot of people walking around. Depressed, disillusioned, negative. I don't want to be like that. Life is entirely too short." She smiled. "And in my line of work, I'm reminded of that fact daily."

After sleeping a few hours, Daryl awoke to a beautiful day, got out of bed energetically, and went for her daily run. The morning sky was clear, and the weather was warm. Daryl could have sworn she even heard the harmonious chirping of birds. This was going to be a very good year for her. She could feel it. When she returned home, she took a shower and threw on a pair of jeans and a sweatshirt. She practically skipped downstairs to make breakfast.

Peering intently at the empty place setting at the other end of the table, she visualized Sheldon sitting there. "It's going to be so nice to have a man around the house," she murmured to herself. She could hear his voice as he complimented her on the western omelette and homemade salsa. She could almost feel his breath on her neck as she envisioned him getting out of his chair and strolling toward her with the intentions of giving her a loving kiss.

Daryl shook her head, sighing wistfully. "Maybe Margo's right. No. No, I can't think like that. It's all going to work out. He'll find a way to reach me—I just know it."

After cleaning the kitchen, she headed upstairs to gather her laundry. Daryl worked steadily and fast to complete the list of chores she'd planned to do during the day. *It's good luck to start off the new year with a clean house,* she mused. A couple of hours later, she was done. She quickly changed into a mock turtleneck and a rayon print wrap skirt in a spearmint color, then headed over to Margo's. They were going to storm the mall and do some shopping, then have dinner.

"Hey," Margo said breathlessly as she opened the door. She moved aside to let Daryl enter. "I just called your house. I thought you might have decided to sleep in or something."

"No, I was up at the crack of dawn."

"Why so early?"

Daryl merely shrugged. "I guess I was too excited to sleep. I got up and cleaned my whole house. I even got the laundry out of the way. Are you ready to go?"

Margo laughed. "Well, let me grab my purse, and we're on our way to do some serious damage to those stores. I've already cooked, so when we get back, all we have to do is warm it up."

Maggie observed her son quietly from the doorway before strolling into the family room, complete with big screen TV, pool table, and wet bar.

"Sheldon, did you sleep okay, son?"

Looking up from the game he was watching, Sheldon smiled at his mother. Although she was in her fifties, she looked much younger. "I slept fine. I hope I didn't wake you when I came in this morning. I saw your light on."

"You didn't. I'd been up a while. Couldn't sleep, so I thought I'd catch up on some reading." She sat down in an old wooden rocker—a chair she'd used to rock Sheldon and his brother, Barry, to sleep when they were younger. She picked up a woven basket that lay beside the chair on the carpeted floor. Retrieving her knitting needles and a ball of yarn, she started to knit. "Have fun last night? I see Tyrell's making these parties of his an annual event."

Sheldon, with his eyes glued to the television, nodded slowly. "It was okay. If I'd stayed home, I wouldn't have missed much." Except Daryl.

He recalled the way her curvaceous body leaned into him, the way her bosom brushed against his chest as they slow danced, and the way his mouth assaulted hers with his lips and tongue. He'd meant the kiss to be friendly, but sensing the white hot flare of desire raging in them both, he'd deepened the kiss. From Daryl's response, she'd enjoyed it as much as he did. She'd pressed her body closer to his, melting into him.

He'd tossed and turned all night thinking of her. Daryl's body filled his night with vivid dreams of hot sexual activity. She'd gotten lusty leers from most of the other men in the club. And the dress she'd worn only served to flaunt her full breasts even more.

Forcing himself to concentrate on what his mother was saying, he turned the volume down on the TV and turned to face Maggie.

". . . You had a phone call last night. From somebody named Mall or something like that. Where do you keep finding these folks with the funny names?" Shaking her head, his mother added, "Can't believe somebody named their child Mall . . ."

Sheldon laughed. "Her name is Malle. You know, like Pal."

Maggie frowned. "And that's supposed to sound better? What is she? She's another white girl, right?"

He didn't respond.

"Boy, I've told you to be careful. Some people don't like to see black folks with white ones."

"Mama, it's not like it used to be. Besides, she and I are only friends."

"Uh huh. That's what your brother always says." She pointed to the rows of photographs on the wall. "See up there. I've got my own rainbow coalition."

Sheldon threw back his head and laughed. "Well, no one can ever call us prejudice, that's for sure."

Joining in the laughter, she said, "No, I don't suppose they can. I tell you, I just wish Barry would at least get married. He's got all these babies by different women. It's just shameful," she said, with a vague hint of disapproval. "Three babies from three different women. Humph."

"He's a grown man, Mama. Nobody can tell him what to do. I think he—like most of my friends—gets bored easily. Why inflict that on a wife?"

"And what about you? Why haven't you gotten married? What are you waiting for?"

Sheldon held both hands up and shook his head. "Don't turn this on me. We were talking about—"

"You," his mother interjected. "Now answer me. What are you waiting on?"

"I have to be honest with you. I don't want to get married, Mama."

Maggie's voice rose in surprise. "Why, for goodness sake? You—"

Sheldon braced himself for the argument he knew was coming. "Mama, don't start. Right now, all the people I know are divorced. Some of my friends cheat on their wives after being married less than a year. They come to me with nothing but problems about their significant others. The way I see it, I'm the lucky one." His voice was firm, final. "I know how Dad treated you—"

"Humph! Let your father rest in peace. As for being the lucky one, I think you mean the lonely one."

Sheldon raised his eyebrows. "What do you mean by that? I can have any woman I want."

"But can they have you? That's the question."

Sheldon turned to face his mother. "What are you talking about, Mama?"

"You go around breaking women's hearts." There was a critical tone to her voice.

"No, I don't. I'm always honest with them. I tell them up front that I'm not looking for a relationship."

"Then you need to stop sleeping with them. One day you might find a crazy one, mark my words."

He gave her a sidelong glance of utter disbelief. "Mama, you shouldn't believe everything you read in the papers about me. Most of it's just a bunch of lies."

"I know you, son. I don't need no tabloid or television show to tell me. I'm the one who gave birth to you. I fed you and changed your diapers." She pointed a needle at him. "Boy, I know you better than you know yourself."

Her tone brooked no argument from him. Sheldon settled back into the comfortable folds of the sofa, preparing himself for the lecture that was forthcoming.

". . . And then with all the diseases out there. I tell you, you'd better leave those fast girls alone. Most of them are probably after your money anyway." She shook her head as if she were unhappy with the thought. "Nothing but gold diggers," she muttered.

Sheldon nodded. He knew better than to try and disagree with her.

"Find yourself a nice girl. One who will love you no matter what. There are still some nice ones out there—course they are few and far between."

"Mama . . ." Sheldon started.

"What is it?"

"Nothing. It's nothing." He had originally planned to reaffirm his decision to remain a bachelor, but decided now was not the time.

Listening to his mother, Sheldon missed the rest of the football game. He wasn't upset though, having set the VCR to record earlier. He'd had a feeling that they would be having this discussion sometime today. They usually did during his visits home.

Finally, Maggie decided to check on her black-eyed peas. Sheldon thought about Daryl. She was really something else. He smiled when he recalled the way she'd left without giving him her phone number. She'd done it as a challenge. Immediately after she left, he'd gone to Ty, who gave it to him without hesitation.

Pulling the number out of his pants pocket, he reached for the phone and dialed. No answer. Her answering machine clicked on. Sheldon debated whether or not to leave a message. Grinning, he decided.

* * *

Four hours later, Margo unlocked the trunk of her shiny red Mercedes. As they packed the numerous shopping bags in the mid-sized storage area, she said, "Daryl, I wasn't going to say anymore about this, but I can't help it. I really don't think it's a good idea to get involved with Sheldon. He probably can't even spell commitment, much less know the meaning of the word."

Sighing heavily, Daryl murmured, "You keep saying that, Margo, and I keep telling you that I'm not going to rush into anything. I probably won't ever see him again."

"You'd be the better for it. Sheldon is the type of man that likes to go from one woman to another." Margo laughed. "You sure showed him—not giving him your phone number. I was so proud of you."

They had just left Montclair Mall and were on their way back to Pomona and Margo's house in Mountain Meadows, a gated community.

Pulling into the driveway of her house, Margo parked her car before she spoke again. "Sheldon's not a bad person. He just uses women as trophies."

Getting out of the car, Daryl interjected, "You know, I got the feeling that Sheldon's not really as bad as he's made out to be. I thought he seemed kind of quiet."

Margo's expression said clearly that she didn't agree, but she said nothing. They carried the bags into the house, dropping them on the living room floor.

"Make yourself comfortable. I'm going to start warming up dinner. Shopping always gives me an appetite."

"Me, too," Daryl agreed. She settled back into the fluffy folds of Margo's sofa. She sniffed the air. "Something sure smells good in there. What did you cook?"

"It's black-eyed peas, smoked ham, and cabbage. It'll only take a minute to warm up the cornbread."

Daryl got up quickly and headed to the downstairs bathroom to wash her hands. She scanned her face, which was completely devoid of make-up, critically for a moment before leaving. Moving to the dining room, Daryl sank down on one of the chairs at the dining room table. "Tell me, Margo, why do you always serve black-eyed peas and cabbage on New Years Day?"

"Because the peas are for good luck, and the cabbage is for money."

She inclined her head. "You really believe that eating a plate of peas and cabbage brings us good luck?"

Margo shrugged in confusion. "Sure, don't you?"

"But isn't it the same thing as what I'm doing? I believe I'm getting a mate for life and I'm standing by that belief."

Margo shook her head. "It's different."

"How?" Daryl challenged.

"Well . . ." Margo thought it over. "Oh, I hate when you do this to me."

She laughed. "Do what?"

"Catch me off guard like this. All I'm saying, Daryl, is just be careful."

"I'm not stupid, Margo." Daryl put a forkful of greens into her mouth. "Mmmmm, these are so good, Margo. I have to give it to you—you sure can cook."

"I—what was that noise? Your pager going off?"

"Yeah." Daryl held the tiny black object up to the light to read the numbers. "Someone called my house and left a message. Probably my mom. I'll check it later. Right now, I'm going to concentrate on all this food."

Margo giggled. "I have to admit—everything really turned out better than I expected. Rob's going to be upset he missed this meal."

"He's not coming over?"

"No, he's with his mother and Kiana."

After dinner, Daryl helped clean the table and wash dishes. Margo put the last plate away and prepared to take the trash outside. "Let me take this out, then we can sit down and watch a movie."

"Margo, it's dark out there."

"And?"

"Taking the garbage out after dark is bad luck. I thought you knew that."

Margo laughed. "That explains why I've had such a bad time of it these last couple of years."

Daryl nodded. "I wouldn't doubt it." She was about to sit down when her pager started to vibrate once more.

"Your pager is just blowing up over there. Maybe you'd better go on and check it now." Her eyes twinkling, Margo said teasingly, "Could be that man you been looking for."

"Ha ha. You're so funny." Daryl headed to the phone and dialed her service. As she listened to her messages, she suddenly looked over at Margo, a big grin on her face. Hanging up, she stated, "Well, believe it or not, you might be right."

"What? Right about what?"

"He called," Daryl rambled excitedly. "I don't know how he got my number, but he did, and he called."

"Who?" Margo's eyes opened wider. "You don't mean Sheldon?"

Daryl nodded.

"Sheldon Turner called you?" She wore a skeptical expression on her face. "I don't believe it."

"You want to hear for yourself?"

"No, it's not that serious." Margo was quiet for a moment.

"Well, I guess he's interested in you. He usually likes the woman to do the chasing." She gestured toward the phone. "You want to call him back?"

Daryl shook her head. "No, I'm going to let him stew for a little bit. I'll call him when I get home."

Margo peered down at her watch. "Where is Audrey? She was supposed to be here by now."

Daryl laughed. "Why don't you try Tyrell's apartment?"

"You don't think?"

Nodding, Daryl said, "Oh yeah I do. I think Miss Thang stayed over there last night. I bet she's spending the day with him."

"You really think she drove back to L.A. last night?"

She nodded.

Grinning, Margo asked, "Think I should call?"

Daryl nodded, a mischievous glint in her eye. "Yeah." She giggled as she watched Margo dial Tyrell's number.

"Happy New Year, Tyrell." She winked at Daryl. "Oh, and tell Audrey that Daryl and I wish her a Happy New Year, too." She nodded. "Yes, put that sneaky heifer on the phone."

Margo laughed when Audrey came to the phone. "You think you're slick, don't you? What did you do—drive all the way back into Los Angeles?" She paused. "He did what? He sent a limo for you? Mmmmm . . ."

Daryl was no longer listening to Margo's conversation with Audrey. Sheldon called. She could hardly believe it. Somehow he'd gotten her number and called.

". . . Well, okay, I'll tell Daryl. Have fun." Margo hung up the phone. "It's just you and me. Audrey's going to spend the evening with Tyrell."

Daryl smiled. "I guess those two really hit it off."

Margo nodded. "Well, why don't you and I carry our lonely butts into the den and watch a movie?"

"Speak for yourself. I'm not lonely."

Margo surveyed her for a moment. "Yeah, right. I bet right now you'd rather be watching a movie with Sheldon than with me."

"And you'd rather be with Rob," Daryl countered.

Putting her arm through Daryl's, Margo grinned before murmuring, "Happy New Year, girlfriend."

That evening, as soon as Daryl walked through the door, she headed straight to the phone. She quickly dialed the number Sheldon had left on her answering machine. When she heard a woman pick up, she froze, until she realized it had to be his mother. Inwardly, she sighed. He wasn't home. Her first instinct was not to leave a message, but she did so anyway, all the while trying to keep the excitement out of her voice.

He had called her. That meant something. Daryl forced herself to be reasonable. It really didn't mean anything at this point. She could not afford to lose her heart to a man with a reputation of being a womanizer. Yet she sensed something else in him. She wasn't sure what it was, but over time, she planned to find out.

Chapter 3

It was after midnight when Sheldon strode quietly through his childhood home, not wanting to disturb his mother. Earlier today, he'd accepted an invitation to join some friends for a couple of drinks.

Standing alone in the middle of his bedroom, Sheldon shook his head as he removed his black leather jacket. Why in the hell did I agree to move back? But he knew why. His father had died eight months ago, and he didn't like the idea of his mother living all alone in this big house—especially with her diabetes. His brother lived in West Covina, a few miles outside of Los Angeles, but Barry and their mother fought constantly. So he'd decided to play the good son and move back to Los Angeles.

Removing his black and white striped shirt, he sank down on the down-filled comforter and removed his black boots. All evening, he'd been forced to lay to rest all the rumors that still circulated about him. Why wouldn't the press just leave him alone? Sheldon's thoughts slipped back to the conversations he'd overheard. *Let's see, so far I've fathered seven children from seven different women.* Somebody had heard that he'd retired because he was infected with the

AIDS virus. He shook his head in disbelief. *Where did people come up with all this stuff?*

Standing up and taking off his black jeans, Sheldon ambled over to a huge pine dresser, retrieving a pair of burgundy silk pajamas. Grabbing a silk navy-colored robe, he padded barefoot down the hall to the bathroom.

After returning to his room twenty minutes later, Sheldon was about to turn down his bed, when he spied the note his mother had left him. Picking it up, he read quickly. Daryl had called him back. He knew she would.

There had been no doubt in his mind that she would call him back. However, he'd surprised himself by phoning her in the first place. Women were usually the aggressors when dealing with him. Daryl was different. In her, he sensed a kindred spirit. Smiling, Sheldon wondered what would come of the attraction between them. She didn't strike him as a clinging female, so perhaps they could enjoy each other without all the complications and demands of a serious relationship.

"Did you have a good New Year's Day, Dr. Larsen?" A young male greeted her as she entered the brightly lit gray and white contrasting room.

"Yes, I did, actually." Daryl adjusted the microphone attached to the front of her pale blue surgical scrubs. Following Curtis, her assistant, around the autopsy room, she said, "I spent the day with a good friend. How about yourself?"

"It was okay. I spent the day with my family." Curtis wiped a lock of sun-bleached hair away from his face. "Long day though. I'm glad the holidays are over. Now we can all get back to some sort of normal life."

She gave a light chuckle. "I'm glad Christmas is over, but I've always liked New Year's. It's a new beginning, filled with hope, love, and prosperity. A new year gives us another chance at getting older and growing wiser."

Curtis grinned as he snapped on a pair of white latex

gloves. "That's a good way of looking at it. But then again, you're always so upbeat and positive."

"You have to be. Being depressed and negative doesn't void the problems—they're still there. Might as well grab your happiness wherever you can. And each new day gives us one more chance to achieve our dreams."

Beneath bright overhead lights blazing down, Daryl slipped on a pair of sterile gloves, then picked up the chart, and started to dictate.

"This is case number LA781–29, Clara Bailey. The body is that of a sixty-eight year old female . . ." After giving a thorough description of length, weight, hair, and eye color, she put the chart down and moved beside the body.

"Rigor mortis is present in the extremities," Curtis observed. They worked quickly, because they had several bodies waiting.

That evening, Daryl strolled into her apartment achy and exhausted. Wearily she took off her clothes and padded nakedly across the floor of her bedroom, heading to the shower. A sigh of pleasure escaped her lips as the hot, soothing water relaxed her tired muscles. Just as she stepped out of the tub, her phone rang. Thinking it might be Sheldon, she ran across the room. On the fourth ring, she picked up. To her delight, she heard Sheldon's deep baritone voice.

"I wondered if I was ever going to talk to you."

She felt a warm glow flow through her as she heard his voice. "Hi, Sheldon. It's good to hear your voice. But how did you get my number?"

He gave a deep chuckle. "You don't expect me to reveal my sources, do you?"

Shivering slightly, Daryl sat on the edge of her bed and wrapped herself within the dry warmth of her comforter, not caring about the water that streamed down her body to the bed. "Yeah, I do."

"Tyrell gave it to me. I hope you don't mind?"

Satisfaction pursed her mouth. "Would it matter if I did?"

"Yes."

Daryl sensed the uncertainty in his voice. Suddenly the man that seemed so confident no longer seemed certain and it thrilled her. "I'm glad you called."

"Really? I have to tell you that I thought after that night you probably wouldn't want to be within five feet of me."

"Why?" She wanted to know. "You mean because of all the rumors?"

"I figured you'd heard them. And I'm sure Margo had a lot to say."

He suddenly sounded aloof. "Are they true?" Daryl asked softly.

"No."

"Then that's all I need to know."

"You mean you aren't even the least bit curious? And I know Margo's not happy with you talking to me."

"Margo and I are very close, but we don't tell each other how to live our lives. We can give each other advice, but it's up to us as individuals whether or not we choose to heed the warnings. I tend not to listen to rumors."

"So then, it doesn't bother you to hear that I've got scores of children around the world?" he teased.

"Do you?" Her fingers tensed in her lap.

"No."

"You don't have any children?"

"None."

"How can you be so sure?" Daryl teased.

"Because I always use protection."

"So these women just make these things up?"

"I guess so. I've always offered to take a paternity test, but they never show up. If I had a child, I'd make sure it was taken care of. As for as the women, I guess it's a money issue—I don't really know."

"I guess it's because you're in the limelight—it makes you more of a prime target."

"I suppose. I hate feeling like I'm living in a glass bowl though."

She was a bit surprised by Sheldon's admission. "I would think you'd be used to it by now."

"Are you into sports?"

Daryl shook her head. "No. I don't like sports of any kind. Sorry. But even though I don't follow sports, I've heard a lot about you. I know that you played pro ball for an ungodly amount of money until retiring last year. And now you're doing what?"

Sheldon could feel the warmth of her smile over the phone. Her perfectly shaped lips—soft, full, inviting—drew a man's undivided attention. He could see them clearly in his mind, curved up at the corners as she smiled.

He laughed. "I'm thinking about starting a program for fathers and sons. I don't think our youth should grow up looking to just sports figures or any other celebrity as role models. I think they should look to the men in their families. I'm hoping I can convince my brother to join me in this venture."

"That sounds like a wonderful idea. I think it'll be great for the children. And the men in their lives. I think we sometimes let our problems and jobs get in the way of what's really important—family."

"I agree. Daryl, do you have any children?"

"No, but I want them. As many as I can afford. How about you? Do you plan on having any?"

"Not anytime soon."

"Not ready to settle down, huh?"

"So, what do you do for a living, Daryl?"

This time she laughed. She hadn't really expected him to respond to her question. "Tyrell didn't tell you?"

"No."

Amusement pursed her mouth. "I'm surprised."

"Well, what do you do?" Sheldon pressed on, as if needing to find out.

"I'm a medical examiner."

"What? Did I hear you correctly? A medical examiner?"

Daryl giggled. "You heard right."

"That's some job."

"Well, it's never boring."

"How can you handle being around so much death?"

"It's something I've always been around. My father owned a funeral home in Moreno Valley and now my mother runs it. However, I must admit that I have a hard time when I have to pick up children. Sometimes, it's a struggle to keep from getting too emotional." She paused for a moment. "Have I freaked you out yet?"

Sheldon chuckled. "No, you haven't. I've just never met anyone in your line of work."

"Well, if it makes you feel better, I've never met anyone in your line of work either." She could hear him laughing on the other end. His laughter warmed her.

"I guess we're even then."

There was a momentary lapse in their conversation. Searching for something to say, Daryl reiterated, "I'm really glad you called."

"I am, too. I would like to see you again, if that's possible."

"I'm free for lunch tomorrow," she offered.

"What time should I pick you up?"

Tapping her fingers on the night stand, she thought about this for a second. "Why don't we meet somewhere? There's a Coco's nearby. They serve a variety of entrees— pasta, meatloaf, and sandwiches. We can meet there, say one o'clock?"

"Sounds good. Give me directions."

Daryl quickly gave him the directions. "I'll see you tomorrow. Right now, I'd better go. I rushed out of the shower without a towel when I heard the phone ringing."

Sheldon's sharp intake of breath made her smile.

He cleared his throat noisily. "Wouldn't do to have you dripping water everywhere."

Daryl grinned. "No, it wouldn't. I'll see you tomorrow." She hung up the phone smiling. "Shame on you, girl-friend," she whispered while toweling her body. "Getting him all worked up."

The sound of his voice did things to her. She could feel

the sexual magnetism that made him so self-confident. Daryl wondered if he could hear her heart pounding over the phone.

The picture Daryl painted in Sheldon's mind left him breathless, and he tried to hide his state of arousal, should his mother venture into the den. Visualizing the water glistening on her sweet skin sent tremors echoing through his body. The heat of desire rose in him quickly, causing his heart to thud loudly within him. Sheldon tried to wrench himself away from his preoccupation with Daryl's naked body, but he couldn't. He imagined her soft in his arms and responsive in ways that would drive him wild. Right now, Sheldon was beside himself with want.

Calling her to mind, he marveled at the soft, satiny texture of her skin. He knew Daryl would feel as good as she looked. Sheldon had seen breathtaking women in his time, but Daryl possessed an unrivaled beauty. She had it all—silky flesh, perfect features, a refined bone structure, and a glossy head of hair. He was enraptured by the vision of her in his mind.

Standing up, he strolled out of his room and down the hallway, careful not to disturb his mother. Noticing the light coming from under her door, he wasn't at all surprised to find Maggie still awake. Ever since he'd moved back home, he had noticed she kept late hours reading or knitting.

In the bathroom, he turned the cold water on full blast. After removing his clothes, he stepped beneath the freezing spray of water, welcoming the cold and painful comfort, in an attempt to cool his ardor. However, the cold shower did very little to lessen the hardness that thoughts of Daryl had aroused.

A full fifteen minutes later, he towel-dried his shivering body. A still-frustrated Sheldon walked quietly back to his room, then climbed into bed. Using a remote control, he flipped through the channels on television. There was nothing on TV that interested him, so he clicked it off. Sheldon turned off the light and closed his eyes. Fleeting images of Daryl crept into his head now and again, but he forced them away. Two hours later, still unable to sleep, he spitefully hoped Daryl was having a hard time falling asleep also.

The next day, Daryl yawned as she pulled into the restaurant parking lot. She was tired. It was all those sexy thoughts of Sheldon that had kept her awake most of the night. His was a face that God had lovingly created. His features weren't haphazardly plastered on his face; they were carved and etched by a sculptor. The word *handsome* seemed sadly lacking in description. Daryl acknowledged that she was fiercely attracted to the man.

Daryl had dreamed of his muscular body brushing against hers, the sensuous feel of his sinewy arms wrapped around her bare legs sending tumultuous waves of shock undulating through every fiber of her being. She felt the heat rise to her cheeks as she recalled the vivid dreams of her kissing his virile and smoothly-muscled body. The sexy way he moaned as she lovingly tantalized him with her tongue . . .

She shook her head. "I've got to stop thinking like this," she whispered. "It's not just about sex." Daryl couldn't remember the last time she'd been with a man. It must have been what? Six years now. Yes, she acknowledged. It's been six long years, but well worth it, she thought.

Just as she stepped out of her car, Sheldon was there. She colored slightly over her aroused state, and swallowed tightly before speaking. "Sheldon, hi."

An escaping reddish-brown curl fell over her forehead. Her hair was a mass of spiral-curled tendrils, clustered around her lightly made up face.

His gaze roved and lazily appraised her body. Returning his eyes to her face, Sheldon's expression beamed approval of her ecru-colored blouse and matching ankle length skirt worn underneath a navy blazer.

"It's good to see you again, Doc."

"You, too. Thanks for inviting me to lunch. How long have you been waiting?"

"I pulled up right before you did."

She looked up into his eyes.

Grinning, Sheldon grabbed her by the hand, leading her into the busy restaurant. They were seated in a booth by a picturesque window near the back of the dining area.

She glanced out, marveling over the colorful parade of cars that swam past the restaurant. When the waitress approached to take their orders, she turned her attention back to Sheldon and found him watching her. After giving the waitress her order, she asked Sheldon, "Did you have any trouble getting here?"

"He shook his head. "Your directions were easy to follow. Thank you."

"It was no problem."

He leaned back, assessing her with his eyes. "A medical examiner," he murmured in amazement. "You really have an interesting career, Daryl."

"Does it bother you?"

"What?"

"That I'm a medical examiner?"

Sheldon shook his head. "No, it doesn't bother me. I guess I'm just surprised that someone so upbeat could work in a place so depressing. I'm sure you've seen some horrors."

"Too many," she agreed. "But it's what I wanted to do."

"So, doesn't it get to you sometimes?"

"I guess it's in the way you look at it. "The dead, no matter how tragic the circumstances that caused their deaths, are really the fortunate ones. I tend to believe that it's comforting to know that they will never know pain, hurt, worry, or anything ever again. They can finally rest. No more bills to worry about—"

"But they won't ever know love or happiness either," he countered.

"That's why we should strive to be happy in life. We only get this one chance. Death is forever—life is not."

Sheldon took a sip of water. "Have you ever lost someone close to you, Daryl?"

She nodded. "Yes. My father died a year ago. And I won't lie to you. It hurt like hell. I was very close to him."

"I lost my father eight months ago. He had lung cancer. I hated seeing him in all that pain. I imagine death was certainly a welcomed release for him."

"My father died in a car accident. I'm a lot like him. He spent so much time around death, he made a point of living his life to the fullest. I thought my mother would just deteriorate after he died; instead she really surprised me. She's still out there doing all the same things she did before. Only now, she's running the funeral home, where before, she basically stayed away from the business. She does a wonderful job, too. My dad would be proud."

"With my mother's diabetes, she has her good days and her bad ones. She misses Dad a lot. That's why I moved back here."

Daryl slowly sipped her soda through a straw. Putting it down, she asked, "Your brother's name is Barry, right?"

Stuffing a single french fry into a pool of ketchup, Sheldon nodded. "Yes. Do you know him?"

She shook her head thoughtfully. "I don't think so, but I have a cousin who dated him in high school. Her name is Renee Cody."

He nodded. "I know Renee. How is she?"

"She's fine. Renee is a psychologist in Chino Hills."

"Really? Boy, I haven't seen her in years. I sure thought Barry was going to end up marrying her."

"She thought so, too. But when he got hurt, he just shut down. She said that he asked her for some space, and then she never heard from him again."

"He shut out everyone, including me."

"I take it that you two are not very close."

"We barely speak to each other."

"Are you going to try to repair your relationship?" Daryl bit into her sandwich. "You should, you know."

Sheldon stabbed his hamburger, attempting to cut it in half. "Believe me, I want to, Daryl. I'm not mad at him."

"Then don't give up on your brother. I've always wished that I had a brother or sister. I hated being an only child."

"You can have mine."

Daryl laughed. "You know you don't mean that."

"No, I don't. I love Barry. He's my big brother and we were very close at one time. I don't know what happened."

"Well, try to get him to open up to you."

"I guess it's worth a shot. I just don't know what his problem is." Sheldon stared at her, baffled. "I don't know what I did."

"It's possible you didn't do anything. Maybe it's your brother—not you. Have you considered that possibility?"

Sheldon shrugged. "Enough about my brother. I want to know something. Why did I have to get your phone number from Ty?"

Daryl rested her chin on her hand, a bemused smile on her lips. "Because you'd collected quite a few numbers that night. I figured you didn't need mine."

"Yours was the only number I asked for," he pointed out. "That's the one I wanted."

"Look around the room, Sheldon. Women are drooling over you." She let out a soft giggle. "Even some of the men are giving you the eye."

Sheldon shook his head laughing before sobering up. "But you know something? None of these people would give me another look if I hadn't played pro ball."

"Oh, I don't know about that."

"Besides, I don't see you lacking. Those two guys over there haven't taken their eyes off you yet. For that matter, neither have I."

"Sheldon—" Out of the corner of her eye, Daryl caught sight of a heavy-set girl walking briskly in their direction.

"Sheldon? Oh my God! It is you!"

Daryl leaned over toward Sheldon. "Is she a friend of yours?"

"She looks real famil—"

"Sheldon, how are you?"

"I'm fine. Do I know you?"

"You don't remember me? Aw, don't tell me that. My name is Clare Daniels. I'm Mike Roberts's cousin. I met you in Atlanta."

"Oh, that's right. It's been a long time."

"Yeah, and I was a lot bigger than. That's probably why you didn't recognize me."

"It's good seeing you."

Daryl bit back a smile when, without asking, Clare slid into the booth, seating herself next to Sheldon.

"Mike said you retired last year. Why'd you do that?"

"I felt it was the right thing for me to do."

"I'm gonna miss seeing you out there. You are one of my favorite basketball players."

"Clare, this is my friend, Daryl Larsen."

"Hey, Daryl. Sheldon and I go way back. We used to have some good times together, hanging with my cousin." She turned her full attention back to Sheldon.

Daryl smiled.

"We should get together sometime. Have dinner or something. Like the good ol' days."

"I . . ."

"Mike will be in town this weekend. Why don't the three of us do something?"

"Er . . . Daryl and I already have plans." He looked over to Daryl for confirmation. He let out a relieved breath when she nodded.

Clare pouted for a minute or so. Shrugging, she said, "Well, it's good seeing you." She hastily wrote down a number. "Here is my phone number. Give me a call sometime."

"You, too." When Clare strolled away, Sheldon said, "I'm so sorry, Daryl. I thought she'd never leave."

"So the three of you were great friends, huh?"

Sheldon chuckled and shook his head. "Mike and I are good friends. Clare kind of invited herself along."

"I thought that might be the case. She struck me as the pushy type."

"Huh! I guarantee you if you were to look up the word pushy, you'll find her picture right there along with the definition."

Daryl threw back her head, laughing. "That's not very nice."

"And she wasn't nice, being rude to you like that."

Daryl waved her hand in dismissal. "She didn't bother me."

"You're not easily intimidated by other women, I see."

"Why should I be? I know exactly who I am and what I want."

"I'm impressed. I've never met anyone like you."

Daryl sat up and leaned toward him. "That's because you've been hanging around with the wrong crowd."

All through lunch, Sheldon was distracted by the tantalizing picture Daryl represented. Her scarlet lips, slightly parted, were full and generous, turning up at the corners in a perpetual smile. He visually traced the shape of her mouth with his eyes. A smile played across his lips as he recalled what hers felt like against his own. When Daryl's tongue flicked out to drag along her sensual lips in an effort to moisten their lushness, fevered desire raged through him, causing him to look away.

"Are you okay?" Daryl's voice traveled to him. "Don't you like your food?"

"Yes, it's fine," he mumbled hoarsely.

"You're sure? You barely touched it." Gesturing with her fork, she said, "You cut up your burger so much, it looks like finger sandwiches."

Sheldon watched beneath hooded lids as Daryl drew back to study him, her questioning expression uncertain. "I . . . um, had something on my mind. I'm fine. Really."

Daryl stuck a fork full of fruit into her mouth. "I suppose I have to take your word for it, don't I?"

"Yes." Smiling, he reached over, covering her hand with his. "I'm really not that hungry. I just wanted to see you."

Daryl returned his smile while gently slipping her hand from his. Sheldon pretended not to notice. He knew she was being cautious, but he didn't mind. Reaching up, he wiped a hand over his chin and leaned back in his chair. "What do you do to have fun?"

Daryl daintily dabbed at her mouth with her napkin. "Well, this is probably going to sound so corny, but it's something I really like to do."

Sheldon leaned in closer. "Come on, tell me. You've intrigued me."

"I like Clue. I really love all types of detective games, but Clue is my absolute favorite."

Sheldon couldn't hide his astonishment. "You're kidding."

Folding her hands across her bosom, Daryl glared at him. "I'm very serious."

He knew she'd misinterpreted his reaction. "Don't get me wrong. I mean, I like playing Clue myself. I have the board game, the Sega Genesis version, and a computer version."

It was Daryl's turn to be surprised. "Really?"

Sheldon nodded. "We've got to get together and play a few rounds."

"Do you really play Clue or are you just telling me this?"

He nodded and laughed. "I really play. Honest."

"Are you any good?"

"I think so."

Daryl was gorgeous by anyone's standards. Although she had a body that would stop a train on a dime, there was something else that Sheldon found captivating. Something in her incredible camel-colored eyes spoke of vitality and hinted at an incredible zest for living.

As they walked side by side to her car, Sheldon put his

hand on her shoulder in a possessive gesture. "I want you to know I really enjoyed myself."

"I did, too."

"So, what do you think? Am I as bad as what everyone is saying?"

"I don't listen to rumors. You shouldn't either."

Sheldon watched as Daryl gracefully slid into her car, her skirt inching up to reveal a sleek, hosiery-clad leg. When she drove away, Sheldon fanned himself as he headed to his car.

Chapter 4

"Is Mama there?" Barry asked as soon as Sheldon answered the phone. Sucking his index finger, he winced in pain. He'd dropped the knife beside a puddle of freshly sliced mushrooms, when he reached for the phone. "Barry? Hey, Man, I've been trying to reach you."

"I need to speak to Mama," Barry insisted.

"It's nice talking to you, too," Sheldon said sarcastically, his dark brows drawing together in a frown.

"Would you please put Mama on the phone?"

Swallowing his anguish, Sheldon turned and handed the phone to Maggie. "It's Barry." He couldn't fathom what he'd done to make his brother hate him so much. Sheldon left the kitchen, his stride purposeful, but not before he heard Maggie chiding her older son for his actions. Although his mother was trying to help, he knew she would only cause the gap to widen farther.

Up in his bedroom, Sheldon found a Band-Aid for his bleeding finger. Figuring that Maggie was still on the phone with Barry, he lay down on the bed, stretching out to his full length. Just as he closed his tired eyes, Sheldon heard his mother shouting for him to pick up the extension in his room.

"Hello," he mumbled into the phone. His eyebrows rose in surprise to find that Barry was still on the line. "Oh, sorry," he said quickly. "I thought Mama was off the phone."

"She is. I wanted to talk to you."

His left eyebrow rose a fraction. "You want to talk to me?" Sheldon asked, the disbelief evident in his tone.

"I-I'm real sorry bout the way I acted. I've been having a hard time lately."

Sheldon sat up, hanging his long, lean legs over the edge of the bed. "No problem, Bro. Anything I can help you with?"

"No. I'll work it out."

"I was hoping we could go out to dinner one night soon." He hesitated for a moment. "I want to talk to you about something."

Barry was quiet. Sheldon supposed he was giving the matter some thought.

"Yeah, . . . I guess we can do that."

Raising his eyes heavenward, Sheldon gave silent thanks for that small triumph. "What are you doing next Wednesday night?"

"I don't have anything planned."

"We can go to El Torito's." Sheldon said the words tentatively. He wasn't sure how Barry would respond. "That's still your favorite restaurant, right?"

Barry gave a small chuckle. "Yeah."

"Around eight?"

"I'll see you then." Barry cleared his throat. "Well, I'd better go. I have some things I need to take care of."

"Later, Bro." Sheldon had barely hung up the phone when it rang again. Thinking it was Barry, he answered it. Sheldon frowned when he recognized the syrupy voice of his caller. "Malle, how are you?"

"I'm missing you dreadfully. Do you miss me?"

Her sickeningly sweet voice grated on him. Sheldon

rolled his eyes. "How was your New Year's Eve party?" he asked instead of answering her.

"Empty without you. I wish you'd stayed with me until after the new year. I even thought you'd at least call me on New Year's Eve, but you didn't. I called you New Year's Day, and you never called me back," she accused.

"I've been busy." Sheldon lay back against the soft pillows, inhaling the delicate powder-fresh scent of the fabric softener his mother used.

"You don't seem busy now. Were you planning to call me back at all?"

"I would've called when I had a moment."

"I have a surprise for you," Malle cooed sweetly.

"And what's that?"

"I'm coming to Los Angeles. Aren't you thrilled?"

Sheldon shot straight up in the bed. "What?"

"I'm coming to Los Angeles the first week in February. Can you pick me up from the airport?"

Sheldon massaged his temple with his right hand. "Why are you coming here?" He hoped she was flying out because of a modeling assignment.

"Because I love you, Sheldon, and I miss you."

"It's not going to work, Malle," he insisted with returning impatience. "I thought I explained that before I left New York."

"How can you just walk out on us?"

"I told you from the beginning I wasn't ready for a committed relationship." His lips puckered with annoyance.

"That's not what your actions said," she countered. "Sheldon, I hope you'll be there to pick me up. We'll be able to talk face to face. Besides, I'll need a place to stay."

"I'm not bringing you to my mother's house. Get a hotel somewhere."

"Please, Sheldon," Malle begged. "I'm coming all this way to see you."

"And I'm telling you to stay in New York, but you're not listening."

"Sheldon, please . . ."

"I'll be there," he whispered harshly, as he reached for a pen and a piece of paper. "Give me the flight information."

"I come in on TWA, flight 524. It arrives at six-thirty in the evening."

He shook his head. "I don't know why you're coming here, Malle. This—"

"I'll see you in a couple of weeks, Sheldon," she interrupted. Then she hung up. Exasperated, he slammed the phone down.

After taking several deep breaths, Sheldon felt somewhat calmer. He pushed himself off the bed and headed back down the stairs to join his mother in the kitchen. He eased up beside Maggie, opening the oven door for her. "I'll get that for you."

"Is your finger okay, son?" she asked. "Looks like you had a deep cut."

"It's fine."

Wiping her hands on her green and white apron, his mother stirred her vegetables once more. Turning to face Sheldon, Maggie assessed her son. "Did everything go okay with Barry? I notice you didn't stay on the phone very long with him."

"As well as can be expected, Mama."

"It's not right—the way he's treating you. It's not your fault." Maggie cleared her throat, making a disapproving sound. "I blame your father. He's the one that caused all this mess."

Sheldon touched his mother's arm to halt her movement. "What are you talking about?"

"Your father always made Barry feel like he didn't matter. Leo treated him like he was invisible." She pointed a large spoon in his direction. "Now you, he doted on."

"Mama, he loved Barry—"

"I didn't say he didn't love his son, but he just didn't . . . treat him so well. He didn't know how to talk to Barry. Leo ended up doing more harm than anything." She turned away and muttered, "Leo did more hurting than he did loving."

"Mama?"

"Huh?"

Her eyes suddenly looked tear bright. Sheldon engulfed her in his arms. "I'm sorry for—"

Maggie waved away his apology. "Son, there's nothing for you to be sorry about. It's not like there was anything you could have done."

"Yes, there was. I could have paid more attention to you. If I had, I would have known he'd been beating you all those years. Did . . . did he ever tell you about our talk?"

Maggie's face twisted in confusion. "What talk?"

"I sat down with Dad a few years back and told him that if he ever laid another hand on you, I would throw him out of the house personally, and I'd stop supporting him. I told him that I'd call the police myself if he touched you again."

Dropping the sauce pan she'd been holding, his mother's body went rigid with shock—or was it anger? Sheldon couldn't be sure.

"Sheldon! How could you say something like that to your father? How could you do it."

"Mama, hear me out. I hated hearing him yell at you for every little thing. I hated catching him with that other woman. I hated him for hitting you most of all."

"You're talking about your father."

"I know, Mama."

His mother raised her hands in resignation. "Leo . . . he didn't mean no harm, son. He tried to be a good husband, but he was the only way he knew to be. It's what he saw his father do. Look at your grandfather—he's nearly a cripple, but he's still trying to chase skirt tails. It's in their blood."

Sheldon's lips twisted into a cynical smile. "And you wonder why Barry and I aren't interested in getting married? What I can't understand is why you put up with it all."

"It's a cross I had to bear, son. We all have 'em."

"But then Dad got sick."

Maggie nodded. "He was once again the man I married when he found out he had cancer. Lord, I remember the day." She shook her head at the memory. "He came home and cried like a baby. Sheldon, he fell to his knees and begged my forgiveness for everything he'd ever done to me."

He was momentarily speechless. "I didn't know . . ."

She nodded. "Sheldon, remember the good things about your father. He was never too busy for his boys. He taught you and your brother how to play basketball, baseball—even golf."

"I know. But then when Barry was about twelve or thirteen, things changed between them."

"Try not to think unkind things about Leo. He was your father and he's gone now. Let him rest in peace. I keep trying to tell Barry the same thing but . . ."

Sheldon reached over and wiped away a lone tear rolling down his mother's face. "You are one in a million, Mama. If I could find a woman like you—I'd marry her tomorrow."

Daryl strolled into her office and found a message on her desk from Sheldon. She hadn't heard from him all week, and she'd been determined not to call him first. She didn't want to give him the impression she would chase after him.

Pressing the pink sheet of paper to her bosom, she closed her door. After dropping down in her chair, Daryl quickly dialed his number. She wasn't surprised this time when his mother answered. She smiled into the phone.

"Hello, Mrs. Turner. This is Daryl Larsen. Is Sheldon home?"

"Hi, Daryl. He ran out to his car for a minute. Can you hold on?"

"Yes ma'am, I can. How were your holidays?"

"Very nice. I have to tell you, though. I'm glad they're over. I'm worn out."

Daryl laughed gently. "I know what you mean."

"Did you enjoy yours?"

"Yes ma'am. I spent Christmas with my mother. We went to Philadelphia."

"How nice. Is that where you're from?"

"My mother grew up there and most of her family still lives there. I was born out here in Los Angeles."

"Oh, I see. I have some relatives in Norristown."

"Really? Have you ever been there?"

"Oh yes. I used to visit almost every summer up until three years ago. My late husband became real sick you know."

"Sheldon told me he passed away eight months ago."

Maggie sighed. "Yes, he did. I miss him so much, but I'm grateful to have Sheldon home again. I don't feel so lonely now."

"I understand. That's why I try to spend as much time with my mother as I can. She manages to stay busy though, so I practically have to schedule an appointment with her."

Maggie chuckled. "Here's Sheldon. It's been great talking to you."

"You, too, Mrs. Turner." Daryl smiled to herself upon hearing his baritone voice.

"So, what were you two talking about?"

"We weren't talking about you, if that's what you're thinking," Daryl murmured, half laughing.

"I'm wounded."

She laughed. "I'm sorry I'm just getting back to you. I've been in meetings all morning, and I had to go over to UCLA to give a lecture."

"You're a very busy lady."

"Not always."

"That's good to hear. I called to see if you're free tonight. I would like to have dinner with you."

Daryl smiled in sheer joy. "As it happens, I am free this evening."

"Good. How about seven-thirty?"

She checked her watch. "That's fine. Oh, Sheldon, where are we having dinner? I didn't bring a change of clothes—"

"I figured I'd drive out to Pomona. We can eat out there. I'll let you decide where we're going since I haven't been out there in a long time."

"Why don't I make us dinner?" Daryl suggested shyly.

"Are you sure?"

"Yes, I'm sure. It gives me a chance to show off my cooking skills."

Sheldon's laughter floated up from his throat. "Should I bring anything?"

"Just a healthy appetite."

"I'll see you later."

Daryl practically floated through the rest of the day. On her way home, she stopped by the grocery store to pick up a pint of spinach dip.

As soon as she'd showered and changed, Daryl set the table, using the antique china her mother had given her.

She'd just turned off the chicken cacciatore when the doorbell rang. Checking herself in a beveled mirror that hung in the foyer, Daryl was satisfied with the way her magenta dress flattered her figure. Combing through the mass of curls once more, she took a deep breath and opened the door. "You're very prompt."

Sheldon leaned down, planting a kiss on her cheek. "I wanted to make a good impression." He checked her out from head to toe. "You look good, Doc. I like that color on you."

Running her finger down her slip dress, she moved aside to let him enter.

"Come in. Make yourself comfortable." As he strolled past, she admired his burgundy twill pants and the ivory collarless shirt he wore. "You look pretty nice yourself."

"Why thank you, Doc." He held up two bottles. "I brought wine. Red and white."

"Thank you." She relieved him of the Cabernet Sauvignon and the California Johannesburg Riesling. "I made chicken in a red wine sauce, so we'll have the Cabernet tonight. We'll have the Riesling another night."

As she strolled to the kitchen, Daryl yelled back, "Have a seat. I'll be right back." She returned carrying a tray of spinach dip, toast triangles, and petite cheese and bacon quiche.

Surrounded by the smooth sounds of jazz flowing around them, they made themselves comfortable in her living room.

"So you made spinach dip. How did you know it's a favorite of mine?"

"I didn't know. It's one of *my* favorites. I wasn't sure you'd like it, that's why I made the quiche appetizers."

He took a bite, closing his eyes as if to savor the taste. "This is really good."

"I can't take the credit for it. It's store bought. Mine doesn't ever come out this good. I don't know what I do wrong."

"Do you put minced garlic, fresh dill, cream cheese, and a dash of basil in yours?"

"No, I just use minced onion, cream cheese, salt, and a dash of pepper."

"My mom adds bacon bits to hers."

"Really? I'll have to try both your recipe and your mother's."

Glancing around the room, Sheldon acknowledged, "You have a really nice place here."

Her eyes darted from wall to wall, admiring her handiwork. The soft lighting from the candles and the fireplace bathed the room in a warm glow. "I'm proud of it." Daryl stood up. "Dinner should be ready. Why don't we head to the table?"

Sheldon followed Daryl into the kitchen. She turned abruptly, practically bumping into him. "You're supposed to be sitting at the table."

"I thought I'd help you."

"You don't have to do that, Sheldon. You're my guest."

"I want to. I'll bring the plates in there. That way you don't have to bring the food to the table. Don't work that hard for me."

She stopped, looking up at him. "You really amaze me."

Grinning, Sheldon asked, "Do I?"

"Yes, you do. I like this side of you."

After they were seated at the dinner table, Daryl closed her eyes as Sheldon whispered a prayer of thanks. She waited for him to stick the heaping fork of chicken into his mouth.

"How is it?"

He chewed thoughtfully.

"Well?"

Sheldon laughed. "It's very good."

He said it so simply, so guilelessly, that it touched Daryl deeply.

"You're a very good cook."

After they finished dinner, Daryl brought out a Boston creme pie. "I hope you left room for dessert."

"I always have space left for something sweet."

She watched as Sheldon tore into his slice. He ate with such relish that it was obvious to her he had a sweet tooth. Daryl was secretly thrilled to find he enjoyed her culinary skills. It wouldn't do to have her future husband hate her cooking, she mused silently.

The light from the glowing embers in the fireplace touched her delicate profile, highlighting the gentle rise and fall of her breasts.

"Dinner was wonderful. Daryl, I really liked the chicken." Tenderly, Sheldon reached down to trace her elegant features. "You know, from the moment we met, I knew we were connected somehow . . ."

"Are we?"

"Mmmm . . . most definitely." Reaching out, Sheldon touched her cheek, then took a lock of her vibrant hair in his fingers, rubbing it softly between them.

He drew her hands over the broad expanse of his chest and settled them on his shoulders. Sheldon's head came deliberately toward hers. His questing tongue traced her soft mouth.

His mouth was strong, as was his chin. Daryl studied the neatness of his mustache. Sheldon's partially unbuttoned shirt revealed a neck as muscular as all the other parts of him. His hands caressed her neck, and his thumbs rested at her throat, causing ripples of excitement to shoot through her.

"You are so beautiful." His lips twisted into a smile.

She could not look away from his lips.

Sheldon loved the feel of her, the heat, the fragrant smell of her hair. Crushing Daryl against his chest, his arms enfolded her, molding her supple curves into his muscular contours.

Desire raised his unruly head, straining against it's chains of confinement, as his lips and hands took on a life of their own. Sheldon lost himself to the delicious taste of her lips. Deft fingers unbuttoned the front of her dress, revealing the lacy cups of her bra.

Before Sheldon realized it, he was pulling Daryl closer. His hands wandered of their own accord, opening the silken folds of her dress wider, discovering the titillating curves and swells of her body. Cupping her breasts, Sheldon lowered his head, kissing the top of each firm, ripe mound. Without shame, Daryl arched her back and lifted herself to him, letting him kiss each breast.

The red glow from the fire played provocatively across her skin, highlighting the sexy contours of her body.

She moaned softly as Sheldon tenderly kissed her throat and moved upward to her mouth. His lips moved slowly, but thoroughly, against hers. Daryl lost herself in his kiss. Sheldon cupped her breasts, placing his palms over their fullness. Her head lulled back in languid submission.

Somewhere in this fog of pleasure, she felt Sheldon's hand travel down to her thighs. He teasingly traced their inner contours, exploring further.

"Sheldon," she whispered against the curve of his shoulder. Her voice caressed him, touching him all over.

"Yes, Baby?"

She looked at him, her camel-colored eyes were dark with heat and longing, her breath coming out ragged in a single short cry. "I . . . I think we should slow down some."

"What's the matter?"

She stilled his hand. "I just want to take it a little slower."

Sheldon gave no argument when Daryl pulled back, looking into his eyes. He merely smiled and nodded his understanding.

"You're not upset, are you?"

He shook his head. "I'm disappointed, but I don't have a problem waiting." Kissing her once more on her full lips, he announced, "Because I know when the time is right, there won't be any stopping us."

His gaze heated Daryl's already flushed body, causing her to stand up suddenly. She needed to be as far away from him as possible right now. He was too intoxicating.

"Daryl?"

He was suddenly standing behind her. She turned to face him. "Yes, Sheldon?"

"Are you okay?"

She nodded. "I'm fine."

Sheldon smiled. "I guess it's time for me to head back to L.A. I really had a nice time tonight."

"I did, too. We're going to have to do it again sometime."

Nodding, he said, "Sometime real soon." Bending, Sheldon kissed her once more before walking in brisk strides to the door.

Daryl placed trembling fingers to her lips as she watched him leave.

* * *

Sheldon broke into a smile when his older brother saun-tered toward their table. "What's up with all this, Shel-don?" Barry gestured around the Mexican restaurant.

Sheldon took a sip of his frozen strawberry margarita before answering. "What do you mean?"

"What's with taking me to dinner? What did you want to talk about?"

A waiter came to take their orders for dinner. Sheldon ordered another round of margaritas.

"I've been thinking about a program designed to bring fathers and sons together. I want you to work with me. The program will be a partnership between us, the Los Angeles Department of Parks and Recreation, and the Los Angeles Housing Authority."

Putting his margarita glass back on the table, Barry leaned forward. "What?"

"I want this to be a joint venture between you and me."

Barry looked suspicious. "Why do you want me involved?"

"Because you're my brother. You're a good father—"

"Sheldon, let's get something straight. I don't need or want your pity."

"What?"

"Man, you're something else. Just because you got mil-lions playing ball, you don't need to feel like you've got to take care of your poor old brother. I invested the money I received as a signing bonus. I've got a nice little nest egg."

"That's not it at all. It's not about money. Damn, Barry. Can't you get it through your head, I miss you. I miss my big brother. What happened to us?"

Before Barry could reply, a young woman of about twenty walked over.

"I'm so sorry to interrupt, but I was wondering if I could have your autograph, Sheldon."

Glancing over at his brother, he saw something in Barry's eyes—something he couldn't identify. "I . . ."

"Please?"

"Sure." Sheldon quickly signed his name to a napkin.

"Thank you!" She practically skipped back over to her table, almost colliding with the waitress as she arrived with plates laden with chicken enchiladas, rice, and sweet corn-bread.

They ate their meals in silence.

After the empty plates were taken away, Sheldon slipped a credit card to the waiter. Leaning back in his chair, he scanned his brother's unreadable face. "Barry, would you please give my suggestion some thought?"

"I don't need your charity. I'm making it by myself."

"It's not pity or charity I'm offering. I just wanted us to do this together. Full partners."

"I have a few hundred thou. Not exactly the kind of money you're talking about."

"We would hold fundraisers to get help with the funding. I know some of the other ball players would—"

Barry shook his head. "I don't want to have anything to do with this venture. You and your rich pro-ballers can handle this all by yourselves. You don't need me."

Sheldon massaged his temple with his right hand. This wasn't going to be easy. "Why are you being so damn difficult?"

"Oh, so because I don't want to be a part of your little make-Sheldon-the-hero scheme, I'm being difficult. That's not it at all. I figure I don't have anything to bring to the game. You're the celebrity. Not me."

"Barry, I'm not trying to fight with you. We're brothers, man," he pleaded. "I want us to be boys. Like we used to."

"Things change for whatever reasons. You should know that." Standing up, he pushed his chair under the table. "Thanks for dinner."

He limped away, leaving a hurt Sheldon in his wake.

At home, Sheldon dropped his keys on the dresser. Tonight had been a failure. Right now, what he needed was to hear a friendly voice. Without a second thought, he picked up the phone and started to dial.

Downing the last of her hot tea, Daryl sat the cup and saucer down in the sink. The phone started to ring about the same time as she selected a book to read.

"Daryl, did I catch you at a bad time?"

She was mildly surprised to hear from Sheldon. "No, I was just about to catch up on some reading. What's wrong?"

"Nothing. I just needed to talk to you."

He spoke in an odd, yet resigned tone and it concerned her. "You sound kind of down. Did something happen?"

"I just had dinner with Barry."

"How did it go?"

"Not too well," he replied in a low, composed voice.

With the cordless phone glued to her ear, Daryl slid gracefully into a love seat. "What happened between the two of you?"

Sheldon's voice was barely above a whisper. "I really don't know. We used to be so close, but after he got hurt— he just seemed to distance himself from the family."

Shuffling around the plump pillows, Daryl settled back, making herself comfortable. "Give it some time. Just don't give up on him."

"He's been like this for a few years. I doubt if he's going to change any time soon."

"He will. Especially if you don't give up trying. So, you can't do that."

"Are you always so optimistic?"

Daryl laughed. "Yes. I always look for the positive in every situation."

"I'm not going to give up on Barry. I'm going to keep right on trying to get through to him. I miss him."

"I'm sure you do, but just wait and see—everything will work out. Your brother's going to come around."

"I don't know why, but when you say it, somehow I believe it'll really happen."

"It's called faith, Sheldon. And yes, I've got lots of it."

"Thank you, Daryl." He felt better just talking to her. Sheldon liked her optimism.

"What did I do?"

Sheldon heard genuine surprise in her voice and smiled. "You've given me hope."

"Just have faith in your brother."

"I do." Sheldon glanced over at the clock. Enough about my brother. I've bored you with my problems long enough—"

"Sheldon, you didn't bore me. I'm your friend. If you need to talk, I'm here."

He smiled. No woman had ever told him that and meant it, but in Daryl, Sheldon felt he'd found a real friend. "Same here. Now as I said, enough about Barry. I'm thinking about checking out a movie this weekend. Interested?"

Chapter 5

Sheldon and Daryl strolled out of the theater hand and hand, into the brisk Saturday night air, to Sheldon's car. Daryl pulled up the collar of her jacket around her neck. "That movie was wonderful. I really enjoyed it."

"I have to admit, it was better than I thought it would be." Sheldon wrapped his arm around her, pulling her close. "How about grabbing a bite to eat before you send me on my way?"

Daryl laughed. "Sure."

They drove to a nearby restaurant. Daryl sank down into a corner booth, glancing around. "BC Café. I've never been here, but this is a fantastic place. Have you been here before?"

"No. I heard about it from Ty. He talks about this place all the time. I think he and Audrey hang out here a lot."

A waitress took their orders.

Their main dishes arrived, and Daryl said grace before they began their dinner. Looking down at her plate, she murmured, "They sure give you a lot of food. I guess I'll be taking some of this home." With a quick smile, she dove into her western omelette.

Sheldon sliced off a piece of steak, stuffing it into his mouth. His lips were firm and inviting; they beckoned to her. Daryl watched as he chewed slowly and evenly before swallowing. Every now and then his tongue would dart out. Feeling a warmth from within, she felt flushed, and had to look away. She never figured watching someone eat could be such a sensual experience.

He impeded her thoughts by asking, "So what's on the agenda for the rest of the evening?"

"Huh? Oh, what do you have in mind?"

"I thought we could just go somewhere and relax . . ."

"Like back at my place?" she asked with a knowing grin.

"If you don't mind. I'm having such a great time with you. I don't want the evening to end just yet."

"I don't either," she admitted. "We can have coffee back at my house. Or something else if you prefer." When she realized what she'd inadvertently implied, Daryl gave an embarrassed laugh. "I didn't mean . . ."

Sheldon cracked up with laughter. "Don't worry, Doc. I know what you meant."

Back at Daryl's house, they made themselves comfortable in her den. While they talked above the soft jazzy tunes that played in the background, Daryl noticed Sheldon rubbing his neck. Concern crossed her face, because she recalled him doing the same thing several times in the theater and again in the restaurant. She also noticed that he seemed to be uncomfortable. "Are you okay, Sheldon?"

He grimaced slightly. "My neck and my back are acting up. I go through this every now and then." He smiled. "Old age, I guess."

"Take off your shirt," she commanded.

Complete surprise on his face, Sheldon asked, "What did you say, Doc?"

"Take off your shirt."

Sheldon swallowed hard. "I thought that's what you said." He did as he was told.

Daryl peered up at the powerful set of bare shoulders. Taking in his tempting, attractive male physique, she practically drooled over his muscular chest that was covered with curling wisps of fine, black hair. "Now stretch out on the floor."

"Now you wouldn't be trying to take advantage of me, would you?"

"No." Daryl laughed at the disappointment on his face. "I'm going to give you a massage. The way to good health is to have an aromatic bath and scented massage every day. At least that's what Hippocrates said."

Putting his hand to his chin, Sheldon inclined his head, asking, "So you have someone give you massages every day?"

"No, but I do get one on a weekly basis."

Sheldon raised an eyebrow. "Really?"

"At the spa, Sheldon," she explained.

He raised his hands. "I didn't say a thing."

"You didn't have to—it was written all over your face. Now you go lie down and try to relax. I'm going to change clothes, and I'll be right back."

When she returned, she had changed into drawstring-waist pants with a matching racer-back tank top. Daryl carried a bottle of massage oil in her hand. Sheldon lay face down on the floor, his eyes closed.

Without opening his eyes, he mumbled in a seductive tone, "Okay, Doc. I'm completely at your mercy."

Daryl poured a drop of the recently warmed oil into her hand. Rubbing her palms together, she leaned over and pressed them on Sheldon's back. Gently at first, she kneaded his flesh with her hands.

"Mmmmm . . . what is that? It smells like apples."

"It's a combination of chamomile, rosemary, and soya oil. It's supposed to relieve muscle pain and stress."

"It does have a calming affect. I can feel the tension leaving my body."

Daryl wanted to bury her face against the corded muscles of his back. She pounded her hands against the contours of Sheldon's athletic body in an experienced manner. While she worked, she silently prayed he couldn't hear her uneven breathing as she continued to massage his sore muscles.

Her own body tingled from the contact of his as she sat astride him. Daryl struggled to maintain her composure. She'd never wanted any man the way she wanted Sheldon, but it was much too soon. If she made love to him right now, she knew she might lose him forever. It wasn't a gamble she was willing to take.

Sheldon closed his eyes languishing in the magic touch of Daryl's talented fingers. The gentle massage sent currents of desire through him, and he felt himself harden. He resisted the urge to flip her under him and . . .

"You're not falling asleep on me, are you?"

"No," Sheldon managed to grunt. Right now, sleep is the last thing on my mind, he added silently. Was she ready to take their relationship to that next step? The sound of Daryl's voice and her feminine scent did strange things to his nervous system. He was sure she could hear his heart pounding as she rubbed his back.

"You can get up now, Sheldon. I'm done."

There was no way he could hide his state of arousal, so he replied, "I think I'll just stay like this for a few minutes more."

"Is anything wrong?" she asked.

"No, it just feels good to lie like this on the floor. I hope you don't mind." Sheldon knew he hadn't convinced her with his lame excuse.

There was a lengthy silence between them.

Daryl cleared her throat before speaking. "I'm going to wash my hands. I'll be right back."

Sheldon stood up slowly, working the kinks out of his shoulders and neck. As he moved his arms and body, he marveled over how much better he felt, thanks to Daryl and her magic fingers.

He looked up when she entered the room. "I feel a lot better." Falling back onto the sofa, Sheldon asked, "Interested in becoming my personal masseuse?"

She laughed lightly. "That depends. How much does it pay?"

Pulling her into his lap, he kissed her, moving his mouth over hers, devouring its softness.

Daryl put her arms around his neck, lowering his head to hers. Parting her lips, she raised herself to meet his kiss. Sheldon felt her shiver and wondered if it was from wanting him as much as he wanted her. His breathing became labored as he deepened the kiss.

Sheldon's wandering fingers found her full breasts and caressed them. Daryl threw her head back and moaned her pleasure. He knew she wanted him to make love to her. Running his hand upward along her thigh, he found her mound.

She suddenly pulled away from him. "Sheldon," she whispered, her voice breathy with passion. Daryl pulled down her shirt. "Let's not . . ."

Her words hit him like a bucket of ice. "What's wrong, Doc?"

"This is too soon," she said quietly. She slid off his lap and onto the sofa.

"I think I'd better go." He stood up for a moment, watching her. "Seems like we've been here before . . ." There was so much he wanted to say, but couldn't. Instead, he smiled, and said, "Goodnight, Doc."

A few days later, Daryl breezed into her office and headed straight to the telephone. She debated over whether or not to call Sheldon. She hadn't heard from him since Saturday night. Needing to know if he were angry over her refusal to have sex, she dialed quickly, tapping her fingernails on her desk. When Sheldon answered on the first ring, she smiled.

"Sheldon, this is Daryl. How are you?"

"Hello, Doc. This is a pleasant surprise."

She felt an eager affection coming from him and relaxed. He didn't seem to be upset over what hadn't happened. "I'm calling to see if you want to have dinner with me. I'm working late, so I thought we could grab a bite before I headed home." Happiness filled her as she talked to him.

"I wish I could, but I've got a friend coming into town today."

Daryl could hear the regret in his voice. "Oh, that's all right. Maybe another time then."

"I definitely want a rain check."

She laughed. "No problem. Have a good time with your friend."

"So where are you going for dinner?"

"Well, I hate eating alone, so I think I'll just head straight home after work."

"Why don't I call you later? To make sure you made it home okay."

She was touched by this small display of concern for her well being. "Oh, you don't have to do that."

"But I want to. I'll call you later tonight."

"I'll talk to you then." Daryl hung up, groaning her dejection. She had been looking forward to seeing him tonight "Oh, well. Another time," Daryl muttered as she picked up a folder, devouring the information it contained. The resonant ringing of her phone jostled her.

"Hey, sweetie. How late you working?"

"Margo, hi. Actually I'll be here for another couple of hours. What's up?"

"I'm still at the office myself. I was wondering if you'd like to have dinner together?"

"That'll be great. I just finished talking to Sheldon on the phone. I was hoping to have dinner with him."

"I take it he declined your invite?"

"Yeah, he's got a friend flying in for a visit."

"A lady friend?"

"I don't know. I didn't ask."

"Why not?" Margo pressed. "I sure would have."

Rolling her eyes, Daryl answered, "Because it's really not my business. We're not committed to each other."

"And you're not the least bit curious?"

She could hear the censure in Margo's voice. "I am, but not going to trip about this."

"You have certainly changed."

She bit back her anger. "What are you talking about, Margo?"

"Well . . . it's just that you suddenly seem to be quite gullible."

Daryl gritted her teeth. "I wouldn't say that. If I can't trust him, then I don't need him in my life."

"That's my point. Can you trust him? Do you really believe that you can?"

"Yes." Daryl believed deep in her heart that she could trust Sheldon.

"I guess you have changed—for the better. You've really grown up, Daryl. You aren't as hot-headed as you used to be. You used to give men hell."

"I think we all have. Not just me. Coming of age isn't just about getting older—it's becoming wiser. Knowing more about ourselves and what we want out of life." And she knew what she wanted. Sheldon Turner. There was nothing or no one who could make her change her mind.

Sheldon muttered curses during the thirty-minute drive to LAX. What the hell was Malle thinking? She shouldn't have followed him here. He would just have to convince her to turn around and head back to New York.

When he arrived, Sheldon found her sitting cross-legged on a bench near the door. Her long flowing blond hair was swept to one side, giving her a seductive look. Her perfect features awarded her the attention of every man in the baggage claim area, from ages nine to ninety.

"Hi, honey." She stood up quickly and wrapped her

arms around him tightly, oblivious to all the curious stares they were getting. "I've missed you so much."

"I've reserved you a suite at the Beverly Wilshire Hotel. Let's go." He drove in record time to the hotel, barely listening to Malle as she spouted all the latest gossip in New York.

Opening the door to the suite, Sheldon stepped aside for Malle to enter. "Well, here we are. I hope you like the room."

She looked around. "This is very nice." Malle sauntered over to the bedroom and peeked in. "Ooooh, Sheldon, this is very nice."

"Are you hungry?"

She shook her head. "No, honey. I'm too excited to eat."

"Excited about what?"

"Being here with you, of course."

"I . . . I have to leave. If you get hungry, just call room service."

She went to Sheldon's side and smiled sexily. "Won't you stay and keep me company?" she whispered huskily. Moving with purpose, yet subtly, she laced her arms about his neck and leaned into his reluctant embrace.

Sheldon managed to gently disengage himself from her hold. "I don't think that's a good idea."

"I came all this way to see you, Honey," she whined. "Won't you stay just for a few more minutes? I really missed you."

Sheldon shook his head. He didn't want to hurt her, but he didn't want to encourage her either. "I'm sorry, I can't. I've had a long day and I'm tired. I'll see you tomorrow, okay?"

"I guess I have no choice in the matter," she pouted.

Downstairs, Sheldon sat in his car for a minute, his hand up to his chin. Smiling, he turned on the car and headed to the freeway.

* * *

The low ringing of the telephone intruded on Daryl's tranquility and jarred her from her reading, as she lay reclining in her bed, propped against a mountain of pillows. "Hello."

"Hello, Daryl, were you asleep?"

She touched her hair, which was wrapped around curlers. It was Sheldon. "N-No. No, I'm up."

"I'm calling to see if I can stop by. I'm right down the street from your house."

Pulling her cotton robe closer together, she asked, "You're calling from the car?"

"Yes. As a matter of fact, I'm pulling into your driveway as we speak."

She jumped up from her bed to steal a peek out of her window. "Oh my God!"

Sheldon laughed. "What?"

Alternately yanking curlers out of her hair and trying to find something to wear, Daryl asked, "Can you please stay in your car for about five minutes?"

"Sure, why?"

Might as well tell the truth. "Because I look a mess. Just give me five minutes, okay?"

Sheldon laughed. "I can't imagine you looking a mess, but take your time."

Running her fingers through the mass of curls, Daryl sighed in satisfaction over her appearance. She'd found a pair of leggings and matching tunic in a lavender color.

She slipped on a pair of cream-colored mules, then ran down the stairs, throwing open the door. The instant she saw him get out of the car, Daryl felt a familiar tightening in her loins. "What are you doing here? I thought you were with your friend." Her body cried out to him. Closing her eyes, she tried to block out her lust.

When she opened them again, Daryl found Sheldon standing before her, a grin plastered on his face. It was as if he knew what she'd been thinking. She colored slightly. "What happened to your friend?"

His wide devilish grin left her breathless. "I just left them at the hotel. I'd planned to go straight home, but I ended up here instead. All evening you were on my mind. I knew I had to see you tonight."

A vaguely sensuous light passed between them, and she smiled. "I'm glad to see you too."

"Am I keeping you up? I know it's late and you have to work tomorrow."

"I wasn't asleep. I'm usually up late reading."

"My mom stays up late reading also."

"It's down time for me."

He seemed to be peering at her intently, causing Daryl to feel uncomfortable in his scrutiny. She placed a hand to her cheek, wondering if she'd left a speck of cold cream on her face. "Why are you staring at me like that?"

"I enjoy looking at you."

Daryl liked looking at him, too, but she wasn't about to admit that particular fact to Sheldon.

Opening the door wider to let him enter, she murmured, "I'm really glad you came by . . ."

"I shouldn't have surprised you like this."

"It's okay," she said quickly. "This is a very nice surprise." Daryl eased up off the sofa. "Would you like something to drink? I still have that bottle of white wine you brought. It's been in the fridge, so it's nice and cold."

Sheldon nodded. "That sounds great."

She navigated to the kitchen, a smile playing across her face. She poured two glasses of wine, then retrieved a couple of peaches from the refrigerator. Slicing them quickly, Daryl arranged them on a small decorative platter. After finding a tray, she placed the wine and the platter on it.

Sheldon was flipping through the TV channels when she approached. He immediately came to her aid, taking the tray from her.

Popping a piece of peach into her mouth, Daryl chewed

slowly, savoring the tangy tidbit. Swirling her wine in her glass, she admired the way the golden liquid rippled. Not meeting Sheldon's eyes, she turned to him asking, "So, what should we do? Now that you've come all this way."

"I know a way to amuse ourselves," Sheldon murmured, his seductive tone suggesting he had a more arousing activity in mind.

"Like what?" Daryl asked, one dark-brown brow arched.

Sheldon blessed her with an impish grin. "Why Clue, of course. What did you think I meant?"

"I . . ." Daryl shook her head. Standing up, she said, "I'll have everything set up in a minute." She hesitated. "Better yet, you set up the game, and I'll make us something else to snack on. I keep the game down there." She pointed to a large drawer on the bottom of her oak entertainment center.

In the kitchen, Daryl made a huge bowl of popcorn and grabbed the bottle of wine. When she walked out, Sheldon circled the table in long, lithe strides to assist her, and she struggled to maintain control of her chaotic emotions.

"Well, let's see how good a detective you are, Dr. Larsen."

"Mr. Turner, I'm a very good detective, but you don't have to take my word for it—I'm going to show you."

Sheldon chuckled. "I'll just bet you will."

Two hours later, Sheldon held up his hand. "All right, I admit defeat. You win."

Daryl found herself engulfed in Sheldon's strong arms. His lips pressed against hers, then gently covered her mouth. His masterful kiss turned her legs to jelly. Tantalizing tremors undulated through Daryl. She never believed it possible to derive so much pleasure from merely kissing a man.

Sheldon's lips brushed against hers as she spoke. "You're the dream I've been having, you know that, don't you?"

Smiling, Daryl thought things were progressing quite nicely.

Chapter 6

Seated in the hotel restaurant, Sheldon buttered his toast slowly and thoughtfully. He'd gotten home late and his body ached from exhaustion. He had no regrets though. Besides being good company, Daryl had to be the most sensual woman he'd ever met. She made no demands of him, so he felt completely relaxed around her. She hadn't pressed him about his *friend*.

Guilt nagged at him for not being completely honest with Daryl. Sheldon wondered how she'd react if she found out his friend wasn't a them, but a female. And one he'd been intimate with over the last couple of years.

Malle took a delicate bite of her apple cinnamon muffin and shifted in her seat.

From her body language, Sheldon knew she was nearly bursting at the seams over something. As he watched beneath hooded lids, she shifted once more. He knew he wouldn't have to wait long before she confronted him.

"I called your house last night. You weren't home."

Looking over at her, Sheldon shrugged nonchalantly. "And?"

Malle sighed her frustration. *"And* that's where you told

me you were going. You said you were tired. As a matter
of fact, you're still looking a bit weary."

Sheldon fought to control his temper. "Malle, don't
start . . .

"You didn't have to lie to me." She took another bite
of muffin. "Have you found yourself a little girlfriend?"

"Drop it." With painful effort, he forced himself to look
straight at his plate, resolving to avoid an argument with
her. However, there was no stopping her. Malle continued
to irritate him.

She gave him a black layered look. "Sheldon, I came a
long damn way to see you. The least you can do is be a
good host. I don't think that's asking too much of you."

"Malle, I can't spend all my time with you."

"I'm not asking you to. I did expect you to at least spend
the first couple of days showing me around."

A shadow of annoyance crossed his face. "This isn't your
first trip to California."

"I know, but I thought I'd get to meet your mother and
your brother—"

"Why would you think that?"

Malle's lower lip trembled slightly as she returned his
glare. "I'm your friend. I thought you'd introduce me."
She placed her coffee cup down gently. "We are still
friends, aren't we?"

Sheldon folded his hands across his chest. "That's all
we are."

Apparently she thought it better to change subjects
because she asked quietly, "So what are we doing today?"
Her commanding gaze was riveted on him.

"We can do whatever you want this morning. I have to
take my mother to the doctor this afternoon though."

"I don't mind going with you to the doctors. Or will
you be taking your girlfriend?"

"Malle . . ." His eyes darkened as he held her gaze.

She threw the cloth napkin to the table. "Fine! I'm not
going to push. You know what? You don't even have to

spend anytime with me, Sheldon," she said angrily. "I have other friends out here. *Lots of them.*"

"That's what I thought you'd do in the first place. I didn't know you were coming all the way here just to see me."

Malle's mouth was set in annoyance as she scanned his face. A consummate actress, she pressed a hand to her forehead, stating, "I'm suddenly not feeling well." She pushed back from the table and stood up. "I think I'll go back to my suite and lay down. Not that it matters to you what happens to me."

"Why don't you try eating a healthy breakfast instead of sweets? You snack too much, Malle."

"As if you really give a damn. If you're so concerned, why don't you just stay here and take care of me?"

Ignoring her dramatic display, Sheldon stood up and said, "Because you're old enough to take care of yourself. Now, after I take my mother to the doctor, I'll call you to see if you want to do something this evening." He doubted anything was wrong with Malle at all. When she couldn't have her way, she always tried to play on his sympathy.

She reached over to grab his hand with her own. "Do you mean it, Sheldon? We're going to spend the evening together?" When he nodded, she kissed his hand. "I'm going to go shopping this morning for something special to wear. I'll also need to get my nails done, then . . ."

He smiled briefly with no trace of his former irritation. Malle seemed to have recovered quickly from her ailment. Standing up, he said, "I'll call you later."

"Hey, Girlie. What's going on with you?" Audrey asked as she smoothed away a wrinkle in her skirt before taking a seat. "I'm so hungry," she stated while picking up a laminated menu.

Daryl put down the menu she was reading. "Nothing much. Just working hard. How about yourself?"

"Everything's great. Tyrell and I are getting closer and closer."

Daryl could see the radiance of her friend's happiness. "You're in love, aren't you?" She pushed a plate of carrots and celery toward Audrey. "Have some."

Audrey nodded. "Yes." She munched on a carrot stick. "I love Tyrell very much. I think he feels the same way."

"Hey y'all," Margo said as she approached the corner table. "Sorry I'm late. Traffic was horrible."

Handing her a menu, Daryl said, "We were about to order without you, girlfriend. Have some veggies."

"Look at you, with your greedy self," Margo teased. "You just get rude when you're hungry. Don't want to wait on nobody."

Daryl laughed infectiously. "Hey, I'm not the one on a diet. I didn't have breakfast this morning."

A waiter approached and took their orders quickly.

Margo turned to Audrey. "I saw you on TV last night."

"Girlie, that fire nearly gutted that whole house. For a minute, I wasn't sure we were going to be able to contain it in those two rooms."

"The fire on Canyon Road?" Daryl asked.

Audrey nodded. "That's the one. I'm glad the family was able to safely get out."

"What's up with you and Rob?" Daryl asked Margo as she pushed the vegetable platter toward her. "Are you two any closer to marriage?"

Sighing in frustration, Margo announced, "I think we're slowly getting there. Rob keeps hedging . . ."

The waiter appeared with their meals.

"Well, whatever you do, don't let him move back in with you," Audrey cautioned.

"I don't plan to, but I have to be honest. I miss not having him to come home to every night."

Daryl chewed thoughtfully. "Margo, Rob really loves you—I don't think it'll be much longer before he decides he's ready to settle down."

"I hope you're right, Daryl. I love him so much, and I want Kiana to grow up with both of her parents."

As they finished their dinner, the three friends spent the evening sharing the latest gossip and small talk. Since Audrey had to be up early for work the next morning, they ended the evening early.

Later, after she arrived home, Daryl was preparing for bed when the phone rang.

"I've missed you."

Her heart skipped a beat when she heard the familiar baritone voice. As usual, his call sent her spirits soaring.

After exchanging small pleasantries, Sheldon said, "I want to apologize for not calling or—"

"You don't owe me any apologies. I know you have a life outside of . . ." She searched for the appropriate word. "Our friendship."

"I don't know why, but I feel bad. Not to mention how much I've wanted to see you. It's been about a week."

"Oh," Daryl responded. "I guess we need to do something about that."

"I was just thinking the exact same thing. How about this weekend?"

Daryl chewed her bottom lip. "Ooooh, Sheldon. I wish I could. I promised my mother I'd help her move."

"Need any help?"

"You really mean it?"

"Sure."

"We can use the help. Thanks." After giving him directions to her mother's house, Daryl hung up the phone. Sheldon really was a very sweet man—nothing like his portrayal by the media. He was not the arrogant, cold ladies man everyone thought. But then, she'd known it all along.

Sheldon carried the last box from the U-Haul truck into the newly built spacious townhouse. Sitting it on the floor in the corner of what would be the dining room, he joined

Daryl and her mother, Maxine, in the kitchen. "Well, that's the last of it," he puffed. Sheldon bent over, trying to catch his breath.

Pushing up the sleeves of her gray sweatshirt, Maxine smiled. "Thank you so much for your help. I really appreciate it."

"It was my pleasure, Mrs. Larsen." Sheldon noticed the striking resemblance Daryl bore to her mother. They looked more like sisters, he thought. "Is there anything else I can do for you?"

"I think we can handle it from here. Daryl and I are going to have dinner out. Would you like to join us?"

"I wish I could, but I need to go home and pack. I have to go out of town." Sheldon registered a flicker of disappointment in Daryl's eyes. "Maybe another time?" he offered.

Maxine glanced over at her daughter, who nodded and said, "Another time it is. Thanks, Sheldon, for all of your help." Daryl kneeled down to rummage through one of the cardboard boxes marked "glasses."

Sheldon waited patiently until she stood up before walking over to stand by her side. Taking her by the hand, he leaned down to whisper, "Will you walk me outside?"

She smiled up at him. "Of course."

When they were outside, Sheldon leaned over and pulled her into his arms. "I hate having to leave like this. I—"

Daryl put a finger to his lips. "I understand. Really, I do."

She looked at him with that raw hunger she had shown him that night at her house. Sheldon recalled how satiny smooth her firm breasts had felt against his palm. He tried to suppress the sudden hardness in his groin. Not wanting her to feel the evidence of his state of arousal, he retreated a step. "I, um . . . , I'll turn the truck in tonight, then head home."

Daryl nodded. "I'll give you a call sometime tomorrow."

"I'm flying out late this evening. I have to go out of

town on business for a few days. I didn't mention it before now because I hadn't decided to go until this morning."

"Okay. Well, have fun."

"It's business." Why did he continually feel the need to explain his actions to her?

Standing on tiptoe, Daryl kissed him on the lips. "I'll see you when you get back."

When Daryl walked back into her mother's new home, she found Maxine waiting with a grin on her face.

Her arms folded across her bosom' Maxine inclined her head. "So, are you going to tell me what exactly is going on with you and this Sheldon Turner?"

Daryl sank down to the floor, pretending to unpack one of the nearest boxes. "We're getting to know each other, Mother."

Maxine smiled knowingly. "I see."

Daryl peered up at her mother, her mouth turning up at the corners. "What?"

"You really like him, don't you?"

"Yeah, I do." She closed her eyes, visualizing him in her mind. When she opened them, Daryl found her mother staring at her strangely. "Mother, I think he's the one."

"The one for what?"

"Mr. Right, Mother."

Maxine suddenly looked worried, and Daryl knew what was coming next.

"Haven't you heard about his reputation?" Maxine shook her head, her gray, shoulder-length hair bouncing. "I don't know if you should get so wrapped up in him. I mean, he seems very nice, but . . ."

"I'm not rushing into anything, Mother. I promise."

Sitting down on the floor beside her, Maxine shrugged. "Honey, I know you've got a good head on your shoulders. If he has flaws, I know you'll find them."

"He has flaws," she smiled at her mother. "But I still

like him anyway," she added softly. "Besides, I don't know anyone, including me, who is without flaws."

Maxine threw her arms around Daryl, embracing her. "I hope Sheldon Turner is aware of the prize he's getting. My problem is that I don't think he is."

"Maybe not right now, Mother, but he will."

Four days later, Daryl still hadn't heard from Sheldon. She sat with one knee up on the sofa, polishing her toenails, as she listened to Audrey's recount over the speaker phone of her most recent date with Tyrell. She wasn't aware she'd sighed loudly until she heard her friend ask, "What's wrong, Daryl?"

Putting the nail polish aside, and her foot on the floor, she said, "I haven't heard from Sheldon since he's been out of town. I thought he'd at least call and wish me a happy Valentine's Day."

"Maybe he has a surprise for you."

"Yeah right. I—"

A clamorous ringing interrupted her.

"Was that your doorbell? Boy, it's really loud."

"Yeah, can you hold on for a minute?"

Daryl's heart leapt erratically in her chest at seeing a messenger with a huge heart-shaped box and the most beautiful bouquet of roses, in a profusion of colors, that she'd ever laid eyes on.

"Daryl, you still there?" Audrey yelled through the speaker phone.

She ran over to the sofa. "I'm here."

"I heard you scream. What on earth happened?"

"Nothing. I just got an enormous bouquet of roses in every color imaginable, and a big box of candy. I mean a great big box of chocolates. Girlfriend, I can feel the pounds jumping on me already. I'm going to have to exercise twice as much."

Audrey laughed. "See, I told you he didn't forget about

you. When is he coming back into town? Tyrell won't be back until tomorrow."

"I thought he'd be back today, but I guess I was wrong."

"So what are your plans for tonight?"

"Don't have any," Daryl said, wishing Sheldon were in town.

"I have an idea. Why don't we get together tonight and have dinner? Maybe Margo can join us."

Daryl shrugged. "Fine with me. I'd hoped to spend the evening with Sheldon but . . ." She wondered once more when he would be returning to Los Angeles. She was sure if he were in town, she would've heard from him by now.

Chapter 7

Malle greeted Sheldon at the door wearing nothing but a white satin robe that left nothing to the imagination, and a smile. "Hi, Honey. I'm so glad to see you're back in town. I don't know why you didn't want me to go with you." She motioned around the hotel room. "It would've been better than staying here by myself." Malle handed him a box wrapped in bright red paper with white hearts all over it. "Happy Valentine's Day."

Mumbling thanks, Sheldon laid the gift on the plush sofa, then sat down beside it. "I told you this was a business trip."

Running her fingers through her hair, Malle sank down beside him, moving the gift to the coffee table. "Well, you've taken me with you before."

"Malle, let's not argue about this. I'm really tired."

She gestured toward the bedroom. "You could take a nap here. As a matter of fact, I'm feeling kind of sleepy myself."

"Then maybe I should leave so that you can get some rest."

"It would be a whole lot better with you here." She

stood up and moved toward him. With her hands on either side of him, Malle pulled him close to her. "I know you have a surprise for me." She pulled away to pat him down. "Well, where is it?"

"Where is what?"

"My Valentine's gift, that's what. You did get me one, didn't you?"

"Malle, I didn't have time for shopping—"

"You know how special this day is," she said tearfully. "I can't believe you didn't get me anything."

"I didn't say that. Look, I just got back into town and I have some things to do this afternoon, but I thought I'd take you to dinner this evening."

"So, what am I supposed to do all day?" she asked angrily. "It's Valentine's Day."

"I know what day it is. You can go sightseeing. Do whatever you want."

"I want to spend the day with you." Pouting, she sighed heavily. "Do you plan on spending any time with me at all?"

"Yes, but I have things to do. Look, Malle, I didn't invite you here—"

"I know that. I came out here on my own, but I thought you'd spend some time with me. Especially today of all days."

"We're going to have dinner tonight, aren't we?" So much for his plans to spend the evening with Daryl. "Besides, Valentine's Day is just another day to me. Nothing more."

"Guess I'll have to settle for that."

"I'll see you later this evening, okay? And thanks for the present."

"Whatever," Malle snapped before stomping off to her bedroom.

"See you later," Sheldon murmured, more to himself than to her, before departing. As much as he wanted to see Daryl, he'd felt guilty about leaving Malle alone when she'd come all this way to visit him. Even if he hadn't invited her. Glancing down at his watch, Sheldon knew Daryl should have received the candy and the flowers by now. He felt Daryl would understand his not being with her today. She wasn't the type of woman to make a fuss, and he liked that about her.

Margo glanced around the crowded restaurant. "I wonder where Audrey is? Maybe she's not coming. Tyrell probably eased back into town to surprise her—"

"Here she comes," Daryl announced.

As soon as she sat down, Daryl grinned and said, "We weren't sure you were going to make our little dinner."

"And why not? This was my idea originally."

"By the way, Margo, how did you get out tonight?" Daryl asked

"Rob and I spent the whole day together, so you two can just stop grinning. I'm not going to forget my girl-friends. She handed each of them a card with a pair of movie passes. To my special friends—Happy Valentine's Day."

Audrey gave each of them a pair of heart-shaped earrings in a lovely red and silver box.

When it was Daryl's turn, she presented Margo and Audrey with small square-shaped boxes of candy.

"How are things going with Sheldon, Daryl?" Margo asked.

"Good so far. He doesn't seem spooked over what I do for a living."

Margo grimaced. "Your job *is* kind of creepy, girl. I don't know how you can handle being around all those dead people."

Daryl sipped her white wine. "I don't have to worry about bad attitudes, smart mouths, or anything. Now your job, Audrey, I wouldn't have it for anything in the world."

Audrey stopped chewing long enough to swallow and asked, "What's wrong with being a firefighter?"

Daryl's body trembled involuntarily. "I don't like being around fires."

"Me neither," Margo added. "Now, I like what I do."

Cutting up her chicken, Daryl looked over at Margo. "You've always liked working in the music industry. Now that you and Tyrell have your own record company, things must really be looking up for you."

Margo nodded. "Things are really going well. As a matter of fact, we just signed a new female group. They remind me of En Vogue. These girls can sing. You've got to hear them."

"When will we get to hear them?" Audrey wanted to know.

"We're going to have a big party later on this year for them. I'll invite you guys. Of course, with you seeing Tyrell now, I'm sure he'll also extend an invitation to you."

"Margo, you need to quit."

"No, seriously, I think he really likes you, Audrey."

"I hope so," she confessed. "I like him a lot."

Audrey glanced over at Daryl. "I didn't realize Sheldon and Tyrell were such good friends. Did you know?"

Daryl shook her head. "I didn't know. What about you, Margo?"

"I knew they went to school together," Margo stated. "But it's only recently that I found out just how close they really are."

Audrey picked up a stuffed mushroom and popped it into her mouth. "Tyrell said Sheldon was one of his closest friends."

Watching Margo closely, she caught the play of emotions on her friend's face. "Margo, you seem to really hate him. I'd like to know why?" Daryl questioned. "And I don't believe it's just because he hurt some friend of yours. I think it's more personal than that."

When Margo and Audrey exchanged glances, she grew more determined to find out what was going on.

"Will somebody enlighten me, please? You both seem to share some deep dark secret. What is it?"

"Margo, tell her," Audrey urged.

"Yes, Margo. You might as well tell me."

"Daryl, it's something that happened a long time ago . . ." she began. "One night, Sheldon and I met at a club in New York. Tyrell was performing. Anyway, he and I left the club together." She looked ashamed.

"Go on," Daryl prompted.

"We slept together. Stupid me, I thought . . ." She shook her head. "I was young and I thought he cared about me. Anyway, the next morning he didn't even remember my name, and he just tossed me two hundred-dollar bills, which I promptly threw back in his face. He's apologized profusely since then, but it won't change the fact that he treated me like a whore."

Daryl didn't respond.

"Are you okay?" Audrey asked her. When she didn't answer, she tried again. "Daryl, are you okay?"

"I—I'm fine Margo, I'm sorry about that. I didn't know."

"No, it's fine. I mean, yes I'm still angry about the way he treated me, but I'm more angry with myself. I should have known better. As much as I want to forget about it, every time I see him, it brings it all back to me."

"Thanks for telling me."

"The only reason I told you this is because I really don't want to see you get hurt. Sheldon can be very cold when he wants to be."

"These are for you." Sheldon handed Malle a half dozen yellow roses. "Happy Valentine's Day."

Her eyes filled with tears as she spoke. "Thank you so much. They're beautiful."

"I'm sorry about earlier. I wasn't in the best of moods. And you're right. I've been a rude host."

"I know you have a lot on your mind. I understand." She whirled around gracefully. "You never said how I looked. Do you like this dress?"

Dressed in a silk tangerine low-cut dress, Malle was strikingly provocative. "You look lovely," he said.

"I thought you'd approve," she replied, favoring him with a radiant smile. "You've always liked this color on me."

"You'd better grab some type of jacket. It's a little on the chilly side tonight."

"Of course." She strolled smoothly toward the bed and bent to retrieve the matching jacket. "What time is our reservation?",

"In forty-five minutes, so we should leave."

"Just let me touch up my face. I'll be out in a minute."

While he waited, Sheldon thought of Daryl. He wondered what she was doing tonight. He'd called earlier but she wasn't home. He hadn't been able to catch up with her to wish her a happy Valentine's Day.

Malle returned, interrupting his musings.

"I'm ready, Honey."

"Let's go, then." He followed her out of the room and down to his waiting car. Malle talked non-stop during the thirty-minute drive to Marina Del Rey. He nodded in agreement several times for lack of anything better to say. How was he going to get her to understand that there was no future with him? Although frustrated with her not-so-subtle manipulations, he compelled himself to remain patient with her. She would soon be on a plane headed back to New York and completely out of his life once and for all.

Seated ten minutes later, Sheldon watched in silence as a waiter walked out of the kitchen carrying a tray laden with plates.

"Honey, I want to ask you something. That is, if I can keep your attention."

Sheldon turned his gaze in her direction. "I'm sorry, Malle. What is it?"

"This is a nice place, Sheldon. I like the atmosphere."

"Malle, we really need to talk."

"Not tonight, Hon."

Her touch, firm and persuasive on his hand, invited more. He had no intentions of succumbing to her sensual overtures, but, at the same time, Sheldon didn't want to anger her. Malle had a quick temper, and he wasn't in the mood to calm down an hysterical woman.

"I told you on the phone that I just wanted to talk."

"Let's just enjoy the evening."

"I didn't come here to enjoy. This is not a date."

Malle played with her water glass, moving it from side to side. "I need to know something, Sheldon. Why did you move in with me?"

He stopped eating. "What?"

Leaning closer, she repeated the question.

"I didn't move in with you."

Anger flashed in her sky-blue eyes. "What do you call it?"

"I spent a few nights—"

"You stayed there a lot. You've still got clothes in my closet. You bought most of the furniture, my car—practically everything."

Leaning back in his chair, Sheldon asked quietly, "What are you getting at?"

"You keep saying that you don't want a commitment, yet you carry a key to my apartment, you practically lived with me—"

"Get to the point, Malle."

"We were acting like a couple. You say one thing and then you do another. Then when you hear those three little words, you take off running." She wiped at a lone tear slipping down her cheek. "Is that fair?"

"You started acting as if you owned me."

"I thought we were in a serious relationship."

"I don't know why." Sheldon shook his head in resignation. "I kept telling you I just wanted us to be friends."

"You kept sending me mixed signals. Why can't you see that?"

"You kept trying to make me change my mind," he argued back. Sheldon held his anger in check. It always came down to this. Women would assure him they understood and accepted the terms, then they changed the rules midstream and blamed him.

Still shaking his head, Sheldon didn't understand why this always happened. Was there a woman on this earth that wouldn't pressure him into a relationship? *Daryl.* Daryl wasn't like that. She would never ask for more than he was willing to give.

"Hey, isn't that Sheldon over there?" Audrey asked. "I thought you said he was still out of town."

Surprised, Daryl dropped her fork and turned around. "Where?"

"Over there." Audrey pointed to the far table in the back of the restaurant. "With that blonde."

"Yeah, that's him, alright," Margo stated. "See, he's never gonna change. Girl, you deserve so much better than the likes of him."

Daryl's fingers clenched the folds of her dress. She turned back around to face her friends but said nothing. She kept telling herself that she and Sheldon weren't exactly a couple. He was free to spend Valentine's Day with whomever he pleased. However, it still hurt to see him with another woman.

Audrey shook her head in sympathy. "Daryl, I have to agree with Margo this time. I don't think he's your Mr. Right."

"Yes, he is," she affirmed quietly. "I know you two don't think so, but I know he's the one for me." Even seeing him with the skinny blonde hadn't caused her to change her mind.

"But how can you be absolutely sure?"

"Because my heart tells me so."

Margo snorted. "Girl, that's just plain nonsense."

"It's Daryl's business. Maybe we should just stay out of it."

"And let her get hurt?" Margo argued, her green eyes flashing with anger. "What kind of friends would we be?"

"Good ones," Daryl said quietly."

"If that's what you want. You're a grown woman."

"Margo, I appreciate your concern. Really I do. But remember when we didn't think Rob was treating you right, and we told you? What did you tell us? To stay out of your business, that's what. You asked us to let you take care of everything. Now I'm asking you to do the same."

"I know. I just really care about you, that's all."

"And I appreciate it, but you can't pick my men for me. I care about you and Audrey. The one thing we've always agreed on is to stay out of each other's lives unless invited."

"You're right. I'm sorry if I've intruded."

"You have intruded. You gave me your opinion—Audrey, too—and I haven't changed my mind. I still believe wholeheartedly that Sheldon Turner is the man for me. My soul mate."

Glancing over her shoulder to the table where Sheldon and his date were eating, Margo shrugged in resignation. "Oookay."

Daryl peeked over once more. It was then that Sheldon looked up and saw her. Caught in the act, she simply stared. When he gave her an embarrassed smile, she turned away.

Daryl's here. Oh God! I know what she's thinking. Sheldon glanced over and caught her watching. He smiled, but she just acted as if she didn't recognize him.

Malle placed a slender hand over his. "I'm sorry. I didn't mean for us to spend the evening together fighting."

"I thought we'd be able to talk, Malle. About your leaving town. Going back to New York."

She sat rigid in her chair. "Suppose I'm not ready to go back? I just may decide to stay in California. What then?"

He shook his head. "I can't force you to go back to New

York, but I have to be honest with you. Even if you decide to stay in L.A., there is no future for us.''

An infuriated growl flew from her mouth. "I thought you cared about me," she hissed.

Sheldon expelled an exasperated sigh. "I do. That's why I don't want to keep hurting you this way. I don't love you, Malle. And I know you want something more than I'm willing to give.''

"Is there someone else? Perhaps one of the women over there at that table. You can't seem to tear your eyes away from them.''

Sheldon's eyes darted to Daryl. "The truth is that I'm just not ready to settle down.''

"I won't rush you, Honey. I'll wait—''

"No, I don't want you to wait for me. Malle, please go back to New York.''

"I don't understand you." A pained grimace tightened Malle's pretty features. "How can you dismiss me like this?''

"When we started hanging out together, we agreed to not let our feelings get out of hand. You weren't supposed to fall in love with me.''

"It's not like I could control it, Sheldon.''

He was about to reply that he couldn't help it if he wasn't in love with her, but thought better of it. "I kept telling you that I didn't want a serious relationship.''

She wrung her hands in surrender. "I know. I really thought you'd change your mind. I mean, we had great sex, good times. I was good to you. I know I'm good for you.''

"I don't want the same thing, can't you understand?''

"I'm trying to." Her tear-bright eyes lifted to the huge painting that hung behind him in the back of the room.

Sheldon suddenly felt guilty for the pain he glimpsed in her eyes. "Malle, I'm sorry.''

"You're not sorry," she snapped angrily. "If you truly felt that way, you wouldn't be doing this to me.''

"Malle . . .''

After eating their dinner in total silence, Sheldon drove her back to the hotel.

"Aren't you going to come in?"

Sheldon shook his head. "No, there's something I need to do."

She tried to smile, but Sheldon could see the hurt and anger in her eyes. "You can do it from here, can't you?"

" 'Fraid not. I really need to go."

"I don't suppose you'll consider coming back tonight." Running soft fingers along the side of his face, she whispered, "We could have such a good time."

Sheldon backed away. "I'll give you a call tomorrow."

"Give me a call!" She looked stunned. "Are you telling me that you don't want to see me?"

"Malle, calm down. I have to take care of some things. I told you about the project I'm working on." He gave her a friendly hug. "I'll talk to you later." Sheldon walked briskly down the hallway toward the elevator, muttering curses all the way. As soon as he got home, he would call Daryl. He hated the fact that she'd seen him with Malle.

Some of the confidence he'd felt earlier dissipated. What if she refused to talk to him? Telling himself that Daryl had no right to be angry didn't exactly convince him. Why did he feel so guilty about tonight? He'd done nothing wrong, he repeated over and over silently. However, it did nothing to diminish the guilt.

He called until she finally answered the phone. "Daryl, it's not what you think—"

"You don't owe me any explanations, Sheldon," she cut in.

He tried to detect any censure in her tone, but found none. Nonetheless, he found himself explaining. "Her name is Malle. She's a friend visiting from New York. There's nothing between us."

"Really? How long will she be here?"

"I'm not sure. Maybe until the end of the week."

"Are you sure she's just your friend? You two looked

pretty cozy to me." Daryl paused. "I'm sorry. I really shouldn't have said that."

"It's okay. We used to date, but it's over now."

"Does she know?"

"I've told her over and over."

"Obviously, she doesn't believe you then."

"She knows it's over. The reason I took her out tonight instead of asking you is because today is a big day for her. Since she was visiting—"

"I realize today is for lovers, Sheldon," Daryl pointed out snidely. "By the way, thanks for the flowers and the candy."

"Are you angry with me?"

She didn't respond.

"Daryl?" When she still didn't respond, he said, "If it means anything to you, I want you to know that it was you I wanted to be with. Not Malle."

"But the fact remains, you were with her."

"Yes, and I can tell it really bothers you."

"A little—no, a lot," she admitted. "I guess I'm a little jealous. Even though we're not lovers, I wanted to spend Valentine's Day with you."

"Can I make it up to you?"

"Don't worry about it, Sheldon."

"I want to see you."

"Well, I'll tell you what. Since Malle's in town, spend time with her. I'm not going anywhere. Give me a call when she leaves. Bye."

"Daryl—"

She had already hung up. Daryl was angry. Sheldon could hear it in her voice, and it made him feel guiltier than hell.

Chapter 8

Over the next couple of days, Daryl deliberated over what Sheldon had told her about his relationship with Malle. Hadn't she tried to convince Margo of her trust in him? So why was she letting disquieting thoughts enter into her mind?

Waging a personal battle within herself, Daryl pushed herself out of bed. Pausing to face herself in the mirror, she asked the one question that needed asking. Are you the one for me, Sheldon? Or am I being a fool?

With fearful clarity, she knew the answer.

"When are you taking me to meet your mother?" Malle asked, while pulling item after item from a Bloomingdale's shopping bag. She was on bag number two out of six. "I've been here three weeks now and I still haven't met her."

"I'm not taking you to meet her." Sheldon knew his mother would throw a fit if he brought Malle to her house.

Dropping a pair of pants to the floor, she asked, "Why not? Are you ashamed of me?"

Sheldon held off Malle's litany of complaints by adding, "No. My mother's not feeling very well, that's all."

"Oh, Honey, I'm so sorry. I hope she feels better soon."

"I do, too."

Shoving the sea of bags aside, Malle stood up to carry an arm load of clothing still on hangers into the bedroom of her suite. Her phone rang and she threw the bags on the bed in haste to answer it.

Sheldon heard her squeals of delight from where he was sitting. As he contemplated the reason for her sudden excitement, Malle hung up and came running into the room.

Dropping down into the chair beside him, she announced, "Well, this should make you happy. I just received a call from the agency. I have to be on a plane to Paris in two hours."

"Really? Big modeling assignment?"

Malle laughed. "Yes, and I'm so excited. It's an opportunity I've been waiting for." She moved closer to Sheldon. "You know I'd love for you to join me."

"I can't. Remember, my mother's sick. But I'm really happy for you."

"Will you miss me?"

Sheldon shrugged. "How long will you be gone?" He ducked to dodge the skirt Malle threw in his direction.

"About a month or so. I should be back the second week in April."

"I know you're going to enjoy being in France."

"I'm sorry about having to cancel the rest of our day together. I'll make it up to you when I get back."

"There's nothing to make up. Now go on and get packed. I'll take you to the airport." He paused. "When you get back?"

"Yes. I'm coming back here. I'm not ready to leave Los Angeles yet."

"What about your career?"

"I can work from here." Malle halted in midstride. "You're sure you're not mad?"

Sheldon smiled. "I'm not mad. Not at all." The truth was that he couldn't have been more thrilled. Malle was leaving. He fantasized that she'd meet a handsome, rich Frenchman and fall madly in love."

"Sheldon?" Malle pulled him up. Pressing her body against his, she whispered huskily, "I bet you were just thinking about the last time we had hot sex? I could tell from that look of pure euphoria on your face." She picked up his hand, pressing it to her breast. He could feel the erect nipple beneath his palm.

It had been a while since he'd had sex, and he fought the desire to strain against her. Ignoring his sexual hunger, Sheldon removed his hand and retreated. "You'd better get ready for your trip."

Malle reached out to pull him to her again, but he stepped out of her grasp.

Her eyes were bright with disbelief. "What's wrong, Honey? I just want a kiss. Besides, what harm can come from one last romp between friends?"

"We can't do this."

"And why not? It's something we both want . . . very badly. Sliding one hand down his stomach, she said silkily, "We are so good together, Sheldon." Malle slowly removed her dress, revealing the sheerest teddy he'd ever seen.

He sucked in a ragged breath at the sight of her exquisite beauty. Bending down, Sheldon picked up the crumpled dress and handed it to her. "I'm serious, Malle. We can't do this. You said yourself you've got a plane to catch."

She walked over to the bedroom, dropping the dress on the floor. When she returned, she wore a satin robe. "I don't understand why you're being this way."

"I can't continue to make love to you—I'd be taking advantage of you."

"No, you wouldn't. I want you just as bad, Sheldon."

"They're not going to hold that plane for you, Malle."

She looked as if she wanted to strangle him. "Fine, Sheldon. I'll be ready in a few minutes." She stalked off to the bedroom, slamming the door.

Sheldon released a long sigh of relief. Malle was leaving. But she would be back. He refused to consider that fact right now. There was someone he needed to see.

"What are you doing here?" Daryl asked when she arrived home to find Sheldon standing outside the door to her house. "You're a long way from home, and I know you can't be lost." She was thrilled to see him but refused to let him know what his being there meant to her. Glancing behind her, she said, "Where's your car?"

"I parked down the street." His eyes twinkled with levity. "I wasn't sure what you would do if you drove up and saw my car parked in front."

Daryl shrugged nonchalantly. "Pretty much the same as walking up and finding you on my doorstep."

"I had to see you," Sheldon stated simply. "I haven't been able to get you out of my mind."

Daryl leaned against her door. "I meant what I said, Sheldon. You have some issues that need to be resolved. I don't want to be a part of whatever is going on between you and Malle."

"I know." It came out in a hoarse whisper as he lounged casually against the door frame.

"Did your friend leave town already?" Daryl turned away, not waiting for an answer.

Sheldon pulled her back to him. "Yes, she's gone."

Daryl's mouth dropped open. "When did she leave?"

"A few minutes ago. I put her on the plane myself. He grabbed Daryl by the elbow, leading her further into the house. "Will you have dinner with me?"

The smile in his eyes contained a sensuous flame, almost rendering her speechless. "Sheldon—"

"Please?"

A thoughtful smile curved her mouth as she nodded. "I guess I do have to eat."

"I'll wait for you to get dressed. We're having dinner at Rillo's."

* * *

Daryl glanced around the empty room that had been gaily decorated in red and white, with heart-shaped balloons floating throughout. Looking up at him, her brow creased with worry, she asked, "Sheldon, why are we the only people in the restaurant?" Daryl turned around to leave. "Maybe they're booked for a private party—"

He pulled her close to his side and they walked together. "Sweetheart, the place is empty because that's the way I wanted it. They *are* closed for a private party—ours."

Standing motionless in the middle of the room, Daryl blinked twice. "Excuse me?"

"We have the whole place to ourselves."

"You're kidding."

Sheldon shook his head, an amused expression on his face. "Come with me." He took her gently by the elbow and led her to a table near the center of the room.

Daryl peered up at him. "More roses?" In the center sat another enormous bouquet of flowers in vivid hues of pink, red, yellow, and white. She bent to inhale their sweet fragrance. "Do I get to take them home?"

"If you want. They're yours." Sheldon pulled out a chair for Daryl. "I know this isn't the same because it's not Valentine's Day, but I was thinking—Valentine's Day is highly over-rated in my book. I thought we'd do something different, like come up with our own holiday. We can call it Daryl and Sheldon's Day. What do you think?"

Her smile widened in approval. "I think it's much better than Valentine's Day."

Seemingly out of nowhere, a waiter appeared with a bottle of champagne and two glasses.

Holding up a sparkling flute of golden champagne, Sheldon announced, "Here's to us. I'm hoping tonight will be the first of many like this. I've grown to care a great deal for you, Daryl. I want you to know that."

She held her flute to his, her eyes never leaving his face.

"And I you. To us." She gloried briefly in the shared moment.

They were still gazing deep into each other's eyes when a waitress came over to take their orders. Looking at Sheldon, she did a double take. It was obvious to Daryl that she recognized him. Smiling widely, she announced, "It's you. I didn't know you were back. How are you?"

Sheldon wore a bewildered expression on his face when he peeked over at Daryl. She put her hand to her mouth to keep from smiling.

"I'm fine," he answered carefully.

"You don't even remember me, do you? It's Brenda."

"Good seeing you."

When nothing more was forthcoming, Brenda pressed further. "I met you when you came home last year, remember?"

"Oh, that's right."

Daryl caught a glimpse of the brief show of disappointment and hurt that played on Brenda's face before she seemed to shrug it off.

"Well, it's good seeing you. What can I get for you and your lady friend tonight?"

Sheldon glanced over at Daryl. "My lady friend and I will have the shrimp scampi."

When she walked away, Daryl leaned over and whispered, "I bet you haven't a clue where you met her."

Sheldon chuckled. "Was it that obvious? I think I may have offended her, but people don't seem to understand that I've met thousands of men, women, and children all over the world."

"I guess everyone likes to think that they've made a lasting impression."

"Does it bother you when people approach me?"

"No. Should it?" Daryl picked up her glass, swirling the contents.

Sheldon watched as her hair swung from side to side. Tonight it was straight and smooth and glossy, picking up the soft lighting and reflecting it back. Sheldon longed to run his fingers through it.

"You're doing it again," she said softly, interrupting his thoughts.

"What?"

"Staring at me. You do it a lot."

Sheldon reached over, touching her silken strands. "It's because you're stunning."

"Thank you."

When he started to pull his hand back, Daryl surprised him by grabbing it. Studying the ring he wore—gold with a square-cut sapphire in the middle, surrounded by diamonds. "Your ring is very nice. I've never seen one like this. I like it."

Sheldon pulled his hand away slowly when their dinner arrived. "Thank you. I usually don't wear rings, but it was a gift from my mother. I never take it off." He gestured with his knife. "I notice you don't wear any. Any reason why?"

"I choose not to. The only ring I'll ever wear is my wedding ring."

"Why is that? Don't you like rings?" Sheldon asked, with a significant lifting of his eyebrows. He'd never met a woman who didn't like jewelry.

"Oh, I love rings, but I believe it's bad luck to wear a ring on the finger where you would put your wedding band."

"Really?"

Her response seemed to amuse him. "You can laugh, but I really believe it."

"Then why don't you wear rings on any other finger?"

"Because I don't think they look right." Daryl picked up her fork and attacked her food with relish.

Sheldon studied her as she ate. She was indeed a very unique lady, and he found that he thoroughly enjoyed her

company. She never questioned him or demanded any of
his time. She seemed content with the times they spent
together. For the first time, Sheldon felt no pressure in a
relationship to move things further. He felt sure Daryl
would never do that to him.

Chapter 9

"Well, Dr. Larsen. Looks like you made someone very happy," Dr. Caroline Hart announced as she walked into Daryl's office.

Without looking up from her monitor, she asked, "What are you talking about?"

"These just came for you." Caroline carried a huge bouquet of mixed flowers and sat them on her desk.

Drawing the fragrance into her nostrils, Daryl knew instinctively that they were from Sheldon. Huge floral displays were fast becoming his trademark. "They're beautiful." She picked up the card and tore open the envelope with enthusiasm. Reading it quickly, she smiled, holding it to her bosom.

Caroline grinned as she leaned against a file cabinet for support. "So, tell me, do I know this special man? The one who's put this big smile on your face."

"You've probably heard of him. Sheldon Turner."

Caroline's eyes opened wider. "The pro basketball player?"

Daryl nodded. "We've been seeing each other since January."

"How'd you meet him? I thought he lived in New York."

"He just moved back to Los Angeles about three months ago."

"So you met him shortly after he moved home. That's great." Gesturing to the flowers, she stated, "I take it he knew it was your birthday?"

"It seems so, but I didn't tell him. I wonder how he knew."

Pointing to the telephone, Caroline suggested, "Why don't you call him and ask?"

She leaned back in her chair, grinning. "I think I will."

"Well, I'll leave you to your phone call." She paused at the door. "Happy birthday. I've a feeling this is going to be one you'll never forget."

"One can hope." Daryl pulled at the neck of her shirt, wondering again how Sheldon managed to find out her birth date. Picking up the phone, she decided, "Only one way to find out."

She opened her front door with a smile. Daryl knew Sheldon would be on the other side. When she'd called him earlier, he'd invited her out. Where, she had no idea. All he would tell her was to wear her best dress. When he entered, she admired the expensive cut of his black double breasted suit. It hung on his muscled frame well.

He leaned down to place a kiss on her full lips. "Happy birthday, Doc."

"Thank you again for the flowers, Sheldon. They're so pretty."

"I'm glad you liked them. However, your birthday celebration is far from over."

"What in the world are you talking about?"

He checked his watch. "We'd better get going. Close your eyes."

"What?"

"Close your eyes. I need you to trust me completely. Can you do that?"

"Sure." Daryl placed both hands over her eyes.

He led her slowly down the stairs and toward the car. The cool air of the March evening washed over her body. She bit her lip to stifle the outcry of her delight as Sheldon helped her into the automobile. Daryl knew they were not getting into his car because she couldn't distinguish the scent of the air freshener that hung in his car.

Sheldon slid his tall muscled frame in beside her. "You can open your eyes now."

They were inside a sleek black limousine. Daryl glanced around. "What? Where are—"

"It's a very special day for you," he interjected. "I thought we'd celebrate the day you were born in grand style."

"But where are we going?"

Sheldon shook his head. "It's a secret."

Her gaze traveled over his face and searched his eyes. "A secret. What are you up to?"

"My lips are sealed," was all he said, leaving Daryl no choice but to settle back and enjoy the feel of his arms around her.

A random glance out of the window caused Daryl to ask, "Sheldon, what are we doing at the airport?"

"We have a private plane waiting for us."

"Heading where?"

"You'll see. You promised to trust me completely, remember?"

She wavered, trying to comprehend what was happening. "You're asking a lot of me. You know that."

"I'm not going to hurt you."

"I know that, Sheldon."

"Then relax and enjoy."

The limousine drove them directly to the plane, where two cabin attendants greeted them. They entered the plane, an L-1011, which had been reconfigured from a 360 passenger plane to luxury transportation for about thirty to forty couples. Fully equipped with wet bar, plush seating, television, and VCR, Daryl thought she'd died and gone to heaven.

"This is incredible, Sheldon." Her eyes brightened with pleasure.

"I'm glad you're not upset."

"Why should I be?"

"Because you have no idea where I'm taking you."

"I trust you, Sheldon."

They sat side by side making small talk as the plane prepared to take off. Once in the air, they were served champagne and chocolate-dipped strawberries. Sheldon selected a movie to watch. He winked when he caught her eye.

"I have to say, you really know how to show a girl a good time."

He grinned. "I try. I'm glad you're having a good time."

Daryl's eyes narrowed speculatively. "Are we going to be in the air long enough to watch this whole movie?"

"I'm not telling."

She punched him playfully. "Curiosity is getting the better of me. Please tell me something."

"Okay," he said, while trying to keep from laughing. "Look out your window."

"Isn't this Las Vegas?"

Sheldon nodded. "I thought we'd take in a couple of shows and dinner."

Daryl felt the beginnings of tears. "This is so sweet. I can't believe you're doing all this for me."

Tenderly, his eyes melted into hers, and Sheldon leaned over and kissed her. "It's your birthday. You deserve it. I also arranged for us to spend the night when I found out you were going to be off this weekend."

"You've arranged for us to spend the night? I didn't bring anything with me."

"I have everything you need on the plane. I took the liberty of doing some shopping for you. You'll have to buy your . . . lingerie, however. He handed her a gift certificate for Victoria's Secret. We'll stop there before we head to the hotel."

"Shopping for me? You continue to amaze me, Sheldon."

"In case you're wondering, I reserved a two bedroom suite for us at the Flamingo Hilton."

Daryl relaxed visibly. "Thank you."

"I admit I want nothing more than to share a bed with you, but I don't want to rush you."

"I appreciate that, Sheldon. Sex is not something I take lightly."

The plane made it's descent and they buckled up. Daryl was still pleasantly shocked over all Sheldon had done to make her birthday special.

Another limo met them when the plane landed and drove them first to Victoria's Secret, where Daryl made her purchases. She made Sheldon promise to stay out of the store while she shopped. A few times, she'd caught him peeking in, during which she shook her fist at him. Their next destination was Bali's where they had dinner.

Three hours later, Sheldon nudged Daryl and asked, "Tired?

She shook her head. "No, I'm having the time of my life."

"Ready to do some gambling?"

"I don't really gamble. I just play the coin machines."

"That's about all I do myself," Sheldon admitted. He pulled out a fifty dollar bill and held it out to her. "Here's some gambling money."

She pushed his hand away. "No, Sheldon. I have some money. You've done so much already—"

"Daryl, I insist. It's your birthday."

"I'll gamble my own money away. Not yours."

A smile tugged at his lips. "You're not going to be difficult, are you?"

"I don't mean to be. Please, let me do this. I don't feel right gambling away somebody else's money."

"Okay." He shrugged in resignation.

Twenty minutes later, Daryl jumped as she hit a small jackpot. Laughing, she and Sheldon rushed to scoop up the silver dollars that rained from the machine.

"See, today is your lucky day. Ready to play some more?"

"No, I think I'll quit while I'm ahead. Do you mind if we call it a night?"

"Let's head to our rooms then."

Daryl felt a moment of panic at those words. Would she be able to keep him at a distance? With the way he made her feel whenever they were together, she wasn't so confident.

At the door to the room she would sleep in, Sheldon surprised her by placing a chaste kiss on her lips before leaving for his own. She listened as he entered the room next door and turned on the television. Shoulders slumped, she stared at the lonely hotel bed she would sleep in.

In the bathroom, Daryl stood in the shower, trying to cool the throbbing ache between her legs. She didn't know how much longer she would be able to refuse Sheldon, her need was so great. *He's used to women giving themselves to him at the blink of an eye. You have to be different,* her mind cautioned her.

Out of the shower and back in her room, Daryl decided sleep was out of the question.

When she assumed Sheldon had settled in for the night, Daryl tiptoed to the door, opening it as quietly as she could manage. Just as she eased past his door, it opened. She turned around.

Sheldon stood in the doorway, shirtless. Her knees went weak over seeing his smooth muscled chest. "I thought you'd gone to bed already, Doc."

"I . . . I wanted to get something to drink." She searched for something to say. "I thought you were settled in for the night."

"I was about to get something to drink too." He cleared his throat. "I was a bit thirsty myself."

Daryl headed back to her room. "You know, I think I'll just head on back to bed. I'm not as thirsty as I thought."

"You're sure?"

"I'm sure." As quickly as she could manage, Daryl returned to her room, closing the door behind her. She missed Sheldon's look of amusement.

Moving to the large window in her room, Daryl stared out into the night. Arms folded across her breasts, she turned and padded across the plush carpet to her bed. Beneath the covers, Daryl shivered slightly. It was going to be a long night.

Visions of Daryl had intruded on his rest all night long, and Sheldon was tossing and turning between the sheets he'd hoped he would be sharing with Daryl. He knew she'd been as ready as he. He had seen it in her eyes before something else had replaced it: Caution.

Nonetheless, Daryl was driving him crazy with the sexy, appraising looks she was always giving him. Sheldon wondered why she kept holding back. *Sooner or later, I'm going to have you.*

Giving up on sleep, he rolled over and peered at the floating red numbers on the hotel alarm clock. Six o'clock. He struggled out of bed and headed to the shower.

An hour later, Sheldon was knocking at Daryl's door. "Wake up, sleepyhead."

She opened the door with a bright smile. To his amazement, she was already dressed in a long, sand-colored apron-style jumper with a tee shirt underneath. To his further surprise, she was already packed. "I've been up for a couple of hours, thank you very much. I'm an early riser."

Sheldon's eyes shone bright with merriment. "So am I. How did you sleep?"

Daryl looked away, not wanting him to see the truth. "I slept fine. What about you? Sleep well?"

He knew she was lying by the way she averted her eyes. "I think you know the answer to that."

Daryl laughed, a mischievous glint coming into her eyes. "Oh, really?"

Sheldon's large hand took her face and held it gently. "You were on my mind all night long."

Putting her arms around his waist and burying her face against his chest, she whispered, "Thanks for being a gentleman. And for a lovely birthday celebration. I've really enjoyed myself." Daryl's body tingled from the contact. At last, reluctantly, they parted a few inches.

Sheldon cleared his throat. "I'm glad. I think birthdays are very special days."

"Yes, they are."

"I hate having to leave so soon."

"I know. Me, too," she moaned.

"We'll have to come back sometime."

"Yes," Daryl agreed. "Sometime soon."

After breakfast, they checked out and headed to the airport.

On the plane en route back to Los Angeles, she realized she hadn't found out when Sheldon would celebrate his birthday.

"Sheldon, when were you born?"

"August twenty-fourth, why?"

"Hmmmmm . . ."

He quirked an eyebrow. "Okay, Doc. What's going on in that pretty head of yours?"

Daryl's eyes widened with false innocence. "You're just going to have to wait and see."

Sheldon strode into the house whistling. Finding Maggie in the kitchen, he planted a kiss on her forehead. "Mama, how're you feeling?"

"I'm doing okay. Just sick of that white girl calling my

house. That Mallie, or whatever her name is, kept calling here looking for you last night and early this morning. She wanted me to tell her where you went. That girl acts like she's your wife. I'd sure hate to see that hotel bill for all those calls here. But then I guess her being a high fashion model," his mother sneered. "Money isn't a problem for her."

"Sorry, Mama," Sheldon murmured while trying to hold back his amusement. "I guess I'm going to have to talk to her."

"I think you need to tell her the truth! She's acting like the two of you are more than friends. Now that other one—Daryl. She's not like that. Always so polite and charming. I like her." She looked up at her son. "Don't you know any girls with normal names?"

Sheldon laughed.

"When am I going to meet this Daryl?"

"Why do you want to meet her? You've never wanted us to bring women here. If I remember you correctly, you said you weren't running a cat house—"

Maggie dismissed his comment with an impatient flick of her wrist. "Because I want to, that's why."

"I see."

"Why don't you invite her over here to dinner. Tonight. What do you think of that?"

"I think that's a great idea."

The phone rang, signaling for someone to answer.

Maggie screwed her face into a frown. "I bet that's that Mall person now."

"In that case, I'll get it." Sheldon reached for the phone. "Hello."

"Where have you been, Honey? I've been bugging your mom to death about where you were."

"And she told you she didn't know. Why'd you keep calling her like that?" Sheldon ripped out the words impatiently.

"I wanted to know if you were safe, that's all. What's so wrong about that?"

"I went out of town. That's all you needed to know."

"Alone?"

"I don't think that's any of your business."

"Sheldon, you don't have to be so rude to me. I'm sorry if I upset your mother. She sounds remarkably well, by the way."

He forced himself to remain calm. "You didn't need to keep calling like that."

"I was worried about you."

"You needn't be. I'm fine. I went out of town, that's all."

"I was thinking . . . why don't you hop a plane and come visit me. Your mother has recuperated, it seems, so you no longer have an excuse."

"Damnit, Malle . . ."

"What? What did I say?"

Sheldon sat up straight. "Listen to me. It is over between us." He ground out the words loud and clear. "What am I saying? Hell, it never started. We had some good times, but now you want more. I can't give it to you, Malle."

"I know you have feelings for me—"

"I care for you as a friend. Nothing more."

"Have you found a new playmate, Sheldon?" Her voice was tinged with anger.

Sheldon was quiet.

"Well, have you? Don't you think I know about your reputation? Everywhere we go, there's some woman throwing herself at you."

When Maggie walked back into the kitchen, Sheldon said, "Malle, I have to go. Just do yourself a favor. Go back to New York when you leave Paris."

"If I agree to go back home, will you answer my question? Are you seeing someone?"

"Yes, I am."

"That's all I needed to know."

Sheldon winced when she slammed down the phone in his ear. Recovering from his session with Malle, he picked up the phone, this time to call Daryl. He was grateful that

Malle had finally gotten the message. Now she would be completely out of his life.

After Sheldon hung up from talking to Daryl, Maggie strolled into the den right behind him.

"I couldn't help but overhear some of your conversation with Mall—"

"Her name is Malle. Oh, I just got off the phone with Daryl. She'll be here in an hour."

"That's good. Now, back to Malle. You need to cut it off completely. I don't think she can tell the difference between love and lust."

"Mama . . ."

"Don't Mama me, son. You need to stop having sex in the name of friendship."

"I'm honest with the women I get involved with."

Maggie shook her head. "Then they're either deaf and dumb, or just plain crazy."

"Things are different since you were young."

"Humph! Boys were still lying to young impressionable girls in order to get in their panties when I was growing up. From where I sit, things haven't changed much."

Sheldon didn't respond.

"I guess I'll go see about dinner." She stood up slowly. Before she left the room, Maggie stood in the portal and said, "I'm telling you, son. Nothing good is going to come out of this relationship or whatever it is you have with Malle. She's too obsessive over you."

Sheldon started to speak, but she interrupted him. "I know what you're about to say, so I'll shut up. I've said all I'm going to say about the matter."

But he knew his mother wasn't done by a long shot.

An hour later, Sheldon had just showered and changed when the shrill whining of the doorbell vibrated throughout the house. Just as he was about to take to the stairs, he heard his mother call out, "I'll get it."

* * *

Daryl hummed happily all the way to Sheldon's house. This impromptu invitation had thrilled her throughout. Her growing relationship with Sheldon seemed to be heading in the right direction, and she found herself becoming increasingly comfortable with him. She supposed he must be feeling the same way, or else he wouldn't have invited her to have dinner with him and his mother.

Pulling into the driveway, Daryl adjusted her rearview mirror to reapply her lipstick. "Here's to making a good impression," she murmured, as she headed up the steps as calmly as she could.

She was met at the door by a stunning woman who could be none other than Sheldon's mother. "Hi, Mrs. Turner, I'm Daryl Larsen."

"It's so nice to finally meet you in person, Daryl. Come on in."

"Same here. Thank you for inviting me for dinner." She stopped just inside the door and handed Maggie a bouquet of wild flowers. "These are for you."

"Well, aren't you sweet, dear. Lord, these are some pretty flowers. Come on in and have a seat." When she heard her son come up behind her, she said, "Sheldon, show Daryl to the den. Dinner's almost ready."

"Is there anything I can do to help?"

"Heaven's no. You're a guest in this house. Just sit down and relax."

Daryl gestured to the pool table before taking a seat on the sofa. "Do you shoot pool, Sheldon?"

"Yes."

From the kitchen, Maggie said, "Sheldon bought that pool table for me and his father. He knew how much we liked to play. Do you play?"

Daryl nodded. "Yes, I play occasionally. It's been a while since I've played though."

"How about a game right now, while we wait for dinner?" Sheldon asked. "Let's see how good you play."

She stood up grinning. "Oh, you sound as if you don't believe I can play."

His long arms folded across his chest, Sheldon grinned. "That remains to be seen."

Daryl slipped out of her jacket. "You're on, Mr. Turner."

After she beat him six out of seven games, Sheldon urged his mother to join them.

"Mama, you've got to come in here and restore the Turner's good name. Doc's killing me."

Wiping her hands on her red apron, Maggie chuckled. "Don't tell me, you let her beat you."

"Okay, I won't tell you—"

"But I will," Daryl teased. Looking up at him, she said, "Sheldon, I thought you could play. You'd better stick to basketball."

"I thought you'd be as bad as I am. I really didn't think you knew how to play."

Daryl leaned back onto a bar stool with her hands clasped over the pool stick. "My dad taught me. Not many people know this, but he was a pool hustler in his youth."

Sheldon and his mother looked at each other before bursting into laughter.

Confused, Daryl asked. "What's so funny?" She had no idea why they were laughing.

"Mama and my dad both did their share of hustling back in the day."

Daryl gazed at Maggie, surprise bright in her eyes. "No way! Did you really?"

Waving her hands, Sheldon's mother nodded and said, "But those days are best forgotten. Actually, that's how I met Leo, Sheldon's father. I beat him out of all his money."

"I bet that was really something to see," Sheldon said. "I know Dad didn't take that too well."

Maggie nodded. "Well, not at first, but as the night wore on, he began to see the humor in it. Besides, he'd just fleeced my brother out of all of his money. And my sorry brother had a wife and children to feed. I couldn't stand by and let Leo take his money. My sister-in-law would've killed him."

"I don't blame you one bit, Mrs. Turner," Daryl acknowledged. "I would've done the same thing."

Sheldon regarded her with amusement. "Really?"

"I sure would have."

Maggie took a peek at the clock. "Well, dinner's almost ready. Son, why don't you show Daryl to the bathroom, so she can wash up?"

Sheldon led the way. "Come this way, Doc."

When Daryl entered the dining room, she found Sheldon doing a last minute inspection of the place settings. "You must have set the table."

He looked up with a smile that melted her insides. "How did you know?"

"By the way you're acting." She moved beside him and patted his arm. "Don't worry—everything looks beautiful. You did a wonderful job."

"My mom told me I had the silverware in the wrong order, so I had to fix it."

"Where do you want me to sit?"

Sheldon pulled out a chair. "Right here."

As if on cue, his mother walked out carrying a bowl of vegetables. He immediately set out to relieve her of them. Daryl noted the way Sheldon was devoted to his mother. She smiled when he finally convinced Maggie to join Daryl at the table, so he could finish bringing out the rest of the food.

"I'm so glad you could join us, Daryl. I know it was short notice."

Placing a napkin in her lap, Daryl said, "It was perfect timing, actually. I was trying to think of where to have dinner when Sheldon called."

After placing the rolls and the garlic herb chicken on the table, SheLdon took a seat across from Daryl. "I don't know about you all, but I'm starving."

"Sheldon, dear . . ."

Daryl hid her laughter behind her hand.

During dinner there was little conversation. Afterward, Sheldon removed the dinner plates, while Maggie went into the kitchen, only to return with a three layer mocha chocolate cake.

Daryl took a bite of hers. "This is so good, Mrs. Turner. I wish I could bake like this."

"It's an acquired skill. It doesn't just happen overnight. It took me years to get a cake to look like this."

Sheldon nodded. "You should see some of the birthday cakes Mama made me."

"I'm sure they were delicious," Daryl countered.

"I never said they didn't taste good—they just were shaped funny."

Pointing at her son, Maggie said to Daryl. "If I hadn't made him and his brother help me in the kitchen when they were growing up, they'd both probably be starving somewhere or eating out every night."

"And I thank you for that, Mama. I don't know where I'd be if it weren't for you," Sheldon pointed out.

Daryl could see the love and respect in his eyes for his mother, and it touched her deeply. "Thank you both for such a wonderful dinner. I'm so full—I'm not sure I can drive to Pomona."

Sheldon pushed away from the table. "Why don't we play a few more rounds of pool? Work off some of that food."

Daryl read the challenge in his eyes. "Sure. But first I'm going to help your mother in the kitchen with—"

"You'll do no such thing, dear. You go on back there and whip my boy into shape."

Smiling, Daryl pushed away from the table and stood. "I'll do just that, Mrs. Turner."

Sheldon lost another two rounds to Daryl.

"You're not ready to give up? Pool is just not your game."

Putting his pool stick away, Sheldon nodded in agreement. "You're right—it's not my game."

Daryl held hers to him. "You get an A for effort though."

"Before I forget: There's a reception being held in my

honor in two weeks. Would you attend with me? Mama's going and I'd like for you to be there as well.''

"Sure, I'd love to go. So, you're getting an award?"

Sheldon nodded. "I tried to just get them to mail it to me."

Daryl laughed. "You're terrible. What's the award for?"

"Recognition for all of my charitable efforts in AIDS research."

"That's wonderful, Sheldon."

Shrugging nonchalantly, he said, "Now that that's settled, I have another challenge for you. How about a game of Clue?"

"You're on. I guess you're in the mood for a good butt whipping tonight."

"I see I'm going to have to stop being Mr. Nice and just show you who's boss."

"Yeah, right. Sheldon, you've already lost and you don't even know it."

Sheldon wondered briefly if she was talking about more than the game of Clue.

Chapter 10

The doors to the crowded movie theater opened and people gushed out. Margo dropped her empty cup into the nearest trash bin. "Daryl, what did you do for your birthday? Audrey and I tried to call you but you weren't home. We wanted to take you to dinner."

Daryl downed the last of her popcorn. The empty carton met the same demise as Margo's cup. "Sheldon surprised me with a trip to Las Vegas for dinner and a show."

"Really?"

She nodded. "We had such a good time. I hated to come back home."

Audrey nudged her on the arm. "Mmmmm, I guess you and he—"

"No, we did not. Sheldon was a perfect gentleman. He and I had separate rooms. We shared a two bedroom suite, however."

"That sounds so romantic," Audrey murmured. "Not the separate rooms, but the trip as a whole."

"It was. I don't think I've ever felt so special." Her smile broadened as she talked.

"Sounds like he's treating you like you deserve to be

treated. I'm impressed," Margo admitted, as she unlocked the doors of her car. "Hop in, ladies."

Daryl slid into the back seat and buckled her seat belt. "Sheldon is not at all like the media portrays him. He's a very sweet person. A very private man."

"Sounds like he's got your nose wide open."

Daryl's mouth twitched with amusement. "I know you're not talking, Audrey. You and Tyrell act like Siamese twins."

"I don't deny it. I'm crazy about Tyrell."

Margo glanced up into her rearview mirror, catching Daryl's eye. "Are you attending that dinner with Sheldon? The one to benefit AIDS research? I heard through the grapevine that Sheldon's going to receive an award in recognition for all his charitable contributions."

Daryl nodded. "Yeah, and I've got to go shopping for my dress. The dinner is next Saturday. Will you two go with me?"

"Sure. When do you want to go?" Audrey piped in. "I'm off until Tuesday."

"How about tomorrow?"

"Well, Daryl, I guess I have to say that I was wrong about Sheldon. First, your own special holiday, and now, your birthday trip. He must really like you."

Grinning, Daryl responded, "I think he's really beginning to care about me. We're finally on our way. There's nothing to stand in our way."

Daryl walked carefully up the steps to Sheldon's house, her royal blue gown clenched tightly in her hands. She didn't want her dress dragging on the ground. When she looked up, she found Sheldon leaning in the doorway.

"How long have you been standing there?"

"Ever since you pulled up." He shook his head slowly. "I have to tell you. You look GOOD, Doc."

Daryl was caught up in his enthusiasm. A delightful shiver of wanting ran through her. "I'm glad you approve. This is your night and I didn't want to embarrass you."

She assessed him as he led her into the den. The formal-wear, a Perry Ellis, looked as if it had been made just for him. Underneath, he wore a sterling-silver-colored vest with glossy treads of black running through it, and a crisp, white collarless shirt. "That tux really is sharp on you. You're going to wow the ladies tonight," she teased.

"The only lady I want to wow is you, Doc." He pulled her into his arms and bent his head to kiss her fully and sensually on the mouth.

The touch of his lips was a delicious sensation, and Daryl didn't want it to end.

"Knock, knock . . ."

Sheldon lifted his head. "Come on in, Mama."

A blush ran over Daryl's cheeks. "Hi, Mrs. Turner. How are you?"

Maggie embraced her. "I'm doing fine." Lowering her voice to a whisper, she added, "And judging from what I just walked in on—you're doing alright yourself. I want you to know that I think you're very good for him."

The two women pulled apart and Daryl smiled her thanks. She averted Sheldon's questioning gaze.

"Mama, you look beautiful."

Maggie's hand flew to her face. She turned to Daryl. "Is my make-up okay? Not too much?"

"It looks great, Mrs. Turner. And Sheldon's right. You look beautiful." Maggie wore a stunning black gown. A simple cut, it was sleeveless and straight with a discreet split centered in the back. The dress complimented Maggie's tall, slender form. The only accessories she'd chosen to wear were a long strand of pearls and matching earrings. Tonight, her hair was piled up on her head in a sophisti-cated fashion.

"Thank you both," Maggie murmured.

Sheldon touched Daryl lightly on the arm. "I'll go check to see if the limo's here."

"I need to repair my lipstick. Mind if I use one of the bathrooms?"

"Follow me, Doc."

Alone in the bathroom, Daryl thanked her lucky stars that Maggie Turner was on her side. She reapplied her lipstick and had just walked out, when she found Sheldon standing right outside the door.

"The limo's here."

Maggie grabbed her black velvet wrap and the trio headed out to the waiting car.

During the drive to the hotel, Sheldon appeared in deep thought. He seemed pensive, disturbed by something.

Daryl reached over to tap him. "Is something wrong?"

"No. I just hate things like this. I mean, I don't mind attending—I just don't want to be the center of attention."

"Sheldon's actually still a very shy person, Daryl," Maggie explained. "He's tried to hide that particular fact, but he's always been extremely shy. That is, until he hits the basketball court."

Daryl had known there was something about him from the very beginning, but she couldn't put her finger on it. "Sheldon, it's going to be fine," she tried to reassure him. "You've done this many times before."

Sheldon nodded and continued to stare out the window.

When they arrived at the hotel, Daryl placed her hand over Sheldon's, who smiled and said, "I'm glad you and Mama are here. It'll make it easier to deal with."

As soon as they entered the reception, Sheldon was assaulted by media personalities. Daryl and Maggie stood silently nearby.

"I meant what I said," Maggie whispered. "You're good for my son."

"I'm glad you think so, Mrs. Turner. I care a lot for him."

"It's good seeing him with a woman of substance. You know, you're the only woman he's ever brought to my house." Maggie neglected to mention that she never allowed her sons to bring women around. She'd always told them that until they found the women they would marry, no women would be welcomed in her home.

"Really?" Daryl tried not to sound so pleased.

Maggie nodded. "Sheldon's one of those men that no matter what you do, you can't change his mind. You have to let him make all of his decisions on his own. His father was that way, and so is Barry, his brother."

Confused, Daryl said nothing.

"I see Mayor Greene and his wife are here. I'm going over to say hello. You wait for Sheldon."

"Where did Mama go?"

Daryl glanced up at Sheldon. "She went to talk to the mayor and his wife."

"Why don't we go get something to drink? I'm thirsty from all that talking."

"I think it all went well. At least it looked that way from where I was standing."

"I don't think I could get through this evening if you weren't by my side."

"Sheldon, I wouldn't be anywhere else." And in that instance, Daryl knew she meant those words more than ever.

While they waited for their drinks, she surveyed the room, filled with celebrities and other prominent people. She caught sight of a face she'd never forget. Daryl nudged Sheldon's arm. "I thought you said your friend was in Paris. And that she would be going back to New York after that."

Sheldon glanced up briefly from his program. "She is."

"I think you better take a look." She nodded to the right. Malle, dressed in a sheer lace dress with solid panels covering her breasts and her hips, employed a drum roll walk as she sauntered toward them.

Daryl heard Sheldon mutter underneath his breath, "What in hell is she doing here?"

"I know why she's here. What I'd like to know is what in the world she has on. From here it doesn't look like much."

Malle stood before them, blocking their way. "Hello, Sheldon." She glanced over at Daryl. "Aren't you going to introduce me to your friend?"

Sheldon's face was unreadable as he made the introductions.

"Daryl, it's very nice to meet you." Malle awarded her with a cool, assessing stare.

"You, too."

Malle grinned. "We're about to be photographed. Why don't we all look nice and cozy. Act like great friends. What do you say?"

Sheldon refused to look at the camera, instead asking under his breath, "What are you doing here, Malle?"

"I thought I'd fly back to Los Angeles early and surprise you. I knew about the award you would be given tonight." She gave a small laugh and downed the last of her wine. "I guess the surprise is on me."

"Malle . . ."

"Don't worry, I'm not going to do something to embarrass you," she glanced over at Daryl. "Or cause trouble. I merely came over to say hello. I'm sure I'll be seeing you later . . . or as early as tomorrow."

"I'll see you later, Malle."

She blew him a kiss. "Of that I'm very sure. It was very nice meeting you, Daryl. It's always a pleasure meeting one of Sheldon's *friends.*"

"Likewise."

Malle stared briefly at her, then burst out into laughter before walking away. But not before Daryl caught a glimpse of the tears that shone brightly in her eyes.

"I'm sorry . . ."

"Don't be. Everything's fine. She's upset over seeing you with me. I can understand that."

"Daryl, I've been very honest with her."

"It's fine, Sheldon. I'm not upset over seeing her. You're with me tonight."

"I've never met a woman like you. You're so understanding."

"Not always," Daryl warned. "Don't put me on a pedestal. That often leads to disappointment."

"I'm a very lucky man, this evening."
For always, Daryl amended silently.

The next day, Sheldon picked up his keys and headed toward the door, when the phone rang. His mother was out and his first instinct was to just let the answering machine pick up, but then he thought it might be Maggie or Daryl.

"Hello."

"Hello, Honey."

Sheldon grimaced at the sound of Malle's sweet, syrupy voice. "I'm on my way out. I'll call you later." His voice hardened ruthlessly.

"I need to talk to You . . . NOW."

"I don't have time for this—"

"If you don't come here, I'll come to your mother's house and wait there until you come home. I mean it!"

"Malle . . ."

"I mean it. I need to talk to you. There are some things we need to settle once and for all."

"I'll be right there, dammit!"

Sheldon was so angry, he could have strangled the living daylights out of her. Tonight he was going to get her out of his life once and for all.

Malle opened the door wide enough for Sheldon to enter. "I see you've managed to tear yourself away from your little friend," she said snidely. "I guess that's why you haven't had much time to spend with me."

Sheldon ignored her comments. "Why aren't you dressed? I thought you wanted to talk. If you asked me over here because you think you're going to seduce me, you can forget it. I'm leaving—" He turned to leave.

"WAIT. I've had a splitting headache all day long, so I spent most of the day in bed." Moving to stand a hairs breadth away, she smiled seductively. "Besides, I do remember a time when you didn't want me in anything else."

Sheldon backed away, shaking his head. "Malle, don't do this. It's over. I've tried to be patient with you, but—"

She shook her head. "It's not over. I love you, Sheldon." Malle planted herself on the sofa, stretching out seductively. "Besides, I really don't believe you that you don't want me anymore. We were so good together."

"Malle . . ."

Her face contorted in anger, Malle sat up abruptly. "What, Sheldon? You just want me out of your life completely? Is that what you came here to tell me?"

"I don't want to hurt you, but yes, I think it's better if we don't see each other anymore. You obviously want more than friendship—"

"Sheldon, please . . ." Malle massaged her temple with her fingers. "I don't want to rehash this. I heard you. Now can we please move forward?"

"Are you okay?" Sheldon wanted to know.

She nodded slowly. "I'm fine. I think I just need to eat. What about you? Are you hungry?"

Sheldon shook his head.

Malle dialed room service. "Hello, could I order a double hot fudge sundae and a coke, please?"

Sheldon frowned. "Are you sure that's what you want to eat right now? I think you eat too much of this junk food, Malle. It can't be good for you. I mean with the headache . . ."

"I've been craving one for days. It won't hurt me. Besides, I took two aspirin right before you came." She sat watching him intently.

"What is it? Do I have something on my face?"

Malle smiled. "No, I just love looking at you. You are such a handsome man."

"Thanks." Sheldon knew where this was leading, and he wanted to stop it before she pressed on. Noting that she still massaged her temple, he suggested, "Why don't you go lie down and rest your eyes while you're waiting for your food. Maybe that'll help your headache disappear. We can talk tomorrow."

"Why are you in such a hurry to leave? Do you have plans for the evening or something?"

"Yes, I have plans."

"With that woman I saw you with last night? Are you sleeping with her now?"

"It's none of your business, Malle." Sheldon played with the ring on his finger, pulling it up and down his finger.

"Can I see your ring?"

"You've seen it plenty of times."

"I just wanted to see if it needed cleaning. You used to have me clean it all the time."

Sheldon removed the ring from his finger and handed it to her.

"I'll clean it after I eat." She sat it on the end table nearby. Glancing down at her hands, she said, "You know, I actually believed that one day I'd be wearing your ring."

"I never told you anything like that, Malle. How could you assume—"

"I thought you'd come to love me. I know you kept saying that you only wanted to be my friend but . . ."

Malle's order arrived. Malle signed the check as the waiter placed the tray on the coffee table in front of her. While she ate, they chatted about Paris as if there were no underlying current of tension between them.

Feeling Malle was in better spirits, Sheldon stood up and prepared to leave. "I have to leave now, okay? I have somewhere I need to be."

She jumped up to block his exit, knocking the tray and its contents on the floor. "Can't you stay a little while longer?"

"I'm sorry, Malle. I have to go—besides, we've already settled everything."

"Do you really think I'll just walk away? Well, it's not going to happen. You can't really think I'm going to disappear so you can carry on with your next victim. Does this

Daryl know how you go around, leaving a trail of broken hearts?"

He moved to step around her. "I'm sorry you got hurt. But I was honest from the beginning. I don't love you, Malle."

She slapped him hard, her long nails drawing blood. "Don't you say that to me," she demanded. "I know you care about me. I know it."

"Don't do that again," he warned.

"And what're you going to do? Hit me back? Go ahead hit me." She screamed hysterically. "You can't hurt me any worse than you already have! You've already broken my heart. Hit Me!"

Sheldon held up both hands, slowly backing toward the door. He hated when Malle had these violent episodes. "I'm not going to lay a hand on you. That's your problem. When you can't have things your way, you become violent, or you try to make me feel guilty. There aren't too many men like me."

When she came at him again, Sheldon grabbed her gently by the shoulders, talking softly. "You can't go around attacking people like this, Malle. One day, some-body's going to hurt you Now, calm down. Let's talk this out, like two adults."

Malle reached out, striking him again and again, each time leaving her mark.

"You're not going to leave me. Not ever."

Sheldon finally grabbed her by both hands and gently pushed her away from him. "I have to go. I can see you're too upset to talk right now. We'll talk when you calm down."

Her eyes glazed over with something he didn't recog-nize. She seemed to suddenly grow weak. Then when she began to stagger, Sheldon gathered her in his arms. "Malle . . . are you okay?" he asked, concern evident in his voice.

"Sheldon, don't do this to me. Please don't leave." Her voice started to grow so faint, he had trouble hearing her, whereas earlier, she'd been screaming to the point of hysteria. Malle grabbed his arm, clenching tightly, as if her life depended on it.

He pried her fingers loose. "Why don't you go to bed. Especially if you're not feeling well." Knowing her penchant for theatrics, he asked, "Do you want me to take you to the hospital?" Malle shook her head no. "Well, let's get you into bed. I'm leaving now so that you can get some rest. I'll call you tomorrow."

"Please don't leave me alone," she whispered.

"I have to go, Malle. I'll check on you tomorrow. I promise."

"I won't be here tomorrow," she said, as she staggered to the bed. "You don't want me, so I might as well get out of your life for good. Here I am sick and you won't even stay with me—"

"All right! I'll stay for just a little while." He stormed out of the bedroom and slumped down into a chair. He was angry at himself for caring one whit about Malle. She was most assuredly faking anyway, he fumed.

"Sheldon . . ."

He was too angry to respond.

Malle called out again. "Sheldon, I need you."

"What do you want?"

Tears ran down her face. "You might as well leave. I can tell you'd rather be somewhere else. You don't care whether I live or die."

"If you're sick, let me take you to the hospital. There's nothing I can do for you. I'm not a doctor."

"Just go! I want you out of my life. I might as well die. Then you'll be free of me."

"You're not going to die, Malle. You've got your whole life ahead of you."

"What do you care?"

Sheldon sighed, throwing his hands up in resignation. "I can't deal with this anymore. I'm getting out of here. I'm sorry you don't feel well, and I hope you feel better."

"Just go straight to hell, Sheldon Turner," Malle shouted, before collapsing in a bout of hysterics. "I hate you!" Sheldon stood outside her room, debating whether or not he should leave her like this. He hadn't wanted their friendship to end this way, but he decided now was not the time to try and comfort her. Sadly, he felt this was the last time he'd see her.

Clutching a napkin to his bleeding face, Sheldon was grateful to find the elevator empty. Wanting to put as much distance between him and the hotel, Sheldon walked briskly through the lobby, only to collide with a slender young man wearing a front desk uniform. "Oh, sir, I'm really sorry—"

Sheldon nodded and muttered a quick, "Don't worry about it." He kept going, his need to get away evident.

"Clarence, are you running down our guests now?"

The young man shook his head emphatically. "No sir. I . . . I didn't want to be late." He had only been working at the Beverly Wilshire Hotel for a week, and he really needed this job. "Sorry, Mr. Boswell. It won't happen again. I'll be more careful."

"Well, then. I suggest you walk back to the time clock and punch in immediately. He checked his watch. "It's approximately two minutes before eleven."

"I'll be right back." Clarence stopped. "Hey, wasn't that Sheldon Turner I ran into? He used to play for the New York Rockets."

Looking down his aristocratic nose, Cecil Boswell nodded.

"Yes, it was."

"Wow . . . hey, I wonder how he got all those scratches on his face. Looks like he was in a fight or something."

"Apparently," Cecil mumbled under his breath. "Clarence, I think you should head to that time clock now. As you stated, you don't want to be late. Your shift starts in one minute."

* * *

Sheldon drove straight home. He and Daryl had a date tonight, but his dealings with Malle had left him drained.

Back at home, Sheldon studied his bruises. Staring at the ugly, bleeding cuts on his cheek, he frowned. Malle scratched him up good this time. She was crazy.

"What on earth—" Maggie's mouth opened and closed repeatedly but no words came. Sheldon hadn't heard her come in.

Sheldon could see the anger in his mother's face. She rushed into the bathroom, moving to inspect his scratches more closely.

"Sheldon, what happened? Did you get into a fight?"

"No, Mama. It's nothing."

"I got eyes, Son. Now tell me what happened."

"Mama—"

"Who did this to you? I want to know."

"I'm fine."

Sheldon grimaced as Maggie applied antiseptic to his face while she talked. "That girl did this to you, didn't she? She made a point of introducing herself to me last night. That Malle, I can't stand her. I could see she was no good just by looking at her. And that dress—that wasn't no dress. That tramp was naked under that see-through whatever you want to call it." She shook her head. "Just shameful."

"Mama, I don't want to talk about it right now."

"That Malle person is crazy." Maggie stopped working on his face. She seemed to be thinking about something.

Sheldon saw her eyes widen with fear as she peered up at him. Maggie pressed her hand to her bosom and leaned back against the wall. "Oh Lord! You didn't hit her, did you?"

Sheldon shook his head. "I didn't hit her. I tried to calm her down. When I couldn't, I left."

"I ought to go over there and calm her down myself.

Somebody needs to tell her that I'm your mama, and I gave you all the beatings you ever needed. She needn't put her hands on you."

In spite of his pain, Sheldon laughed.

Daryl paced back and forth. Where was Sheldon? Had something happened to him? she wondered. He was over three hours late. *And here I am acting like a fool by still waiting for him. Girl, he'd better be worth all this trouble*, she whispered to herself.

Finally, she realized he wasn't going to show. Daryl went upstairs and took off her clothes. She'd just settled into her bed with a romance novel she'd been planning to read for weeks, when the phone rang. Her first impulse was to just let it ring. When it looked as if the caller wasn't going to give up, Daryl picked up.

"Daryl—" Sheldon began.

"I guess you forgot about our date tonight." She threw the words at him like stones.

"No, Sweetheart, I didn't. I had to take care of something. I know I should have called, but when I got home, I just wasn't in the mood to be good company."

"It's just as well, I'm kind of beat anyway," she lied.

"Hard day at the morgue?"

Daryl chuckled softly. "Yeah, you could say that."

A clicking sound could be heard. "Hold on a minute, Sheldon. I've got another call." When she returned, she said, "I've got to go."

"What's up? Is something wrong?"

"I just got a call from my office. I need to get to a crime scene. I'll talk to you later."

"How about breakfast tomorrow morning? To make up for tonight."

"I'll let you know." Daryl hung up and called her office.

Dragging herself out of bed, she quickly dressed in a pair of jeans and a denim shirt. She picked up her keys and her purse. Sighing, she slipped into her car. She had to drive to the Beverly Wilshire Hotel. They had found a dead woman in one of the suites.

Chapter 11

Treading through the mass of curious bystanders, Daryl eased into the luxurious suite swarming with cops and detectives. Careful to stay clear of all potential pieces of evidence, she eyed the opulent room from one end to the other. She had to admit the room was beautiful and the furnishings sumptuous.

"She's over here, Dr. Larsen," a policeman called out to her.

She greeted him with a smile. "How're you doing, Sam?"

"I'm fine."

A body clothed in a silk chemise lay sprawled in line with the end of the king size bed. The telephone lay on the floor just within her reach. Kneeling beside her, Daryl touched her. She wasn't breathing, and her body was cool to the touch. She hadn't been dead that long, she estimated. Smoothing her long blond hair gently from the dead woman's face, she gasped in surprise. It was Sheldon's ex-girlfriend. "Oh my God," she murmured softly.

A policeman next to her picked up a ring, placing it carefully in a plastic bag.

"Wait! Let me see that." She couldn't believe her eyes.

It was Sheldon's ring. She glanced down at the dead woman, then back at the ring. What was she doing with his ring? Sheldon said he never took it off. Surveying the ransacked room once more, Daryl caught sight of shattered glass near the doorway. What in the hell happened here?

"Hello, Dr. Larsen," a detective greeted her.

His name was Brian Stinson, and she disliked him immensely. "Detective Stinson."

"The deceased was registered under Malle Vincent. She's some high fashion model from New York. The manager said that Sheldon Turner was a frequent visitor here. That would be the Sheldon Turner that you've been seen with. As a matter of fact, your boyfriend was here earlier tonight. And when he left, several guests said that he had scratches on his face. The manager said that they got a couple of complaints earlier tonight from other guests on this floor. Apparently, there was some kind of fight going on in here."

Daryl didn't like where he was going with his story. Standing with her arms folded across her chest and her face impassive, she asked, "So, you're saying what, exactly, Detective Stinson?" Inside, she was dying. Sheldon wouldn't have hurt Malle. He wasn't capable of such violence.

"Miss Vincent managed to call the front desk a few minutes after he left, and it seemed she had some trouble talking. The only thing she managed to get out was his name. They sent someone from security up here to check on her. When she didn't respond to his knock, he used his key to get in. This is the way he found her. The guard administered CPR while waiting for the paramedics to arrive."

The other detective, a man that reminded Daryl of a modern-day Sherlock Holmes, nodded and said, "Looks like we're going to have to have a little talk with Mr. Turner." He turned to her. "Any idea how she died, Doc?"

Daryl shook her head. "Not yet, but as much as I hate to disappoint you, it appears Miss Vincent died of natural causes. There are no wounds, no bruises, nothing that would indicate her death was otherwise.'' Her vision swirled dangerously. She stood up slowly and leaned against the door to steady herself. They were wrong. Sheldon couldn't have done this. There was no way he could have murdered Malle. Besides, she reasoned, she couldn't venture a guess at the cause of death right now. ''You'll have to wait for the autopsy report.''

''By the way, Dr. Larsen. Where were you tonight?''

She stared Detective Stinson straight in the face. ''I was at home.''

''Alone?''

''Yes.''

He exchanged glances with the modern-day Sherlock Holmes, before saying, ''Can you prove it?''

''Of course I can. I received a call approximately one hour ago to come here. I live in Pomona. That's why it took me so long to get here.''

''You could have had your calls forwarded. Perhaps to Mr. Turner's house?'' Detective Stinson sneered.

She smiled then. ''Perhaps. One problem though, Detective.''

''What's that?''

''I don't have call forwarding. Feel free to check my phone bill . . . or anything else.''

He moved to stand in front of her. ''You know what, Dr. Larsen? I think this young lady did not die of natural causes. I think something else happened. It's too much of a coincidence that she and Sheldon Turner were overheard arguing in here. Apparently, there was some sort of physical altercation—''

''As I said earlier, we'll know more after the autopsy.'' Turning away from Detective Stinson, Daryl asked, ''Sam, are you done with the body?''

Not looking up, a bespectacled man replied, ''Yeah. You can have her.''

''I'll see you later.'' Nodding to Sam, she said, ''Let's

get her out of here.'' She wondered how Sheldon was going to take the news of Malle's death.

"Sheldon, honey, come quick!" Maggie called from her room.

Thinking Maggie was feeling ill, he leapt out of bed and ran the short distance to her room. "Mama, are you all right?"

"Yes, son. I'm fine, but you need to see this." She turned up the volume.

"The body of a young woman was found in a room at the Beverly Wilshire Hotel . . ."

Maggie switched to another channel. "The body has been identified as that of Malle Vincent, a New York model . . ." Another reporter was saying.

Sheldon felt as if he'd been slammed in the chest with a sledge hammer. Falling to his mother's bed, he put his hand to his mouth.

"I'm just as shocked as you, Son. Right now they don't know how she died."

"I don't believe this. I was just with her . . ." Sheldon looked wild eyed at his mother. "This is a mistake. Malle's not dead. She can't be."

The phone rang and Maggie answered. She handed it to Sheldon. "It's Daryl."

"Hello, Doc. I guess you just saw the news. They're wrong—"

Daryl closed her eyes. "No, Sheldon. It's Malle."

"It can't be! I just left her not too long ago—" he stopped suddenly. He hadn't told her about his seeing Malle earlier. That she was the reason he'd decided to cancel. "Daryl, I'm sorry. It wasn't . . ."

"It doesn't matter right now. I just wanted to let you know . . . about Malle. I didn't want you to hear it on the news, but I guess I'm too late."

"The call earlier. It was . . ."

"Yes. I'm really sorry about . . . her death."

"Daryl—"

"Sheldon, I have to go. I'll try and call you later."

Maggie placed a comforting arm around him. "I wish I knew what to say, Son."

"I was so mean to her earlier. She kept talking about dying."

"Do you think she killed herself?"

Sheldon shrugged. "I don't know. But according to the news, the police haven't ruled out foul play." Shaking his head, he murmured, "I'm going to lie down."

Back in his room, Sheldon paced back and forth in his room. Malle was dead. She died shortly after he left her at the hotel.

Emotionally drained, he fell to the bed in a slump. There was still a part of him that couldn't believe Malle was gone. She would never again grace the covers of magazines or the runways of New York and all of Europe. In spite of their disagreement, she was still a friend.

"Oh, Malle . . . I didn't . . . I didn't want this for you." Tears of grief slipped down his face. "I wanted you to go on with your life—find some happiness. That's all I wanted."

He massaged his throbbing temple. "What happened after I left? How did you die? Why did you die?"

"Sheldon, honey?" Maggie stood in the doorway. "Son, are you okay?"

"Mama . . ."

Maggie eased down beside him. "Why don't you try to get some sleep?"

"No. I keep replaying everything that happened in Malle's room last night. I keep going over and over it in my mind . . ."

"Once they have the autopsy report, they'll know a lot more."

"Mama, how can this be happening? When I left the hotel, she was alive. She died right after I left. Oh, God, what if I'd stayed a few minutes more? She'd asked me to stay." His voice broke.

Sheldon, I want you to get in this bed and try to get some sleep. You're going to need your strength for the battle up ahead."

"I can't sleep—"

"Then just lie there and rest your eyes."

Sheldon reluctantly did as he was told. But instead of sleeping, he stayed up most of the night trying to make sense of Malle's death.

Daryl's footsteps sliced into the silence of the solemn autopsy room. Malle's body lay on a cold steel table. Even in death, she was still very beautiful. Daryl picked up the photographs of Malle dressed and the ones of her nude. "What happened to you?" she whispered.

Picking up the chart, she began her notes.

"I thought you went home earlier," Caroline said, walking briskly into the room. "I just heard what happened. I can only imagine what this is doing to both you and Sheldon. So, I thought I'd come in and help."

"I really appreciate it. This is Sheldon's ex-girlfriend lying here. He's devastated. And the police are trying to find a way to pin this one Sheldon." Daryl returned the photographs to the counter nearby.

"Why? What would be the motive?"

Daryl shrugged her shoulders. "Well, I guess they'll say she followed him to L.A., wanting to rekindle their relationship. Earlier tonight they had a fight, and he stormed out. Now she's dead." She bit her lip until it throbbed like her pulse.

"Daryl, I'm so sorry. It can't be easy for you, either."

"I'll be fine. It's Sheldon I'm worried about." Her gaze returned to Caroline's face. "I believe she died of natural causes—we just have to prove it."

Caroline nodded. "We'll go over everything with a fine tooth comb."

"Hello, ladies," Curtis called out, as he entered the room. "You wanted to see me, Daryl?"

Daryl tapped her fingernails on the counter. "Yes. Have you examined the nightgown?"

"Yes, and the fibers have all been sent to the lab."

"What about the hair and skin samples—"

"Done. Fingernails, too. Relax, Daryl."

"Curtis is right. If Malle Vincent died of natural causes, we're going to do everything we can to prove it. And if she didn't, we'll prove that also."

Daryl smiled. "Thanks, Caroline." She took a deep breath. "Let's get started. We need to find out what happened to Miss Vincent."

Snapping on her microphone and latex gloves, she moved slowly, paying careful attention to her work.

"All the tests have been ordered, Daryl. We should have an answer sometime tomorrow."

"We need to know why she went into cardiac arrest." She stretched and yawned. "I think I'm going to go have some coffee. Want to join me?" Daryl asked sleepily.

"Sure. We've done all we can do in here," Caroline mumbled.

Chapter 12

Daryl struggled to sleep, but couldn't. Sheldon stayed on her mind. He was so grief stricken. A part of her felt jealous, but she fought to keep it at bay. Malle was dead. And Sheldon cared a great deal for her. She was his friend.

She wondered why he'd felt the need to lie about where he'd been. Well, he didn't lie exactly, she amended. Sheldon just hadn't bothered to tell her where he'd been. It was obvious that something went on in that suite, but Sheldon—capable of murder? No way. She would not believe that.

Tomorrow she would have the test results in her hand. Daryl tried to wish away her feelings of nervousness and anxiety. Everything would be all right, she kept telling herself over and over. So why am I not believing it? She couldn't get rid of the sinking feeling in her stomach, that's why.

The next day, Caroline knocked on Daryl's door. "The tests all came back." In her hand, she carried a large 12 X 14 inch envelope that Daryl assumed contained all the

photos, the autopsy report, and other information perti-
nent to the Vincent case.

Motioning for her colleague to enter, Daryl noted that
Caroline closed the door before sitting down. Taking a
deep breath, she reached for the results of Malle's autopsy.

"Oh my God! There was an excessive amount of insulin
in Malle Vincent's blood, which led to cardiac arrest."
She looked up at Caroline. "Her liver wasn't diseased or
damaged. And I examined the pancreas very closely. There
were no tumors present." Daryl knew there were two
known causes of excessive natural insulin created in the
body. One from insulin-producing tumors in the pancreas
and the other from a disorder of the liver caused by alcohol-
ism. Neither of these conditions were found in Malle Vincent.

"Maybe she was diabetic?" Caroline offered. "We don't
have her medical reports yet."

"The amount's so much . . . it can't be natural." Daryl
closed her eyes, feeling utterly miserable, and her heart
began to beat wildly. "I didn't see any needle marks, did
you?"

"No. I'll check her again though. Maybe we missed
them."

"I'm sure we didn't," she whispered. "We searched
every inch of her body. Give me your expert opinion. Do
you think she was injected with insulin, Caroline? Do you
think the police are correct? That someone killed Malle
Vincent by injecting her with insulin?"

"As you well know, the facts are that Malle died because
of insulin overdose." She lowered her voice a notch. "Do
you know if Sheldon had access to insulin? Is he diabetic?"

Daryl wasn't sure what to think. She knew Sheldon's
mother was a diabetic, and she needed a daily injection
of insulin. Shaking her head, she tried to force her accusa-
tions out of her head.

"Daryl, you still with me?"

"Huh? Oh yeah. I'm sorry, what were you saying?"

"I asked if Sheldon had access to insulin? The reason I

ask is because there wasn't any evidence of insulin in the suite. The police found a bottle of aspirin, a bottle of Valium, and some multi-vitamins.''

Daryl rubbed her throbbing temple. Something wasn't right about this case. Looking up at Caroline, she asked, "I wonder if Malle was ever diagnosed with reactive hypoglycemia?"

Caroline shook her head. "I don't know, but even if she was, I don't know of a case in my experience in which reactive hypoglycemia caused someone's death."

Daryl was deep in thought.

"What's going on in that head of yours?"

Something tugged at her memory. "Seems like—" she sighed in frustration. "It'll come to me late—" She stopped short.

Detective Stinson walked into her office without so much as a knock.

"This was a closed meeting, Detective."

"Dr. Larsen, do we have the results of the Vincent case?"

"It's right here, but . . ."

"But what?"

"We're not through with our investigation."

"Why don't you give me what you have?"

"Because it's not complete."

"How did Malle Vincent die?"

"She died of hyperinsulin. Insulin overdose."

"We found no evidence of insulin in her suite. Any needle marks?"

"None."

"Any history of diabetes?"

"We're still waiting on her medical report—"

Curtis walked in. "Daryl, this just came in over the fax. It's Miss Vincent's medical report."

"I'll take that." Detective Stinson said, snatching the papers from his hands. "Hmmmm," he said, as he scanned the documents. "I don't see any evidence of her being a diabetic." Folding his hands across his chest, he asked.

"Now, Dr. Larsen, how do you suppose all that insulin got into the victim's body?"

Daryl stood, her body shaking with anger. "Detective Stinson, my colleague and I still have some work to do. As soon as I have the full report ready, I'll let you know. Now please leave my office."

He stopped at the door. "Think I'll go have a talk with your boyfriend. You know, you thought you were too good to go out with me . . ." He laughed nastily. "I guess you couldn't do any worse."

Daryl was so angry, she could have spit at Stinson's back.

"What an idiot!" Caroline announced.

"Among other things. He's going to try to pin this on Sheldon. I just know it."

"Do you really believe he's innocent, Daryl?"

"Yes, I do. There's got to be another explanation. I know there is."

Caroline scanned the medical reports. "She was diagnosed as having reactive hypoglycemia."

Daryl and Caroline left her office and headed back to the autopsy room. Once again, they checked Malle for needle marks.

The phone rang, interrupting them. Smiling apologetically, Daryl said, "I'd better take this."

Caroline nodded. She busied herself by reading her notes in the Vincent report.

"Mrs. Turner. How are you? WHAT?"

Caroline looked up in concern.

"I'll be right there. Bye."

"Thanks, Caroline. I hate to cut this short, but I've got to run." Daryl grabbed her purse and headed out.

"What? Where are you going?"

"The police have arrested Sheldon. They found an empty bottle of insulin in his car. I'll be back as soon as I can."

* * *

Daryl followed the guard to the cell where they were holding Sheldon. Her heart went out to him when she found him sitting with his face in his hands. "Sheldon?"

He looked up, his eyes filled with sadness . . . and fear. "Daryl, I'm glad to see you." He stood up slowly and moved to stand before her, iron bars separating them.

"How are you holding up?"

"I'm as well as can be expected. Sweetheart, I need you to believe me. I didn't kill her. Although, the way I treated her, I might as well have."

"Don't talk that way, Sheldon."

"The police found an empty bottle of insulin in my car. My mother is a diabetic, Daryl. She must have left it in there. They said Malle died because of an excessive amount of insulin in her system."

"Did she seem all right that night? Did you notice anything different about her?"

Sheldon shook his head. "No . . . wait a minute. That night she said she'd had a bad headache all day, but then she ordered a double hot fudge sundae and a coke."

Daryl digested what he'd just said. "Hmmm, did Malle eat a lot of sweets?"

"Yes."

She pulled a small notepad out of her purse and began to take notes. "Did she ever take anything to control her weight? In her career, all the junk food could work against her."

Sheldon shook his head thoughtfully. "Malle always said she could eat pretty much anything and not gain weight. I'm pretty sure she didn't take anything."

"So you don't recall ever seeing bottles of insulin in her apartment?"

"No. What does this have to do with controlling her weight?"

"We had a case once where a woman injected herself with insulin to control her weight. Did Malle take anything for her headache?"

"She took aspirin. I believe that's what she said. I . . ."

"Sheldon? What is it?"

"Right before I left, Malle suddenly became weak. She almost collapsed. Even her voice sounded strange."

"Strange how?"

"Kind of weak. I could barely hear her. I offered to take her to the hospital—"

"You did? Did you tell the police that?"

"No, it didn't seem really important at the time."

"Make sure you tell your lawyer just what you've told me."

"I will. Do you think it'll help? I thought she was faking. If I'd known . . . maybe she'd be alive today."

"Sheldon, I'm so sorry you have to go through this, but there really isn't anything you could have done to save her. I'm not clear on what happened, but I'm still working on it. I need you to remain strong." She lowered her voice. "I'm going to leave now, because I have some research to do, but I'll be back."

The guard reappeared. "You're real popular, Mr. Turner. You have another guest."

Sheldon's mouth dropped open. "Barry, what are you doing here?"

"I thought you might need someone to talk to." Barry glanced over at Daryl and held out his hand. "I'm Sheldon's brother."

Daryl shook his hand. "I know. It's nice to meet you. I'm Daryl Larsen, Renee Cody's cousin."

"Really? Tell her I said hello. Haven't seen her in a long time."

"I'll be sure to tell her."

"Barry, I didn't kill her." Sheldon clenched the bars as if his life depended on it.

"I know that, little brother. There's no way you would have hurt that girl. They got it all wrong."

"The police are trying to pin this on me."

"They won't."

"How is Mama holding up?"

"She's fine. She's more worried about how you're doing."

"Barry, I need you to do me a favor. Would you walk Daryl out? Don't let the media anywhere near her."

"Sure." Barry looked down at her. "Are you okay with it?"

"Whatever Sheldon wants."

As soon as Daryl and Barry burst through the doors, a reporter approached them.

"Barry, what do you have to say about your brother's arrest?"

"He's innocent! That's all I have to say. Now if you will excuse us . . ."

"What about you, Dr. Larsen? It was your findings that landed your boyfriend in jail."

Barry stopped. "What in hell are they talking about?"

"I'm the M.E. assigned to the Vincent case."

"Is your boyfriend speaking to you, Dr. Larsen?" someone called from the back.

Barry grabbed her by the arm, pulling her until they were out of hearing range of reporters.

"How long have you and Sheldon been seeing each other?"

"Since January."

"You are the person that put my brother behind bars?"

"It's not like that, Barry. Now, please listen to me. Sheldon is a celebrity. So was Malle. The police are being pressured to make an arrest." She held up her hand when he started to speak. "Please hear me out. I believe Sheldon is innocent. However, I'm required by law to report my findings to the police. In this case, I'm still working on it. Detective Stinson jumped the gun as far as I'm concerned. I'm going to do everything in my power to clear your brother."

"You really care for Sheldon."

"I care very much. Just bear with me. I think I'm on to something, okay?"

Barry nodded. "How . . . how is Renee doing? Did she ever get married?"

"No. She's still single. She's a psychologist in Chino Hills."

"Really? That was always her dream." He seemed wistful.

"Sheldon really needs you right now, Barry. He's so scared."

"I'm not going to abandon him. I know he didn't kill that girl."

Margo was parked in front of her house when Daryl arrived home.

"Are you avoiding me?" Margo asked, displaying her judgmental furrow.

Daryl shook her head. "Now, why would I do that?"

"You haven't been returning any of my or Audrey's calls."

"I've been busy."

"Daryl, do you really believe that Sheldon's innocent?"

"Yes, don't you?"

Margo shrugged. "I don't know. He had scratches on his face and neck—"

"Because she jumped on him."

"Did it ever occur to you that maybe he hadn't meant to kill her—things could've gotten out of hand. She starts fighting him and he gets angry. For goodness sake, they found an empty bottle of insulin in his car. What more do you need for proof?"

Daryl held up her hand. "I know where you're going with this, and Margo, I have to tell you that I don't like it. Sheldon did not kill Malle Vincent."

"I know you want to believe that. I do, too."

"He didn't kill her."

Margo folded her arms across her bosom. "There is absolutely no doubt in your mind? Be honest, Daryl. Do you really believe Malle killed herself? She was a top model and could have any man she wanted. Can you look me in the face and say that there's not one tiny part of you that thinks Sheldon could be guilty?"

Her eyes met Margo's. "He didn't do it." Deep down, Daryl believed Sheldon was innocent. So they had a woman dead because of excessive insulin in her blood, no injection, and neither of the two classic sources for that insulin present. She admitted that it was unusual, but maybe not unique . . . Margo's voice interrupted her thoughts.

Margo sighed in frustration. "I know you love him, Daryl, but you've got to be prepared."

"I hate to cut off our visit but I've really got to run. I need to stop by the USC library, and I have an appointment with one of my professors." She headed to the door.

"Daryl . . ." Margo called from behind her. "What are you up to?"

"We'll talk later," she yelled back, walking as fast as she could.

"Caroline, when you're done, could you meet me in my office? You too, Dr. Murdoch."

"Sure, we'll be there in a few minutes."

Daryl tapped her fingernails impatiently on her desk. Silently, she prayed they were close to finding out the truth.

"What's up, Daryl?" Caroline asked as she breezed into the office. Dr. Murdoch followed on her heel.

"I think there's another natural cause for excessive insulin that could result in death."

"And what might that be, Daryl?" Dr. Murdoch asked.

"I don't know, but in medical school, I remember doing a case study on the mysterious death of an eight-month-old baby in Northen California. Are you familiar with it, Dr. Murdoch?"

He pulled off his glasses as he gave her question some thought.

"What about you, Caroline?" she asked.

Caroline thought about this. "I . . . think so. Now that you mention it, I do remember something . . . wait, they found something similar to the Vincent case."

Dr. Murdoch nodded. "This theory was used by the defense in another case. A C-Peptide test was never ordered when she was taken to emergency. If it had been, it would've disclosed if the excessive insulin found in her body was natural or had been injected. It was a high profile case at that—the Sunny von Bulow case."

Daryl nodded. "That's right. That poor woman is still in an irreversible coma. And there was one more case. In Alabama, a sixty-year-old black woman died. I just have to gather more—"

Dr. Murdoch cleared his throat loudly. "Daryl, I know how much this case means to you, but I think I'd better take you off it right now."

"What? You can't be serious."

"I'm very serious. Daryl, when we write the autopsy report, we don't want anyone to question it. Now, I know you're one of the best ME's around, but you're much too close to the case. You've done the work. Let Caroline and I take it from here."

That evening, Dr. Murdoch knocked on her office door. Dropping the large envelope containing Malle's report and other documents, he sank wearily into the chair closest to the door. "Malle Vincent died of natural causes. It's a condition called Islet cell hyperplasia. The islet cells start multiplying and increase in numbers, producing excessive insulin—"

"Which pours over into the blood, and the person goes into a coma or dies," Daryl finished for him. She fell back into her chair. "He's innocent. Oh my God. Sheldon's innocent."

Dr. Murdoch laughed. "You knew it all along. Even when the facts showed otherwise."

"Have the police—?"

He nodded. "I'm on my way over there now. I wrote the official report myself."

She stood up. "Thank you, Dr. Murdoch, for not giving up. For finding the truth."

"We're supposed to find the truth, no matter what."

Chapter 13

"You got here in record time. Where did you call from?"

"I called from my car." Audrey embraced Daryl tightly. "Hey, how are you doing? You look wonderful."

"I'm fine."

Audrey climbed onto a bar stool and made herself comfortable. "Have you heard from Sheldon since he left town?"

Daryl shook her head no. "I thought I would have by now. I guess he's really taking Malle's death and the arrest harder than I thought. I think a trial would have killed him."

"I guess he really cared about her."

"I suppose. You know, Audrey, I really don't want to talk about Sheldon or Malle right now."

"What's wrong, Daryl?"

"Nothing's wrong," she lied.

"Something is wrong. I can see it on your face."

"I'm just really worried about him." Daryl stood up and walked over to the huge kitchen window. Looking out, she pretended to be interested in the scenery outside.

"I'm sure he's okay."

Turning to face Audrey, Daryl folded her arms across her chest. "I'm not so sure. You didn't see the look of devastation on his face when he found out she was dead and that the police actually thought he had something to do with it."

"I'm sure it's affected him greatly."

Daryl turned back to peer out of her kitchen window. "Even though she died of natural causes, Sheldon still blames himself for her death."

Audrey was quiet for a few moments. "I don't know why he would feel that way. It's not his fault."

She turned around, gazing into Audrey's eyes. "I hope you really believe that."

"I know it's not his fault, but there are going to be some people who will always believe the worst. They thrive on it."

"I wish I could convince him of that."

The phone rang, and Daryl motioned for Audrey to answer.

"Hello. Hi, how are you? Yes, she's here." She held out the phone to Daryl.

Daryl assumed that it was either Margo or her mother. "Hello? Sheldon, what a surprise! I was worried about you."

"I'm fine. Daryl, I'm leaving New York in a couple of hours."

"That's wonderful, I—"

"Only," he interrupted, "I'm not coming to Los Angeles. I'm going to Palm Springs."

Daryl was disappointed. "Oh. Well, when will you be back in L.A.?"

"I was hoping you'd be able to meet me in Palm Springs. What do you think?"

"I think it's a wonderful idea. I have some days off coming to me. I'll call and explain that I need to take an emergency vacation."

"Great. I'll be staying at the Desert Springs Resort and Spa. Call and let me know when to expect you."

"I'll talk to you later tonight." She was grinning from ear to ear when she hung up.

"I take it you and Sheldon are about to spend some quality time together?"

"Yes, Audrey, we are. I have to call and get the time off, and then I want to go shopping. I need to pick up a few things before I leave. Will you go with me?"

"Sure, I've got nothing better to do. I don't have to meet Tyrell for another three hours. That gives us plenty of time to do some damage."

The next day, Daryl was excited about the prospect of seeing Sheldon. She pulled up to the front of the resort. Jumping out, she practically threw the keys to the valet parking attendant. Not paying attention to the beautiful desert scenery, Daryl grabbed her overnight bag and walked briskly into the hotel to a waiting elevator.

She counted the minutes until she'd see his handsome face. Sheldon had been gone for the last month, and it seemed more like forever. Now in a few mere seconds, she'd see him again.

Nervously, Daryl knocked on Sheldon's door. She ran trembling fingers through her hair, smoothing it down.

"You made it."

She smiled. "Yes. Traffic wasn't bad. I got here earlier than I expected." She wanted to touch him, but was hesitant to do so. Tentatively, Daryl reached out a hand and brushed it softly against his cheek. She was pleased when he covered her hand with his.

All of a sudden, Sheldon pulled her into his arms, whispering, "I'm so glad to see you." He embraced her closely.

Tender, loving emotions swirled through her and she was somewhat startled by their intensity. "Me, too. You had me worried, Sheldon. When I didn't hear from you, I didn't know what to think."

"With everything that happened—I needed some time to myself."

Looking up at Sheldon, Daryl found his worries were etched clearly on his face. Concerned, she asked, "How are you? You look like you haven't had much sleep."

"I'm okay."

Daryl gently pushed out of Sheldon's arms and moved around him to put her purse on a nearby table. Turning back to face him, she said, "I'm so sorry about Malle."

Grabbing her hand gently, he led her over to the sofa. "Her mother blames me.

"She's grieving, Sheldon. And she wants to blame someone."

"I wouldn't have hurt Malle in a million years. I was honest with her, Daryl. I tried to explain that to her mother, but she wouldn't listen."

"Don't be so hard on yourself, Sheldon," she replied, patting his hand consolingly.

Sheldon shook his head. "I don't know," he sighed deeply. "Her mother used to like me. I never thought she'd say the horrible things she said to me. She wouldn't let me attend the funeral."

"She's hurting, Sheldon."

"I'm not jumping for joy here. Hell, I still can't believe Malle's really gone."

"I wish there was something I could say to make you feel better." Wanting to comfort him, Daryl put her arms around him and drew him against her.

"You're here. That's all that matters right now."

Sheldon bent his head and she met his lips halfway. He kissed her tenderly, but with an undercurrent of passion. Sliding her hands about his neck, Daryl responded eagerly.

"I'm glad you called me," she said happily. "I really missed you."

"Sweetheart, I missed you, too. And I know you must be hungry. I thought we'd grab a bite to eat, if you feel up to it."

"I'm starving. Just give me a few minutes to shower and change."

"Great, I'll call and make reservations."

* * *

Daryl and Sheldon were seated quickly at the Italian restaurant.

"So, what have you been doing while I was away?"

Daryl shrugged. "Not a whole lot of anything. Mother and I went to San Francisco and did some shopping one weekend. And I got caught up on some of my reading."

Sheldon waited until the waitress had taken their orders before responding.

"How is your mother doing?"

"She's fine. She stays so busy—it's still hard for me to keep up with her."

While they waited for their food to arrive, Daryl and Sheldon made small talk.

". . . and then the woman just sat up. I'd never seen a person take off and run like that."

Sheldon threw back his head laughing. "I can't say I blame her. I think I'd run too, if a dead woman sprang up like that. Is she still interning?"

Daryl shook her head, her eyes full of laughter. "No, she quit. Said she didn't think this was the job for her."

Their food arrived.

Daryl smiled as she observed Sheldon. He was finally beginning to visibly relax. He'd seemed so forlorn earlier.

"Aren't you going to eat?" Sheldon asked, motioning toward her plate with his fork.

Picking up her knife and fork, Daryl smiled and nodded. As she sliced off a piece of her veal, she stated, "I see Barry's been staying with your mother."

"Really?" Sheldon was surprised by the news.

"Yes, I stopped over there a couple of times and he was there. And your mother mentioned it on the phone."

"I'm glad to hear that. I was kind of worried about her. I know all of what happened bothered her."

"Your mother's fine. Just worried about you."

"I didn't mean to worry either one of you. I just needed to get away."

"I know, Sheldon." Daryl smiled. "How's your pasta?"

"Wonderful. What about your veal?"

"Very good."

Sheldon watched her for a few seconds more be concentrating on the plate in front of him.

After a sumptuous dinner, they returned, arm in arm, to the hotel room. Daryl leaned into Sheldon. "Dinner was wonderful. Thank you for a lovely evening."

"It's just beginning."

"Really? Now what else do you have planned?"

"Just wait and see."

Letting Daryl's hand go, but continuing to maintain eye contact, Sheldon shrugged out of his shirt. As he undressed, he watched her tongue dart out and moisten her trembling lips. Sheldon watched her eyes widen as he pulled off his underwear. Licking her lips once more, Daryl boldly reached out to touch him.

"Don't you think something's wrong with this picture?" he asked, while trying not to explode from the way she was caressing him. "Aren't you a bit overdressed?"

Daryl looked up into Sheldon's face. She was ready to take their relationship to the next level. "You have no idea how much I've wanted you."

"Not nearly as much as I want you, Sweetheart."

She quickly slipped off her pants and her shirt, revealing a black lace bra and matching thong panties. Sheldon could hardly contain himself seeing her dressed in so little. Huskily, he asked, "Do you always wear . . . ?"

Standing with her huge breasts proudly jutting forward, and her hands planted firmly on her hips, Daryl nodded. "Do you like what you see?"

He practically growled out the resounding, "Yes."

Daryl did a slow strip tease. Sheldon practically choked when she removed her bra. She laughed throatily when she eased the lace panties over her hips and down her thighs—never once taking her eyes off Sheldon. "What about now? Do you still like what you see?" He could only groan. Taking him by the arm, Daryl led him to the bed. She crawled in first, with Sheldon in her wake.

He rolled to Daryl's side, planting a series of enticing kisses over the nape of her neck. Fire burst through her arms and shoulders before spreading to her lower limbs. Sparks of pleasure shook her body.

He nuzzled his way along the curve of her full breasts. "So beautiful. A fantasy come true," he murmured, giving soft kisses along her neck. The touch of his fingers against her bare breast caused Daryl to cry out her pleasure.

A low moan escaped from deep in Daryl's throat, as Sheldon continued his titillating exploration along her abdomen to the heart of her sex. "Oh, Sheldon, don't stop." His kisses caused her body to tremble with pleasure until she thought she would scream with need. Her breath was coming in rapid pants, and she turned her face into the king-sized pillow to muffle another groan that threatened to erupt from her swollen lips. Wave after wave of unutterable pleasure assailed her as she climaxed.

Getting up off the bed, Sheldon bent to retrieve his wallet out of his pants pocket. Returning, he placed the wallet on the night stand and climbed in bed beside Daryl. In his hand, he held a condom.

Frantic with wanting him inside her, she lifted her hips and invited him into her body. She embraced him tightly, and together they began to rock in the ancient rhythm of lovers. When their eyes met, Sheldon kissed her forehead, then her mouth. The kiss was hungry and fierce. Daryl strained back to accept Sheldon's deep thrusts, then leaned away to coax him back into the folds of her snug warmth. His thrusts were strong and slow, building tension, until Daryl shook with pleasure.

Sheldon lovingly caressed her huge breasts with one hand while his other hand slid between her legs to further fuel the blazing inferno in her body.

Together, their fulfillment came with an intensity that defied description.

As they lay in a tangle, their chests rising and falling

rapidly as they fought to recover from their fervid lovemaking, with shadows of the candle-lit room dancing over the bed, Daryl turned to face him, her eyes filled with emotion. "In all my dreams, I never imagined it would be so wonderful."

Sheldon seemed to regain his strength enough to shift over onto his back. "What is so wonderful, Sweetheart?" Daryl settled along his side, her head on his shoulder, her hand on his damp chest. "Tell me."

"Making love with you. I've thought about it for months now."

"Really?"

She nodded. "I knew we would be good together, but I had no idea it could be like this."

"We are good together, aren't we?"

"Yes." Laying her gently against the pillows, he kissed her forehead. "I'll be right back. Nature calls."

"Okay; while you're in the bathroom, I'll call my mother. She wants to make sure I made it here safely."

Sheldon started the shower. He was about to ask Daryl to join him, when he found her still on the phone with Maxine.

"Mother, I'm fine. We had a delicious dinner and then we came back here." Daryl paused. "Mother, I can't believe you just asked me that. But since you did, I'm going to be honest with you. Yes, I'm staying in the same room with him."

Sheldon smiled in amusement.

"Mother, I'm a grown woman. Besides I love him. I've loved him from the moment we met."

Her declaration sobered him like a pail of ice cubes. Sheldon eased away from the door, closing it quietly. He sat on the edge of the tub, his mind reeling. *Daryl was in love with him.*

There was a knock on the door. "Can I join you in the shower?"

Standing up, Sheldon opened the door with a grin. "Just waiting for you to get off the phone with your mom."

"I'm sorry it took as long as it did. She had a lot of questions."

"She's just trying to protect you." With good reason, he thought.

Daryl studied his grave expression and it worried her. "Are you okay, Sheldon?"

Pulling her into his arms, he said, "I want you to know that I care for you more than I've ever cared for any other woman." He leaned over to kiss her gently.

After their shower, Sheldon and Daryl made love once more before falling asleep, their bodies entwined.

That spasm of guilt he'd felt all last night tightened in his belly. Long after she'd fallen asleep, Sheldon had lain in bed watching her. He should've known this moment would come. He should've suspected they would have to confront what their relationship—how he hated that damn word!—was going to be. Lowering his head, Sheldon didn't want to examine his thoughts too closely right now.

Seated at a corner table the next morning, he and Daryl waited in silence for their breakfast to arrive. She could feel the tension in the air between them and could see it in the tight set of his jaw. She looked up to find him watching her, a strange look on his face. "Sheldon?"

"I was just thinking that you're a very special lady, Daryl. I don't think I've ever met anyone quite like you."

She smiled and tried to relax. "I guess I could say the same about you."

"Really?"

Their food arrived.

Noticing how serious his expression had become, Daryl asked quietly, "Sheldon, is something wrong? And please don't tell me it's nothing. I can tell something's bothering you from the way you're acting."

"How am I acting?"

"You've seemed so withdrawn lately. I know you've been through a lot with Malle's death . . ."

"For the first time in my life, I was scared. Really scared. That last night I saw her—the look in her eyes . . ." He shook his head. "I don't think I'll ever forget it."

"I sense that you're still blaming yourself somehow. It wasn't your fault."

"I never loved her." He choked out the admission. "I took her feelings and walked all over them."

"I think you're being too hard on yourself."

"No. Malle's death has forced me to face the truth."

Tentacles of anxiety curled along her spine. "What truth?"

"I need to be more sensitive to the feelings of others. I didn't love her, but I never told her until recently. Instead, I let her think that there could be something more between us. More than sex."

"Sheldon . . ."

He held up his hand to stop her. "No, please let me finish. I don't want to make the same mistake with you, Daryl. I meant what I said about caring for you, and I don't want to hurt you."

"Sheldon, I can take care of myself." Daryl studied his pain-racked face for a long time. "I really appreciate your concern, but you don't have to worry about me. We'll continue to take one step at a time. Baby steps." Reaching over, she covered Sheldon's hand with her own.

"You've been a good friend to me, Daryl."

"I'll always be there for you. Remember that."

Sheldon glanced down at his watch. "We should probably get on the road."

A week went by after their return from Palm Springs, and Daryl still hadn't heard from Sheldon. He'd been silent through most of the drive home, which she attributed to his grieving for Malle.

Unable to take the suspense of not knowing how he was doing, Daryl gave into her heart and called him.

"Hi, it's me."

"Daryl . . . how're you doing?"

She gave him a brief recap of her day, then dove right to the purpose of her call.

"Sheldon, would you have dinner with me tonight? I thought I'd make us a delicious meal and we could enjoy the rest of the evening here."

"Sure. What time should I come?"

"How about eight o'clock?"

"I'll be there."

The rest of the afternoon, Daryl spent cleaning her house, shopping for groceries, and preparing dinner. One glance at the clock told her that she should get dressed.

After a long, luxurious bubble bath, she slipped into a red satin bra and matching thong panties beneath a red body-hugging dress. Running her fingers through the shining mass of curls and appraising her make-up, Daryl approved. She wanted to look sexy, because tonight she planned to seduce the unsuspecting Sheldon.

Stealing a peek at the crystal clock, she quickly covered the bed, which had clean sheets on it lightly sprayed with a musk-scented mist.

That evening, Sheldon poured himself a glass of wine. He'd done the right thing by not going to her house tonight. He didn't want to hurt her this way, but he felt backed into a corner. Sheldon watched the clock as it ticked closer to the appointed hour. He wondered briefly if she would call to inquire why he never showed. Shaking his head, he decided she wouldn't. It wasn't Daryl's style.

Barry crossed his mind. He and Barry were slowly moving toward rebuilding their relationship. Sheldon doubted they would ever be as close as they used to be. His brother hated him—for some unknown reason. Something had happened long before the accident that took away Barry's dream.

Right out of high school, Barry had signed with Philadelphia to play professional basketball. During his first season, on the way to practice, Barry had been in a car accident that left him with a permanent limp. Sheldon felt his brother's antagonism toward him grew even more when he himself was drafted by New York.

Feeling guilty, Sheldon picked up the phone and called Daryl.

"I was so worried about you. What happened?"

"I . . . I don't think I'll be good company tonight. I have a lot on my mind."

"Sheldon, are you okay? You sound strange. Have I done something to upset you?"

"I just think I need some time alone, that's all."

"I see," she said quietly.

In an effort to assuage his guilty conscience, Sheldon suggested, "Why don't we get together during the Memorial Day weekend?" That would give him a week to pull himself together.

"That's fine."

Sheldon hung up the phone, thankful that he'd been able to pull that off.

Daryl hung up and surveyed the intimate setting she'd so painstakingly created. Dejectedly, she put away the oysters. Just as she closed the refrigerator door, a thought occurred to her. She picked up the phone, punching speed dial.

"Margo, what are you doing?"

"Nothing. Rob's got Kiana, so I'm just relaxing. What's up?"

"Sheldon's not feeling well and had to cancel our dinner date. I've got all this food over here and nobody to help me eat it. Want to come over?" she asked hopefully.

"I'll be right over."

While Daryl waited for Margo to arrive, she contemplated Sheldon's recent behavior. Something wasn't quite right, and she felt reasonably sure it had nothing to do with Malle's death.

She opened the door to Margo, who appraised her up and down.

"Mmmmmm, I guess you had some plans for Mr. Turner. He's going to be upset that he missed you looking so hot."

"You need to quit, Margo. Come on in here and let's eat."

Margo stood, watching Daryl from behind. "Somebody had to spray paint that dress on you because I don't see how you were able to get it on otherwise."

Chapter 14

"So, how was your romantic getaway? And don't you dare leave anything out." Audrey settled herself against the counter in her kitchen, waiting for the water to boil.

"It was nice, but I have to admit it didn't turn out the way I thought it would," Daryl said, as she smoothed back her hair and caressed her temples, trying to quiet the cacophony of thoughts.

"What happened?"

"Sheldon's still upset over Malle's death. It really shook him up."

"Daryl, I'm so sorry," Audrey said, as she placed a cup of hot tea in front of Daryl before joining her at the dining table.

"Don't be," she said, while flicking an imaginary speck of lint from her dress. "I'm not tripping over this. I'm just worried about his state of mind."

"But if he's that distraught over her death, he obviously cared a lot for her." Audrey wore a sympathetic expression. "More than he's led you to believe."

Daryl shook her head. She was lost in a whirlwind of conflicting emotions, but she responded, "I don't think so. Sheldon feels guilty over his treatment of her. It doesn't help that Malle's mother is blaming him."

"What?" Aubrey was clearly surprised. "But I thought foul play had been completely ruled out. Didn't she die of natural causes?"

"Yes, Malle Vincent died of Islet cell hyperplasia. Additional tests proved that the excessive insulin in her body was produced naturally and had not been injected."

Audrey laid a comforting hand on hers. "He'll come around. He just needs some time."

Daryl made a slight gesture with her right hand. "I know."

Audrey grinned slyly. "So, tell me. Did the two of you finally do the horizontal tango? Margo and I believe that you two finally got together."

She grinned then. "I'll never tell."

"You don't have to. I can see it written all over your face. Things will work out for the two of you—just wait and see."

Daryl decided to change the subject. "What are your plans for the Memorial Day weekend? You and Tyrell going somewhere?"

"No, we're just going to hang out at my house. What about you?"

"Well, Sheldon and I are supposed to go to a barbecue. It's at the mansion of some basketball player. I hope he's in better spirits by then."

Daryl checked her watch for the fifth time. Sheldon was over one and a half hours late. What in the world was his problem? Could traffic be that bad?

Recognizing the loud rumbling in her stomach, she navigated to the kitchen and made herself a sandwich. While she ate, Daryl continued to watch the clock. An hour later, she finally conceded that Sheldon wasn't coming. He'd stood her up a second time. Daryl decided she deserved to be treated better than this. This would be the last time.

Having had enough, Daryl grabbed her car keys. She couldn't begin to understand what Sheldon was going through, but she was determined to get some answers today.

Daryl arrived at Sheldon's house in record time. She trembled out of pure anger over seeing his car still parked in the driveway. Daryl had half hoped she was wrong about the situation. With her heartbeat racing and her temples throbbing, she sat in her car for a few minutes debating over whether she should confront him. Having made her decision, Daryl hopped out of her car and headed up the steps to the ornate front door. She forced a pleasant smile when Maggie answered her knock.

"Hi, Mrs. Turner. Is Sheldon home?"

"He's back in the den." Maggie moved aside to let Daryl enter. "Come right on in." Giving her a quick hug, she stated, "It's good to see you, dear."

"You, too." Daryl found Sheldon stretched out on the couch. He looked up at her, not quite meeting her gaze.

Moving to stand before him, she asked, "Have I done something to offend you?"

"No," was his response.

Sheldon seemed to shut down right in front of her eyes. "Then would you mind explaining to me what in the world is going on?"

"There's nothing going on."

"Then why do you make plans with me, and then not bother to show up?" Daryl folded her arms across her chest. "It's really rude and disrespectful."

Sheldon looked up at her, his eyes full of sadness. "Daryl, I'm sorry. I just didn't feel like doing anything today."

She sat down beside him. "And you couldn't have called me to cancel? I could have made other plans." She scanned his face. "Are you trying to push me away from you? Is that what this is all about?"

Sheldon played with her fingers. "Daryl, I was wrong about the way I treated you, and I'm sorry. I should've called."

Pulling her hand away, Daryl pleaded with him. "Sheldon, would you please talk to me? Have I done something to make you act this way?"

He shook his head, his eyes shut tight. "It's not you. It's me. I think we need to put some distance between us."

Looking down at her hands, Daryl mumbled a soft, "I see."

Sheldon opened his eyes and stared into the depths of hers. "I just want to be your friend. I'm not looking for anything more. Although we set fires in one another, I'm not the marrying kind."

She was suddenly angry. "And you couldn't just tell me this? You had to stand me up a couple of times, not to mention the lame excuses you gave—"

"I know I went about it the wrong way."

"You certainly did. I deserved at least a kiss off via phone or mail." She tried to keep her face impassive, in spite of the searing pain in her heart.

Sheldon looked ashamed. "I'm really sorry, Daryl. Ever since Malle died, I've been going through some changes." Her death made me take a good look at myself and I didn't like what I saw. Malle's dying has changed me forever."

"I can see that."

"We can be friends, right?"

Daryl nodded. "Sure." Standing up slowly, she said, "Well, I guess I'd better be going."

"You don't have to leave. We can watch a video, play Clue—"

"Sorry, but I really do have to go," she lied. "After you didn't bother to show up, I made some other plans."

"Doc, wait." Sheldon stood up. "I never meant to hurt you," he said quietly, then wondered why he spoke the lie. He'd already hurt her. He'd hurt every woman he'd ever been involved with.

"Take care, Sheldon." Mustering up her dignity, Daryl strolled to the door without so much as a backward glance. More so because she didn't want Sheldon to see her cry.

From her car, Daryl placed a call to Margo. She made

an attempt to sound cheerful. "Hey, girlfriend. What are you doing?"

"At the last minute I decided to cook out. You and Sheldon want to stop by? There's plenty of food for everybody."

"I'm on my way," Daryl said. Glancing up at Sheldon's house, she added, "I'm leaving L.A. right now, but I'll be alone."

"Did you and Sheldon have a fight?"

"I'll tell you all about it when I get there." She hung up and drove to Mountain Meadows, where Margo lived.

Her friend met her at the door. "What happened, Daryl? You sounded horrible on the phone."

Daryl waved her away. "I don't want to depress you. Let's just enjoy the party."

Margo grabbed her by the arm. "No, I think we should talk. The food's not going to burn. Rob's back there cooking."

"Who's here?"

"Audrey, Tyrell, Rob, and now you."

"I'd better leave. I don't think I can take the couples scene. Not right now." She turned to leave.

"Daryl, wait," Margo begged. "Please, let's just go to my room. We can talk there."

"There's not much to say. Sheldon just wants to be my friend. Nothing more." Water ran from her eyes, Daryl quickly wiped them away.

With her hands on her ample hips, Margo asked, "And he's just now getting around to telling you this?"

She could read the anger in Margo's eyes. Wiping away more tears with the ball of her hand, Daryl replied, "It's okay. He told me the truth. Now, I'll have to live with it."

"Will you stay?"

"Daryl shook her head. "No, I think I'll go on home. I'm not the best of company right now."

Margo embraced her. "If you need me, just call. I wish you'd stay though. I hate you being alone right now."

"I'll be fine. Thanks."

"Daryl, I didn't know you were here." Audrey threw herself in her arms. "It's good to see you."

"Hey, Audrey."

Turning to Margo, Audrey said, "Your honey sent me to find you. He needs you."

"Daryl, will you stay until I come back?"

"Sure." She ran her hands over her face.

Audrey glanced around. "Where's Sheldon? Didn't he come with you?" She scanned Daryl's face. "What's wrong? Why have you been crying?"

"I might as well tell you, too. Sheldon and I aren't seeing each other anymore."

"I'm sorry, Daryl."

"It's okay."

Margo returned, asking, "You're sure you won't stay and eat with us?"

"I don't feel up to it, but thanks anyway."

"Then, at least let me fix you a plate to take home."

Daryl forced a smile. "Okay. I'll take a plate."

"I'll be right back."

Audrey placed a comforting arm around her. "You know, Daryl, I really believe Sheldon's gonna come to his senses real soon. He'll be back."

She smiled. "We'll just have to believe that, won't we? I learned a long time ago that you can't make someone love you. When Sheldon's ready, I'll be here waiting. I just hope he doesn't wait until it's too late."

Sheldon stood watching Daryl as she sat in her car talking on a cellular phone before driving away. Uneasiness settled in his stomach, as, once again, he tried to reassure himself that he'd done the right thing.

Maggie's voice came from behind him. "You sent her away, didn't you, Son?"

He turned around to face Maggie. "I didn't feel like doing anything today. Daryl made other plans, so she left."

She placed her hands on her hips, and stared up at him.

"And you mean to tell me that Daryl drove all the way from Pomona to Los Angeles to tell you this? I think a phone call would have accomplished the same thing." Maggie pointed her finger in accusation. "I'll tell you what I think. I think you stood her up, and I know it's not the first time. You stood her up because you're letting Malle's death eat you up."

"Mama, I really don't want to get into any of this. I did what I thought was best for everyone." Sheldon held up his hands in resignation. "I'm sorry you don't agree, but . . ." He looked forlornly back toward the door.

"I know it's your life, Sheldon Jerome Turner. But I hate seeing that nice young lady hurt—especially after she stood by you when everyone was saying you were a murderer. She was the one that proved you were innocent."

He knew Maggie was angry, because that's the only time she ever called him by his full name. "I realize if it weren't for Daryl, I would still be in jail. Mama, I know that, and I appreciate all she did for me. But she wants a serious relationship. I can't handle that right now. I need some time to myself." Sheldon strolled to the den, slumping down on the sofa. Maggie followed.

Sitting down in her old rocking chair, Maggie suddenly looked weary. "It's not your fault—what happened to Malle."

"Mama, when we were in Palm Springs, I overheard Daryl tell her mother that she was in love with me."

"What were you doing listening to her conversation?"

"I didn't mean to—it just happened. The point is . . . I don't want to hurt her. She wants more than I can give her."

"Son, you've got so much love to give to the right woman. If you'd only let yourself."

"I told you before. Marriages are no longer made in heaven, Mama. Everybody I know seems to be getting divorced."

"What's that got to do with you, Son?" Maggie wanted

to know. "You young people need to take time to really get to know each other. Build a friendship first. That's the foundation for a good marriage. You two really need to like each other—not just jump into bed with each other . . ."

"Mama—"

"Well, it's true. People get married for the wrong reasons, Son. A marriage can't work by itself. It takes two people."

Sheldon considered what Maggie was saying. "You're right, Mama. But the hard part is finding that special someone."

"Humph. It's real hard when you keep running away with your tail stuck between your legs."

Maggie's rebuke had taken the wind out of him.

"Son, you don't have to stop for love. It will kindly stop for you." Having said that, she pulled herself out of the rocker. "Think I'll check on dinner."

Daryl waded into the Precision Club. Ladies Night was always crowded, but tonight seemed more so than usual. Daryl supposed it had to do with college students out for the summer.

Margo greeted Daryl with a bear hug. "I'm glad you agreed to meet me here. I have someone I really think you should meet."

"Margo, I don't need you setting me up with anybody. If I'd known this was what you were up to, I would've stayed home." The last thing she wanted right now was a blind date. She hadn't seen or heard from Sheldon in a month, so she supposed it was over. But had it ever really begun? she wondered.

Margo was still talking. "He's not just anybody, Daryl. Sidney is a real nice guy. And I had no idea he'd be here. I didn't even know he was back in town."

Daryl glanced around the room. She was searching for some sign of Sheldon. Returning her gaze to Margo, she said, "I don't know. I don't think I'm ready—"

"Shhhh, here he comes now. Just meet him," Margo pleaded in a whisper. "I know the two of you will hit it off."

"Okay, fine," Daryl muttered. She eyed the light-skinned man with beautiful gray eyes. Tall and slender, he was fashionably dressed and extremely attractive, she acknowledged silently. But he wasn't Sheldon.

"Sidney, this is my good friend, Daryl Larsen. Daryl, this is Sidney Moore. He's a model."

"I've heard many good things about you. It's nice to finally meet you." Lifting her hand to his mouth, he kissed it softly.

Not impressed, Daryl retreated a step, trying to avoid his probing gaze. "You, too."

"I really like this song. Would you like to dance?"

"Um, sure." Daryl pushed her chair away from the circular table. "Why not."

Sidney pulled her close to him—so close she could smell the faint fragrance of his spicy after shave, combined with the musky scent of his cologne.

"So, are you enjoying yourself?" His voice was deep and scratchy.

"Yes, I am," she lied.

"Now you wouldn't lie to me, pretty lady, would you?"

Apparently, Sidney thought his smile would have the same devastating effect it had on other women. "No, why would you say that?"

"Because you look a little troubled."

"I'm fine."

After one song, she pushed out of his arms and headed to her table. "Thanks for the dance," she mumbled, not wanting not to encourage him in any way.

As soon as she sat down, Margo leaned over. "Well, what do you think?"

Daryl's eyes clouded over darkly. "About what?"

"About Sidney."

Daryl shrugged. "I guess he's okay. He seems like a nice guy."

"He might be your Mr. Right."

Daryl shook her head. "I don't think so. I don't feel it in my heart."

"Your heart was wrong about Sheldon, remember. Maybe it takes longer than a first meeting."

Daryl could feel Sidney's eyes on her. Looking up, she found him standing just a few feet away. She granted him a brief smile, then turned away.

"Why don't you ask him to join us?" Margo whispered loudly.

"Why don't you, Margo?" Daryl snapped. "You're the one who seems to be so interested in the man."

"You don't have to snap. I was just trying to help."

"I don't need your help. I'm so sick and tired of—"

"Mind if I join you, ladies?" Sidney's voice cut through the air.

Margo gestured for him to sit down. "No. We don't mind at all. Daryl was just about to ask you to do so, weren't you?"

She opened her mouth to deny it, but changed her mind. What good would it do?

Sidney signaled for the waitress. "What are you ladies having? I'm getting this round."

Daryl shot him a quick glance. "I don't want anything, thank you."

"Come on, Daryl. Let's have a good time," Margo pleaded.

"I don't need to drink to have a good time."

Sidney looked wounded and Daryl regretted her comment. "I'm sorry. I didn't mean for that to come out the way it sounded."

"Why don't we go dance?"

She smiled. "Lead the way." She decided that she might as well make an effort to enjoy her evening. It wouldn't do her any good to take her disappointment with Sheldon out on Margo and Sidney.

* * *

Sheldon headed out to the club. The first thing he noticed was Daryl dancing with some pretty fellow.

He was plagued with jealousy—at least, he supposed it was jealousy. It was a new emotion that he had never experienced before. Sheldon didn't like feeling this way. He felt waves of anger on one hand and on the other hand, he felt pain. Seeing Daryl with another man had hit him hard. When he initially saw them dancing, she in his embrace, Sheldon felt he should have turned around and left. But he had been unable to do so. So he just stood there watching.

It didn't take her long to get over me, he thought bitterly to himself. Sheldon knew deep down that he couldn't blame her for going on with her life. Daryl had every right, especially after the way he'd treated her.

Waves of guilt washed over him as he recalled their weekend in Palm Springs. He never should have made love to her.

Daryl was positive, upbeat, and a very independent woman. She would survive. But then he'd thought the same about Malle—and she shocked him by dying. Her last words to him haunted him day and night.

Sheldon continued to watch Daryl. Smiling and laughing as she danced. She seemed to really be enjoying herself. Without him.

He wanted nothing more than to right then and there pull her out of Pretty Man's arms. Sheldon moved to stand behind a huge column, hidden from her view. Daryl was so busy having a good time, he could probably stand right in front of her face, and she wouldn't see him.

There wasn't a man with eyes in his head who wasn't watching her as she moved to the sensual vibrations of the song playing. He was in too foul a mood to chuckle at the man who'd just been elbowed after his date caught him leering at Daryl.

Wanting her more than he cared to admit, Sheldon drained the last of his cognac and headed to the nearest exit. He'd seen enough.

Sheldon didn't stop driving until he'd driven all the way to Pomona. Without fully realizing it, he was on his way to Daryl's house. Parking two houses away, he sat in his car trying to comprehend why he'd driven twenty miles out of his way.

Daryl carefully scanned her surroundings before getting out of her car. The night was quiet, the only sounds were coming from the few cars that passed her house at this late hour. With a firm grip on her keys and her can of mace, she quickly unlocked her door. Just as Daryl was about to step into her house, something caught her eye. She glanced down to find a note lying on the floor. It must have been sticking in her door. Although it wasn't signed, she knew instinctively that it must have come from Sheldon. She glanced around quickly, searching for some sign of his car.

Unlocking her door, Daryl keyed her code into the alarm system. Securing the lock, she rekeyed her code, then headed upstairs to her dimly lit room.

"He must have been at the club tonight." Had he seen her with Margo's friend? She stripped out of her clothing, leaving them in a pile on the floor of her bedroom. After a quick shower, she dressed for bed.

Once she'd settled beneath the covers, she dared to reread the note:

I saw you tonight. You looked so beautiful. I wanted to come say hello, but realized it was probably not the right time. Rest well.

"You, too, Sheldon," she whispered. "We're meant for each other, but you can't see it right now."

Chapter 15

Resolving to get on with her life, Daryl reluctantly agreed to have dinner with Sidney. She drove to the Italian restaurant that had been agreed upon.

Sidney greeted her with a smile. "You look lovely tonight."

"Thank you, Sidney."

Throughout the appetizers, Daryl fought to control her temper. She didn't like the way he stared hungrily at her breasts. There were times she felt like kicking him to bring his attention to her face.

"I'm glad you accepted my offer for dinner tonight."

She shrugged slightly. "I wasn't looking forward to sitting at home alone."

"I thought afterward we could go by the Precision Club and have a few drinks—maybe do some dancing."

Daryl shook her head. "Not tonight. I have that drive back to Pomona, and I'm not really looking forward to it."

"You don't have to drive out there. You can stay at my place," he suggested huskily.

"I—I don't think that would be appropriate, Sidney. Thanks anyway."

He brushed his fingers across hers. "You sure you don't want to go home with me tonight? We could get to know each other better."

"I'm positive." Daryl leaned back in her chair. "Sidney, I think we need to understand each other. I'm not looking to play. I like taking my time and getting to know a person before I even think about intimacy."

He shrugged nonchalantly. "Can't blame a man for trying. You're a very sexy lady."

"Well, you've tried. It didn't work, so I hope we can now enjoy dinner."

Sidney observed her for a minute. Then he burst into laughter. Daryl didn't know if she should be offended or not. "What's so funny?"

"You are. You're sitting here trying to be tough. I like that."

"Really," she responded dryly.

"I'm sorry. I—"

She cut him off. "Shall we order?"

Daryl let out a long sigh of relief as she drove out of the restaurant's parking lot as fast as the law allowed. Sidney had gotten on her nerves. She didn't like his sense of humor at all. *Why did I let Margo talk me into this mess?*

Stopping at a gas station, Daryl sat contemplating while a service attendant tended her car. In all fairness, she had to admit there was nothing really wrong with Sidney. He just wasn't Sheldon.

"Daryl, what are you doing here? You're just getting off work?"

Daryl whipped her head around to find Sheldon standing beside her car. Had she dreamed him up? No, there was no way she would have goose bumps, or feel the heat of desire pulsating through her body like this. He was real. He was at the gas station.

He moved closer to her. "Daryl? Did you hear me? You all right?"

"N—No, I didn't work late. I had dinner with someone."

"Oh."

Looking up at him, Daryl asked, "What are you doing here?"

He laughed. "I just stopped to get some gas."

She glanced away in embarrassment. "That was a stupid question, huh?"

"No, it wasn't. Actually, I was about to ask you the same thing, but you beat me to it."

Sheldon looked at her as if he really meant it. His lips were beckoning, and Daryl struggled to ignore the urge to kiss him.

The attendant was done and Daryl handed him a credit card.

"Well, it's late, and you should be getting home. Drive safe." He turned to walk away.

"Sheldon, wait!" Daryl called. She pulled her car into a nearby parking space and got out. Moving to stand before Sheldon, she asked, "Did you leave a note in my door one night last week?"

"Yes. I stopped by the Precision Club and I saw you— you and your date. Looked like you were having a good time."

"I was," she lied. "Why didn't you come say hello?"

"I didn't want to interrupt your date."

His eyes were unreadable. "Oh."

Sheldon moved closer to her, his voice a hoarse whisper. "I have to admit it bothered me seeing you with that guy."

Daryl looked down into her lap. "I don't know why it should."

"I care a lot for you, Daryl."

"I see."

Sheldon drew back to his full height. "Why do you sound so cold?"

"I'm sorry, Sheldon. It's just that you confuse me sometimes. One minute you're fine, then the next minute you're hiding behind a self-imposed wall."

"I didn't mean—" He seemed to struggle for something to say.

Daryl shrugged. "I'd better get on the road. Take care of yourself, Sheldon."

"You, too."

Daryl drove home, tears rolling down her cheeks.

Sheldon couldn't concentrate on his game of Clue. Losing once more to the computer, he decided to give it up. It was time that he stopped lying to himself. He hated the fact that Daryl was dating another man. After seeing her last night, Sheldon could not deny that he wanted her to himself. A knock caused him to turn around.

Barry stood in the doorway. "Sheldon, you wanted to see me?"

"Yes, I do. Come on in."

Taking a seat on the edge of Sheldon's bed, he asked, "What is it?"

"I want to thank you again for sticking by me. I really appreciate—"

Barry waved him off. "You're my brother, Sheldon. Even though we have our . . . times. You're my blood."

Sheldon nodded. "I agree. And I think it's time we start acting like it."

Barry reared back. "Man, what're you talking about?"

"I'm trying to tell you that I miss you, big brother. I need to know something. Why do you hate me?"

"I don't hate you, Sheldon."

"Over the past few years, we would barely speak to one another. Something's wrong. I just don't know what it is."

Barry checked his watch. "I've got to pick up my son.

You want to ride with me? We can go back to my place and talk.''

"I'll follow you in my car. That way you don't have to bring me back.''

Barry stood up, keys in hand. "Sounds like a plan. Come on.''

Both Barry and Sheldon whizzed past Maggie, who carried a neatly folded stack of fresh laundered towels. "Where are you two headed?''

"I'm following Barry to his house. I'll be back later. You need anything?''

"Just some of Barry's gumbo. I know he's got some in his freezer.''

Barry laughed. "I'll send it back with Sheldon, Mama.'' He kissed her cheek. "See you.''

"Call me if you need anything, Mama,'' Sheldon whispered before kissing her other cheek.

Neither one of them saw Maggie raise her eyes to heaven and express her thanks for reuniting her two sons.

As soon as Barry put his son down for a nap, he returned to the living room where Sheldon sat thumbing through numerous CDs.

Sinking down on the soft, custom-designed leather sofa, he stated, "I was thinking about what you said, Sheldon. We should talk. Get everything in the open.'' Barry handed him a beer.

"I'm glad you feel that way.''

Barry took a long sip of beer before speaking. "First of all, I don't hate you, Sheldon. I've just been angry about some things. And maybe a little jealous, too.''

Sheldon's mouth opened in surprise. "Angry about what? Me playing pro ball? Your getting hurt during your first season? What?''

"That's part of it. A big part of it. I admit I was jealous. But what made me angry the most was how you let Dad treat Mama. You were their favorite son—you could have done something.''

''What are you talking about?''

''All the beatings Dad gave Mama.''

''Barry, I swear, I didn't realize what was happening until I was about to go off to college. I came home early one day. I made Dad leave the house.'' He gazed into his brother's eyes. ''How long have you known?''

''I think I've always known something wasn't right. I caught him beating her real bad when I was twelve. Before I could think about it, I jumped on that man and tried to kill him.''

''Where was I?''

''You spent the weekend with Grandma. That's when they told you Mama had a real bad fall. I think I would've killed him if Mama hadn't taken a strap to me.''

''What?'' He could see the hurt in the depths of his brother's eyes.

''Here I was trying to protect her and she's whipping me like I did something wrong. Dad was through with me then. He never said much to me after that. Just ignored me.''

Sheldon was shaking his head in astonishment. ''Barry, man. I never knew. A few years ago, I had a serious talk with Dad myself.''

''Did you know about the women?''

Sheldon nodded. ''I caught him one time with a woman. Right before he found out he had cancer.''

Barry whistled. ''Just one time? Man, I used to see him all the time. And when I'd tell Mama, she'd just get pissed off with me. Said I was interfering where I shouldn't. I'm trying to protect her. But I get punished.''

''I guess she didn't want to be protected.''

Barry took another sip of beer. ''I couldn't understand how she could let him treat her that way. I still don't.''

''Have you ever tried to talk to her about all this? You need to tell her how she made you feel.''

Barry shook his head. ''I can't talk to Mama.'' He sat

up straight. "Want something to eat? I can whip us up something."

Sheldon stood up, straightening his jeans. "I'll help." He laughed. "Mama always said we'd better learn to cook in case we couldn't find anybody to marry us."

"Yeah, Mama seemed to know what she was talking about, huh?"

In the kitchen, Sheldon sliced up an onion while Barry prepared the thick steaks and the potatoes.

"So, Sheldon, tell me. How many of those kids are yours?"

"None. I don't have any children." He elbowed his brother. "Unlike a certain brother of mine."

Barry laughed. "Want to know something? I don't have any myself."

"Then who are the three children plastered all over Mama's den?"

"They're mine, but they are not my biological children."

"Then why are you claiming them?"

"Because they need fathers. Cameron, my oldest boy— his mother was raped and chose to keep the child. She was pregnant when I met her. Even though things didn't work out for us, I'm still his father."

"And the other two?"

"Hailey's father ran off before she was born. Her mother and I are good friends. I was her Lamaze coach and ended up delivering Hailey myself. She was born at home."

"Couldn't make it to the hospital or did you two plan it that way?"

"Couldn't get to the hospital in time. My youngest, Joshua, now that was kind of tricky. I thought he was mine, but a blood test says he isn't. My name was already on his birth certificate, and I'd already established a bond with him. He's my son. I love all three of my children."

"I can see that." Sheldon shook his head. "Man, much respect to you. Three children and none of them are yours biologically."

"They're mine in here." Barry pointed to his heart. "Children need both a mother and a father. I know I did."

"Mama doesn't know this, does she?"

"No, and I don't want her to know. I was thinking about the program you were talking about. I'd like to be a part of it—if you still want me."

"Yes, I want you. As a matter of fact, we're having a fundraiser next weekend. It's a dinner, and I'd like for you to come."

Chapter 16

Beneath the hot August sun, Sheldon inspected the rims on his car. It was time to take it to a car wash. Right before he started up the steps, a car pulled up. A teenage girl got out, carrying a package. He thanked the messenger and handed her a five dollar tip. Sheldon examined it with curiosity as he entered the house.

"What you got there?" Maggie asked from behind him. "Looks important."

"I think it's a card, Mama. A birthday card."

Maggie read the label. "Looks like it's from Daryl. How is she these days?"

Sheldon laughed. His mother was so obvious. "I'm sure she's fine." He tore open the envelope. Inside was a beautiful custom birthday card. Sheldon opened it and read it. Suddenly he started grinning.

"What's put that crazy look on your face? She tell you a joke or something?"

"No, she made a donation in my name to the AIDS Foundation and the American Diabetics Foundation."

"I knew she was a sensible girl. She's going to make some man a wonderful wife."

* * *

Daryl tried in vain to concentrate on her work. Pushing the report aside, she leaned back in her chair. Today was Sheldon's birthday. She wanted to call, but her brain cautioned her against doing so. She'd promised to give Sheldon all the space he needed. She jumped when the phone rang.

"Hi, Doc. Thanks for the birthday present. It's the best one I've received."

"For the man who has enough money to last several lifetimes, I didn't know what to do in the way of a present, so I thought I'd make donations in your name. However, I do have something else for you."

"Really? What is it?"

"You'll have to drive all the way out to Pomona for it."

"Hmmmmm, you've got me curious."

Not wanting to mislead him, she said, "Actually, I thought I'd have a catered dinner brought to my home tonight. I know how much you hate public displays."

"I appreciate your sensitivity to my needs."

"It's your birthday, Sheldon. I want you to enjoy every minute of it."

"I've got a feeling that I'm going to," he murmured. "I'm looking forward to seeing you this evening. It's been a while."

"Yes, it has. Oh, and Sheldon, please dress for dinner."

He laughed. "Until this evening."

"Wow!" was all Sheldon could mutter when he saw Daryl. She looked stunning in her black calf-length body-hugging dress. As she walked, a leg, clad in sheer black hosiery, showed. "You look great."

"Why, thank you. You look quite wonderful yourself." Sheldon wore a black silk suit that made her mouth water. "Come on in. Make yourself comfortable."

Sheldon glanced around the room, lavishly decorated with black and gold helium-filled balloons, candles, and streamers. "Everything looks wonderful. You certainly out-did yourself."

In the center of an old-fashioned cherry wood buffet sat an ice carving of a basketball, surrounded by shrimp.

"Would you like an appetizer?" Daryl asked.

Pulling her to him, Sheldon said, "What I want is to kiss you, Doc."

She slid her arms beneath his and pulled him close. "Then what are you waiting for?"

He kissed her, opening his mouth with hers. Daryl held her breath as his tongue met hers. Tonight, she wanted to love him, freely giving and taking what they both desper-ately wanted.

"I've missed you so much, Doc," Sheldon whispered, as they reluctantly parted.

Daryl was thrilled over his admission. "I missed you, too." Sticking her arm through his, she led him over to the table. "Now have a seat. I know this is not as extravagant as what you did for me, but—"

"Doc, this is perfect." He scanned the room once more. "I couldn't wish for a better birthday."

"I'm glad you're pleased." She led him to a chair. "This is where I want you to sit."

All through dinner, Daryl and Sheldon gazed at each other. She didn't want to tear her eyes away from him. "Would you like dessert now, or later?"

"That depends."

Grinning, Daryl asked, "Depends on what?"

"Depends on what dessert is."

Shaking her head, she burst out laughing. "You're bad, Sheldon. I meant the birthday cake. I even have ice cream . . ."

"I can think of a few ways of having that ice cream." He stood up and came around the table to stand by her side. "What do you think, Doc?"

Suddenly feeling very warm, she nodded slowly. "I . . ."

Pulling her up, Sheldon could not contain his laughter. "I've never seen you speechless. Did I shock you?"

"N—No." Daryl broke into laughter. "You've got to stop talking that way."

"Why, am I turning you on? Putting thoughts of my licking ice cream off your—"

Daryl playfully pushed him away. "Stop it, Sheldon." He was right. She was turned on—so turned on, she wanted him to take her right then and there. "Why don't we go back into the living room?"

"After you, Doc. I'll do whatever you want."

She couldn't stand it any longer. Turning to him, she stood with her hands planted on her hips. "Whatever I want? You mean it?"

"Yes."

"Take off your clothes," she commanded.

Sheldon grinned. "As you wish."

He stripped slowly. Daryl sank down on the sofa to keep from falling. Her legs felt like jelly as she watched him remove his bikini briefs.

Standing up, Daryl removed all of her clothes. "I want you to make love to me right here. Right now." Her body burned with need. Together they fell to the floor. Covering her mouth with his, Sheldon's kiss was deep, passionate, needful. His head bent to her neck, dropping a trail of kisses all the way to her thighs.

When neither one could wait any longer, Daryl braced herself to receive all of him. All thoughts fell away as they joined with each other. Sheldon was impetuous, mindless, and passionate in taking her. For the rest of the night, they made love.

The next morning, they had ice cream and birthday cake for breakfast. Daryl spooned the last of her ice cream on Sheldon's chest. Pushing him down on the bed, she proceeded to lick it off him, igniting their passions once more.

Later that morning, when Sheldon drove away, Daryl collapsed on the edge of her bed, holding her head in her hands. How could she have thrown herself at Sheldon like that. Worse, she'd made a liar of herself. There was no way she could continue making love to him and just settle for his friendship.

"I wish I could blame it on the champagne, but I can't," she whispered. She'd drunk very little last night during dinner and nothing afterward.

Daryl wiped away a lone tear, evidence of her shame. Unless Sheldon was willing to commit to her, she could not become his lover.

A week later, Daryl opened an envelope to find an invitation. Sheldon and some of the other NBA basketball players were sponsoring a dinner to benefit the Fathers As Role Models program. Holding the formal invitation to her breasts, she slid into a chair. "I wonder if I should go."

Images of Sheldon drifted into her mind. How badly she wanted to see him. Smiling, she nodded. "Yeah. I'm gonna go. Maybe once he sees me, he'll decide he really misses me in his life." Daryl frowned. "Girlfriend, you really need to get a grip. Sheldon is not going to fall all over himself just because he sees you."

Running her fingers lightly across the top of her sofa, Daryl tried to analyze Sheldon's feelings for her. At one time, she thought he might be falling in love with her, but then Malle's death changed everything.

He blamed himself, long after it was proven that she'd died of natural causes. I don't know if I ever really knew you, Sheldon. Daryl pushed strands of shining hair away from her face. You've confused me so much. The night of his birthday dinner, she'd felt some of those same vibes— the ones she received from him before Malle's death.

"I wish I knew what was going on in your mind, Sheldon."

"Did you invite Daryl to the dinner?" Maggie asked.

Sheldon bit back a grin. "Yes, Mama. I invited her and she's coming."

"I'm glad. You know, you never told me about your dinner with her—for your birthday."

"I remember." He laughed. "And I'm not telling you what happened that night."

Maggie frowned. "Son, I'm not stupid. I know what happened between you two."

"Then you know all you need to know." He pulled himself up from where he'd been sitting reading. "I'm going out to Barry's house. Want to come along?"

"I don't think I should," she said quietly. "He didn't invite me to come."

Sheldon saw the hurt in her eyes. "Mama, he did invite you. Please come. He's making a special dinner."

"Really? You're not just saying that, are you?"

"I wouldn't do that to either one of you. How long before you're ready?" he asked.

Maggie touched his arm. "Wait a minute. If Barry invited me, then why didn't he call me himself?"

"Because he thought you'd say no."

"What?" Maggie was genuinely surprised.

"You two need to sit down and have a long talk, Mama."

"He won't talk to me. I'll be just a minute."

While he waited for Maggie to get dressed, Sheldon's mind traveled back to the night of his birthday. He and Daryl had made wild, passionate love. It was a night that would forever be stamped in his memory. He could still recall the way she smelled—like wild lilacs.

He'd wanted to call her, but couldn't force himself to do so. Before he left, he caught a glimpse of something in her eyes. Sadness. She wanted more of him than he could ever give.

Sheldon shook his head. Deep down he wished he could make her happy, and give her the commitment she needed. Truth was, he didn't know how. Or if he could. Could he spend the rest of his life with her? With anyone?

When Daryl walked into the elegant ballroom of the Beverly Hills Hotel, it was like stepping into another country. The room had been transformed into a street in Paris, France.

"When the invitation stated the theme as An Evening In Paris, I had no idea that it would be like this," Renee whispered. "I feel like we've been transported to Paris."

"It sure feels that way." Daryl pointed to several men and women attired in french fashions lined up along the sidewalk. "They even have artists painting pictures of the guests." She glanced around the room. "This is incredible."

Renee covered her mouth to stifle her giggle. "They even have the Eiffel Tower carved in ice."

"Sheldon should be proud. They really did a wonderful job on the decorations." Daryl stroked her knee-length cocktail dress. "Thanks for coming with me, Renee. I really didn't want to come by myself."

"By the way, where's Margo? I know Audrey will be here with Tyrell. Will Margo come with Rob?"

Daryl shook her head. "No. Margo and Rob went to Hawaii. She thinks he's going to propose while they're there."

"Really? That's wonderful. Looks like moving back to L.A. was the right thing for her to do."

"Looks that way," Daryl agreed. "I hope it works out."

"Rob seems to love her. I wouldn't be surprised if they come back married."

"I wouldn't either."

They headed to the banquet table, where Daryl quickly

spotted Sheldon. He was surrounded by people, but when he spotted her, he headed in her direction.

"Hi, Sheldon."

"Hello, Doc. Renee, it's so good to see you. How have you been?"

"I'm fine. How are you?"

"Taking one day at a time. It's been a long time since I've seen you . . ."

Renee nodded. "Yes, it has."

Daryl helped herself to a golden Brie beignet, stuffed zucchini blossoms, and champagne grapes.

Renee excused herself, murmuring something about seeing an old friend. Daryl believed she just wanted to give her and Sheldon a chance to talk.

Popping a grape into his mouth, Sheldon asked, "Where's your date?"

"No date. Just me and Renee."

"I'm with Barry. Same here."

She was surprised. "That's great. I'm glad to see you haven't given up on him."

Sheldon nodded to where Barry and Renee stood talking. "Look over there. Renee and Barry look like they're happy to see one another. She sure looks good."

Following his eyes, she agreed, "Yeah, she sure does. She still cares a lot for Barry."

"Maybe this will be a new beginning for them."

Daryl nodded. "Maybe. Everything looks wonderful. You did a great job putting all this together."

"You look very nice tonight."

Casting her eyes downward, she murmured a soft, "Thank you, Sheldon." Trying to appear interested in the selection of French cuisine laid attractively before her, she said without looking up at him, "Please excuse me, but I'm starving." She had to keep her guard up. She was still too vulnerable to Sheldon. Daryl piled a Roquefort-stuffed chicken breast on her plate, pasta with Chevre and walnuts, and an assortment of cheeses.

"Well, I guess I'll be seeing you around."

Daryl looked up then, her heart breaking over the hurt she saw in his eyes. "Take care of yourself, Sheldon."

"What did he say to you?" Audrey asked as she joined Daryl at the buffet table.

"Just small talk. We really don't have anything to talk about."

Chapter 17

Renee eased up behind Barry, putting her hands over his eyes. "Hello, stranger." Recognition hit him like a kick in his stomach. He turned around. "Renee!" Her eyes were the same camel color as Daryl's and her generous mouth still as sexy as ever. Regret followed recognition. Regret for how he'd just walked out of her life, never looking back.

She smiled. "Yes, it's me. In the flesh."

Barry leaned over to place a kiss on her cheek. "I can't believe it."

Renee stared up at him, her camel eyes searching his, as if she were afraid he wasn't real—an illusion. "It's very good to see you, Barry. I've missed you."

Barry felt like the worst person over his hurtful treatment of her. The way he broke her heart. "I've missed you, too. I . . . I'm so sorry about—"

"There's nothing to be sorry for. It just didn't work out," she said quietly. "I didn't come over here to rehash the past. I wanted to say hello. I hope we'll be able to renew our friendship."

Complete happiness shone brightly in his eyes. "I'd like

that very much. I don't deserve your friendship, but I'm not going to turn it down."

Renee picked up two flutes of champagne. Giving one to Barry, she then held her flute to his. "To friendship."

Sheldon's heartbeat quickened over having seen Daryl. Her scent, the sound of her voice, made his pulse leap with excitement. He admitted silently how much it bothered him to have her act so distant. Especially after . . .

Someone walked up and tapped him on the shoulder. Sheldon glanced her way once more before turning his attention to Tyrell.

"Man, why are you treating Daryl like that? She's cool people."

"I know that, Ty." He shook his head regretfully. "We just want different things. She's looking to get married. I'm not."

"Well, I used to be that way."

"What are you talking about, Ty?" Sheldon found himself very curious, seeing the change on his friend's face.

"I'm thinking about marrying Audrey."

His eyes widened with astonishment. Sheldon cleared his throat before speaking. "That's great, Man. Congratulations."

Tyrell held up his hand. "It's not definite yet. We're still getting to know each other. If things keep going like they are—I plan to ask her at Christmas."

Sheldon nodded. "That's all right."

Leaning closer, Tyrell asked in a low whisper, "If it's so all right, how come you're not itching to do it?"

He shook his head. "I don't think I'd be good at being a husband."

"Why?"

"All of my friends that are married are now either getting divorced, or they're having affairs. The way they tell it, after marriage, boredom sets in."

"You're nothing like them, Sheldon. Most of them shouldn't have gotten married in the first place."

"I know. The other reason is that I just haven't met the one woman who could make me hear wedding bells."

"You have to stop listening up here," Tyrell stated, pointing to his ear. "You have to listen with your heart."

Sheldon laughed. "You sound just like a man in love."

"Let's hope one day you'll be so lucky," Tyrell said, before walking off to join Audrey.

Sheldon glanced over to where Daryl was sitting. She looked up, catching him. He smiled and his heart did a flip when she smiled in return. He was relieved she didn't seem to hate him.

When the band played a favorite tune of Daryl's, he glanced her way again. He was about to head her way, but halted when he found someone else had beaten him to her. He watched jealously as she danced very closely with a complete stranger.

When Daryl excused herself and headed toward the door, Sheldon released a deep sigh of relief. Just as he was about to follow her, a woman with waist-length braids approached him.

"Hi, you're Sheldon Turner, aren't you?"

"Yes, I am."

"My name is La Vonne. I'm a big fan of yours. Could I please have your autograph?"

"Er . . . sure. I don't have . . ."

"You could just sign this napkin."

As Sheldon signed his name to the white cottony paper, he was aware of her bold, assessing perusal.

"You sure look good. It's always been my dream to meet you. You're not seeing anyone, are you? I've been watching you most of the night. I thought we could go somewhere. Get to know each other. What do you say?"

"I'm—I have someone. Someone I care a lot about. I'm even thinking of marrying her—" He stopped short when he spotted Daryl standing nearby. From the expression on her face, he knew she'd heard what he just said and misunderstood. "Excuse me, please. I need to talk to someone."

"Daryl—"

"Sheldon, please get away from me," she snapped angrily. "I'm tired of this mess. Just leave me alone."

He grabbed her gently by the arm. "No, you misunderstood."

Daryl pulled away. "I don't think so. My hearing is very good."

"It's a lie. I told her that to get away from her."

Did he really think that would make her feel any better? Daryl shook her head sadly. "Sheldon, it really doesn't matter."

"Yes, it does. I haven't lied to you. I haven't been seeing anybody else."

"You want me to believe you're telling me the truth, even though you've just lied to the other woman. Is that it?"

"Daryl. I didn't know what else to say to her. I didn't want to be rude. The truth is, I'm not thinking of marrying anyone. I don't have a special someone."

"Excuse me. I have to go." She stalked off.

Sheldon had no idea why she was still so angry.

Daryl held her tears in check. She refused to let Sheldon see how much his words hurt her. Lifting her chin defiantly, she plastered a smile on her face when she spied Renee coming her way.

"Thanks so much for inviting me, cousin. I really had a good time."

"I'm glad, Renee." From the excited look on her cousin's face, Daryl could tell that their conversation had gone well.

"Did you know Barry was going to be here?" Renee asked.

She shook her head. "No, not really. I was hoping though. I think you two have some unfinished business."

"So, how did it go with Sheldon? From the look on your face, it doesn't look like it went well."

Daryl's bottom lip trembled. "Sheldon and I can only be friends. I just have to accept that, Renee."

"I don't agree. He looks just as miserable as you right now. I think he's fighting his emotions, but I wouldn't worry, Daryl. If it's meant to be, love always wins. You'll see."

"Where's Daryl? I thought I saw her over here with you," Barry asked as he offered Sheldon a glass of cognac.

"I think I made her angry."

"What did you say?"

He shrugged. "To tell you the truth, I'm not so sure. She overheard me telling another lady that I was involved with someone—someone I wanted to marry. I tried to explain to her that I was only saying that. It was a lie. Anyway she still stormed off in anger."

Barry put his hand up to his mouth to hide his laughter.

Sheldon scowled at his brother. "What's so damn funny?"

"You're in love with Daryl, man."

Sheldon frowned. "You've got that all wrong. I'm not in love with anybody."

"Sheldon, you can't be that dumb, Bro."

"What are you talking about?"

"You upset her with what you said. She's jealous. And hurt."

"It was a lie, Barry."

"In a way, but it's the same thing you're telling her. She wants a relationship with you and I think you feel the same way—only you haven't realized it yet."

Sheldon shook his head. "Man, you're crazy. I can't deal with marriage. It's not like it used to be—they barely last as long as the wedding ceremony."

"Marriage isn't easy, but I wouldn't write it off."

"Then why haven't you gotten married?"

"Waiting for the right woman. I had her at one time, but lost her." He glanced over to where Renee stood with Daryl. "But you know something. I think if given another chance, I'm going to do the right thing. I won't lose her a second time."

Sheldon followed his brother's eyes. "You're serious, aren't you?"

"I sure am. I never stopped loving her."

Sheldon watched Daryl. She looked up to find his eyes on her. She promptly turned her head. *She's beautiful.* "I wonder what it's like to love someone enough to want to spend the rest of your life with them."

Barry laughed. "Bro, I think you're going to find out the answer to that very soon."

"Congratulations to the bride and the groom. I knew you two were going to come back married." Daryl hugged Margo tightly. "I'm so happy for you."

"I still can't believe it," Margo gushed. "I suspected he might propose, but he had the wedding all planned."

Audrey rushed toward them. "Congrats again, girl-friend." Putting her hands on her slender hips, she declared, "You is married now!"

The three friends laughed as Margo recounted how Rob almost passed out during the ceremony.

"I practically had to hold him up."

"He loves you though. It sounds so romantic." Daryl shook Sheldon from her thoughts. She would not let her unhappiness intrude on Margo's night.

"How are you and Sidney doing?" Margo asked.

"To tell you the truth, he's getting on my last—"

"Shhhh, he's coming this way," Audrey whispered under her breath.

"Hey, baby. I've been looking all over for you."

Daryl groaned inwardly and rolled her eyes heavenward. "I've been right here. What did you want?" She ignored Margo's look of disapproval.

"I thought we'd take a spin out on the dance floor."

She tried to smile. "Maybe later."

Sidney suddenly grabbed her by the arm none too gently. "I know you want to stand here and yap with your girls, but you came with me. I'm ready to party."

Snatching her arm away, Daryl stared him down. "Excuse me?" She glanced over at Margo. "I think you'd better inform your friend that he's just overstepped his bounds . . ."

Margo touched Sidney's shoulder. "I think you'd better apologize."

"For what?"

"Going forward, do not, and I repeat, do not grab me like you did a moment ago. You don't own me."

Sidney suddenly appeared apologetic. "Baby, I didn't mean anything by it. I'm real sorry it came off that way."

Daryl scanned his face, trying to discern if he were sincere. He seemed to be.

"Come on. I'm sorry. I didn't mean anything by it."

She felt some of the earlier irritation leave her body. Intensely aware of Margo and Audrey watching, Daryl smiled evenly. "I accept your apology. If you want, we can have that dance now."

"Let's party."

She followed him to the dance floor, but not before Margo stopped her, whispering, "Thank you. I know he didn't mean to be so aggressive."

"I'll forgive him this time," she whispered back.

When the music stopped, Sidney escorted her back to their table. As he held her chair out, he said once more, "I hope you know I'm sincere."

"Forget it. I already have." She looked away, not wanting him to see the sadness in her eyes. Perhaps Margo was right. She wasn't giving Sidney a fair shot because she still had Sheldon in her system.

"I really like you, Daryl."

"I'm kind of thirsty. Could you please get me something to drink?" When he walked away, Daryl closed her eyes, wishing she could escape. She opened her eyes to catch Margo and Rob in a tender moment with their daughter, and her eyes filled with tears. She struggled to ignore the inner stirring of envy that stabbed her insides.

Chapter 18

Over the weekend, Daryl groaned as she lost another round of Clue to the computer. She was about to pick up the phone to call her mother when it rang. It was Sheldon. Surprised, Daryl stared at the phone in astonishment before speaking. "Sheldon, hi."

"You sound as if you're surprised to hear from me."

"Well, I am, actually," she admitted. "I wasn't quite sure where things stood."

"Why?"

"Well, it's been a while since we've talked."

"I knew you were mad at me and I know you're involved—"

"I'm not involved with anyone, Sheldon."

"I see. Are you still mad at me?"

"No, I'm not mad."

"So, you're not involved with whats-his-face?"

Daryl smiled. "You don't have to sound so pleased."

"I'm sorry. It's just that I don't think that guy is right for you."

"It's none of your business, Sheldon," she chided him gently.

"You're right. I'm sorry."

"Is that why you called? To dictate—"

"No. Doc, I called to ask you to have dinner with me. I thought we'd maybe, take in a play or something afterward."

Daryl opened her organizer. "When did you have in mind?"

"What about this weekend?"

"I'm off on Saturday."

"Great. Is it a date?"

"Yes. I'll have dinner with you. Call me on Friday with all the details."

"Doc?"

"Yeah?"

"I really miss you."

"I'll see you this weekend." Daryl hung up with a grin plastered on her face. "He wants to see me. That's good," she whispered. Maybe there was still a chance for them. She hoped with all her heart that Sheldon had finally realized his feelings for her.

Sheldon stood in the doorway of Daryl's house. "You're breathtaking, Doc."

She smiled. "Thank you."

Taking her by the hand, he led her to the car. "I thought I'd take you to Vincente's for dinner."

"Great. I haven't been there in a long time."

They drove in silence the short distance to the Italian restaurant. Pulling up, the valet attendant opened the door for Daryl.

They were seated almost immediately. Under the romantic lighting, Sheldon's gaze never wavered.

Daryl leaned forward. "Why do you just watch me like that, Sheldon?"

He shrugged. "I don't know. I love looking at you. Does it bother you?"

"No."

"You do something to me, Daryl. I don't know what it is, but you do something."

She didn't know what to say. Once again, Sheldon was giving out mixed signals. Daryl decided it was best to remain neutral. Throughout dinner, she ignored all his innuendos. She would not let herself be drawn under his spell.

As soon as they were back at her place, Sheldon reached out and pulled her into his embrace. His mouth came down on hers quickly, giving her no chance to turn away.

Daryl tried not to respond, but his kiss was too persuasive, and the demanding pressure of his lips destroyed her defenses. She felt her hands relax, where they had been curled into small fists by her sides. Surrendering, she wrapped her arms around him, returning his kiss with ardor. Her better judgement once again attempted vainly to intercede, but she thrust it to the far recesses of her mind. She loved Sheldon with her whole being.

Encouraged, he turned his head, moving to her ear. "I want you," he whispered hoarsely. "I want to make love to you."

Not one shred of logic remained in Daryl's thoughts as he swooped her into his arms and carried her upstairs. Taking her to her room, Sheldon set her gently on her feet, wrapping his arms about her, and kissed her fiercely. Then, taking her hand, he led her to the huge, inviting bed. The only light came from a lone lamp that Daryl had left on before leaving for the evening. It's glow illuminated the bedroom in a soft, romantic light.

For a blissful moment, Daryl was totally happy, but then reality set in, and it was like a splash of ice water in the face. He doesn't want a relationship, remember? she thought, almost angrily. It's just sex he wants. She sensed he cared for her, but what she hadn't sensed in Sheldon was love. He didn't love her.

She whirled on him. "I can't do this." There was a touch of sadness in her voice.

Sheldon looked down, confused. "What's wrong, sweetheart?"

Daryl's arms were wrapped tightly around her, beneath her bosom, as she took shallow breaths. "You need to make up your mind, Sheldon. I can't go back and forth like this."

He looked at her in confusion. "What are you talking about?"

"One minute you want me, and then the next you just want to be friends. What is it that you want?"

"I want you. I want to make love to you."

Daryl folded her arms across her bosom. "I don't sleep with my friends, Sheldon."

"Are you trying to corner me into a relationship?"

"No, I'm not."

Sheldon shook his head, baffled. "I don't understand women. Why do you always go around trying to put labels on things?"

"What on earth are you talking about?"

"I enjoy your company. We have a good time, and we're attracted to each other. I know you want me as much as I want you. Making love doesn't imply that we've committed ourselves to each other—just to the pleasure of the moment."

"So what you're saying is that I shouldn't believe in happily ever after. I should give up making love in favor of just hot and wild sex?"

"What I'm saying is, why can't we just take our time with this? I think you know I'm crazy about you. I'm not ruling anything out, but I want to take things slow. You know, see where it goes. I—"

Daryl held up her hand to interrupt him. "That's a crock! Sheldon, I'm not a fool by any means. We're adults here. You want to have sex with me, but you're not looking for anything serious. I want a long-term relationship—one that will lead to marriage. I want a man willing to give me the sun, moon, and the stars. Because I deserve it. You just want a warm body whenever the mood hits you. We want two different things."

"Daryl—"

"It's fine, Sheldon. I know where you're coming from. I care a lot about you. I even thought we were destined to be together, but I was wrong." She headed to her bedroom door. "I think you'd better leave."

"Just like that?" he asked.

"Just like that. I'm not going to lie to you by saying that I can accept being your friend and have casual sex."

"You make it sound as if I just want sex—"

"Are you going to tell me that you want more than that?"

"Yes, I want more. I want us to be friends—"

"You mean lovers, don't you?"

"As you stated earlier, we're both adults. Adults who are very attracted to each other sexually. As long as we're consenting adults, that's all that matters."

"You don't get it, do you?"

"Get what? I've—"

She held up a hand. "Please, Sheldon, let me finish. You were honest with me, and I with you, but you need to understand that I must also be honest with myself."

"Honest with yourself?"

"It's very hard for most women to give themselves sexually without becoming emotionally involved. A few won't give themselves *until* they are committed to that person." She pointed a finger at herself. "I'm one of those women. I have to really care about someone before I give my body to him. I'm not into casual sex."

"I'm not sure I'm following you, Daryl."

"Oftentimes, women think that making love is just as emotional for the man, but it's not."

"That's why I'm honest and up front with my feelings," Sheldon blurted out.

"I realize that, Sheldon. But we women could save ourselves a lot of pain and heartache if we're honest, too."

"Huh?"

"I have to be honest with you. I don't think I can just be your friend. At least not right now. My feelings are much too strong for you. Making love to you would only make things worse."

"I don't see how it would be so bad."

"Because, Sheldon, I would be making love and you'd be having sex. You can't make love unless you're in love." She held out her hand. "I hope you understand. I won't lie to myself, as much as I want you."

"I really care for you, Daryl. I thought you knew that."

"It's not the same, though. I'm not going to settle, Sheldon. I deserve a man who cares just as much as I do."

"So we can't be friends?"

"I'm not ruling it out eventually—just not right now. I can't handle it."

"I understand."

"Do you really?"

Sheldon shook his head. "No, but I'll respect your wishes. I wish it didn't have to be this way."

"It doesn't. You made a choice and so have I."

"Take care of yourself."

"You, too, Sheldon."

He stopped at the door. Without turning around, he asked, "Can I at least call you sometime?"

"I don't think that's a good idea." When Sheldon left, Daryl fell to the sofa. "I did the right thing," she professed tearfully. "So, why does it have to hurt so bad?"

Fall leaves crackled under Sheldon's boots as he climbed out of his car and headed up the steps of his house. He was met by a tiny ghost, a ballerina, and a pint-sized Batman.

"Trick or Treat," they chorused.

Laughing, Sheldon reached into his pocket and pulled out a wad of five dollar bills. He placed one in each of the bags. "I'm not much on giving kids a lot of candy, so I'll give you money instead."

"Wow! Thank you. I like money. I'm gonna put it in my bank. I already have ten dollars saved," Batman announced proudly.

"I'll save mine, too," said the ghost.

The ballerina tugged on his hand. "Me, too. I'm gonna save mine, too."

Maggie appeared with a huge basket of candy. "My, my, don't you all look precious. I have something for you." She lowered the basket. "Just take a handful."

As the happy trio bounded down the steps heading to the next house, Sheldon wrapped an arm around Maggie. "Boy, I sure remember those days." He laughed. "And I sure don't miss them, but they looked cute, didn't they?"

"They sure did." She elbowed him gently. "Come on into the house, son. If you'll listen out for the trick or treaters, I'll have dinner ready in about an hour. I don't feel like cooking, so I'm kind of dragging around."

"Have you started?"

"What?"

"Cooking."

"No. I'm about to start now."

He halted her by grabbing her arm. "Forget about cooking, Mama. I'm going to take you for dinner."

Maggie waved him away. "You don't have to do that. Why don't you take Daryl? You young people go on out and have a good time."

"No, Mama. You're my date for tonight. Now march on upstairs and get into your best dress."

"Son . . ."

"Don't make me wait too long. I'm starving."

"I'll be ready shortly."

Sheldon hated like hell what had happened between Daryl and himself. Every fiber in his body called out to her—he missed her warmth. As he dressed, Sheldon couldn't stop his mind from arguing with his heart. He cared more for her than he wanted to admit. Now that he'd blown any chance with Daryl, Sheldon silently conceded that he was falling in love with her. And it scared him.

Chapter 19

Margo gently massaged Daryl's shoulders. "You're so tense. What's wrong?"

"Nothing's wrong. I can't seem to stop thinking about Sheldon. I still love him. It's not something that's going to just disappear."

"I know that, but what about Sidney? He really cares about you."

Daryl turned around to face Margo, "Is that what you really think? I think he just wants to jump my bones."

Margo's eyes opened wider. "He really likes you, too." She sounded defensive.

"I know he's your friend, but I don't believe you know him as well as you think you do."

"Why do you say that?"

Daryl shrugged. "I don't know. It's just a feeling I have. And he's always making sexual innuendos."

"What if it were Sheldon making those same comments? Would you still be so worried?"

"That's different, Margo, and you know it," Daryl snapped.

"All I know is that you're not giving Sidney a chance. It's not fair—"

"I don't want anything other than friendship with him."

"He's a nice guy."

"Then you date him." Daryl grabbed her purse and stormed out of Margo's office. She knew what she had to do.

Daryl knocked lightly on Sidney's door. He greeted her with a grin. "I was kind of surprised to receive your call. I'm glad you're here."

Easing down on the sofa, Daryl folded her hands across her lap. "Sidney, I don't think we should continue seeing each other. I don't want to mislead you in any way."

"I thought we were friends, Daryl?"

"We are. But that's all I want it to be."

"I want to be more than just your friend, Daryl. I want to get to know you better." He leered lustily at her breasts. "Much better. We could be real good together."

"I've already told you that I'm not interested in a sexual relationship, Sidney."

"What's wrong with you, girl?" he asked in a terse voice.

"Nothing's wrong. I just don't hop into bed with just anyone."

"I bet you didn't say that to Sheldon Turner."

Daryl snapped her head around to face him. "What?"

"Yeah, I know all about you and Sheldon. He got what he wanted from you and dumped you. Now you're trying to keep it on lock down. What for?"

She pushed up off the sofa. "I'm leaving."

Sidney grabbed her arm pulling her back down. "Wait a minute. I'm not through talking to you. You owe me."

Her eyes filled with fury; Daryl snatched her hand from his. "I don't owe you anything. And if you lay another hand on me, I'll cut it off."

Sidney stood up, towering over her. "Now you wait a minute. You don't come in my house threatening me like this." Grabbing her roughly, he pulled her against him. "You and I know the real reason you came here."

Daryl tried to swallow her rising panic. "Sidney, let me go!"

"You've been teasing me for too damn long. I'm tired of the chase." He held both her hands in his. "Now why don't you just take a deep breath and calm down. I promise you, you won't be disappointed."

Daryl was really scared now. Sidney was going to rape her! Fighting with all her might, she struggled against him to free herself. "Let me go, Sidney! If you don't, I'm going to scream and somebody will call the police."

Shoving her on the couch, he hovered over her, his gaze deadly. "And if you as much as open your mouth, I'll strangle the life out of you. You came over here. I didn't go chasing after you."

Fearing for her life, Daryl started to cry. "Please, Sidney. Just let me go. I won't mention this to anyone. Just let me leave."

"When I'm done, you can go to hell for all I care." He started to undress. "You've treated me like a second class citizen to that womanizing bastard."

"Sidney, I never meant to hurt you. I—"

"I don't want to hear your mouth. Just stand up and take your clothes off," he demanded.

Daryl watched his every move. There was no way she'd let him have sex with her. Standing up slowly, she unbuttoned her top. Sidney's eyes nearly popped out of his head, as he stood ogling her breasts. Estimating the distance between her and the door, Daryl then waited for her chance. Finally it came. She kicked Sidney with as much force as she could in his groin.

She didn't hang around long enough to see him collapse on the floor in agony. Leaving his door wide open, Daryl ran as fast as she could. With no time to button up her shirt, she held it together with her hand. She was thankful that she'd had the foresight to leave her purse in the car, otherwise she would've had to leave it. Luckily, her keys were in her pants pocket. As she neared her car, she unlocked it with her remote. Daryl jumped in and drove quickly into the dark night.

When she was about two miles away from his apartment, only then did Daryl permit herself to cry.

"I'm glad you called and invited me over. The Martin Luther King Center is very excited about the FARM program."

Sheldon offered Linda a glass of wine. Seated at the dining room table, they had papers spread everywhere.

Pushing her long curling tendrils away from her face, Linda put on her glasses to read the proposal for the fall basketball program. "I like this, Sheldon." Placing the folder flat on the table, she leaned back. "We've got twenty fathers and sons signed up already. And we have a few big brothers who've signed their little brothers . . ."

"I'm glad to hear that. If the program goes well at the MLK Center, then we'll be implementing it in all of the recreational centers throughout LA county."

"I think it's a wonderful program, Sheldon."

"I hope everyone else will share your sentiments. My brother and I have worked hard on this."

"Well, I need to cover one more thing."

While Linda searched her notes, Sheldon thought about Daryl. He hadn't spoken to her in a few weeks. He decided he'd give her a call when his meeting with Linda ended.

Maggie entered the room. "Excuse me. Sheldon, someone is here to see you."

Perplexed, he asked, "Who is it?"

"It's Daryl."

Daryl was here? He turned to Linda. "Will you excuse me? I'll be back in a second."

"Take your time."

He found her standing in the living room, her back to him. "Daryl?" He called to her softly. He still couldn't believe she was here. He was surprised by her expression when she turned around. She looked like she'd been crying.

"Hi, Sheldon."

"What's wrong? Did something happen?"

"I know I should have called, but I really needed to talk to you. I—"

"Excuse me, Sheldon. I should leave," Linda announced from the doorway.

Daryl gasped.

"Daryl . . ."

"Oh, Lord." She took a step back in an effort to steer clear of him. Her heart was beating rapidly, her entire body rigid, and she felt terribly sick inside. She could barely find her voice to ask the obvious. "Why didn't you tell me you had company?"

Sheldon swallowed heavily. "I—"

Instantly, Daryl's pain was ripped away by anger. "I can't believe I just made a fool of myself like this."

"Daryl—" He reached for her.

"Don't you touch me!" She backed away, a crazed expression on her face. "Don't you dare put your hands on me. I don't even know why I came here." She turned and fled out of his house before Sheldon could stop her.

"Are the two of you involved?" Linda asked.

He shook his head. "No, we're not."

"Didn't appear that way to me. It's not my business, but I think you should go after her. She's very upset about something."

"I think she was about to tell me something." He put his hand to his mouth. "I could see it in her eyes. Something happened to her."

"I agree," Linda stated. "That's why you need to go after her now. I think we've covered everything. If not, give me a call at the office."

"Thanks, Linda."

"It's for the kids, Sheldon."

His thoughts right now were centered on Daryl. He was worried whether or not she would make it home in the condition she was in.

"Sheldon . . ."

He came out of his daze. "Huh?"

"I hope she's all right. Take care."

"Let me walk you out. I'm leaving right behind you."

"I always knew she'd be the one to settle you down. I knew it the first time I saw you two together."

"What?"

"New Year's Eve. Tyrell's party."

"I wouldn't say she's settled me down—"

"She has. Take my word for it." Linda tiptoed to kiss his cheek. "I'll see you around."

"Sheldon, could you come here, son?"

Sheldon turned around to face his mother. "Mama?"

"If you're on your way to see Daryl, you don't want to forget this." She handed him a package.

Walking to his car, Sheldon decided Linda was right. In a way Daryl had spoiled him for other women. When he saw her tonight, he'd literally ached to hold her close. Sheldon wanted to feel her heart beating next to his, and it was Daryl he wanted to kiss. His need to be with her struck him so powerfully that it rocked him to the core.

As he drove to Pomona, Sheldon recalled something in her eyes. Fear. He'd seen fear in her eyes tonight. Had something happened to her? Sheldon reached for the phone.

Daryl lifted her chin proudly, looking at him with contempt. She asked calmly, "What are you doing here, Sheldon?"

"I thought we should talk. About what happened tonight."

She walked away from the front door, leaving it open for Sheldon to enter. "I would rather just forget about it."

Closing the door behind him, he walked over and took a seat beside her. "Linda is just a friend, Daryl."

"I really don't care," she lied. "Now please leave and don't worry about ever coming back."

"Why are you acting like this?"

"Because I don't like public humiliations. I made a big fool of myself dropping over like that."

"I could tell you were upset. What happened tonight?"

"Just forget it, Sheldon."

"No, I won't. I'm not leaving until you tell me what happened."

"I just got a little freaked that's all."

"How?"

"I went to Sidney's place tonight. I went to tell him that I didn't think we should go out anymore . . ." Unable to finish, Daryl looked away.

Sheldon covered her trembling hands with his. "And what happened?"

"He tried . . . He tried to . . ."

"What?" Sheldon demanded. "Did he try to rape you?"

"He wouldn't take no for an answer. He said some horrible things to me."

"That bastard! Wait til I get my hands on him—" He made a move to stand up.

Pulling at him, Daryl pleaded with him. "No, Sheldon. That's not why I came to you. I just needed to feel safe."

Wrapping his arms around her, Sheldon pulled her close. "I'm so sorry, sweetheart."

"I made such a fool of myself."

"You didn't make a fool of yourself. I'm sorry he put you through that. I'd better not see him anytime soon."

"Sheldon, I hate to ask this, but can you do me a big favor? Will you stay here with me tonight? You can sleep in the guest room."

He nodded. "I'll stay." Motioning to the telephone, he asked, "Has he called you?"

She shook her head. "No. And if he does, I'm calling the police and pressing charges."

"Doc, why don't you go take a nice hot shower and get your pajamas on. I'll make you some hot tea. I can see the tension in your body."

"Yes, I think I'll do just that." Daryl stood up. Looking back at Sheldon, she said. "I'm glad you're here. I really didn't want to be alone."

"I'll have the tea ready by the time you're done."

An hour later, Daryl was curled up on the sofa with him, sleeping like a baby. Smiling, Sheldon laid her down gently. Running upstairs, he retrieved a blanket from the linen closet and brought it down with him. After covering her up, Sheldon stretched out on the floor in front of the sofa. He was asleep in a matter of minutes.

The next morning, Sheldon had breakfast ready by the time she'd awakened.

Smiling, Daryl shook her head. "You really didn't have to do all this, Sheldon."

"You had a hard night. How are you feeling this morning?"

"I'm fine. Much better, thanks to you."

He checked his watch. "I'm going to have to leave. Think Margo will come stay with you?"

She nodded. "She and Audrey will most likely be here shortly. We're supposed to do some Christmas shopping today."

"Speaking of Christmas, I brought you a present. He handed her a small brightly wrapped package. I went out to the car and got it this morning while you were still sleeping."

Daryl was touched. "You didn't have to—"

"I want you to have it."

"Sheldon . . ."

"Please take it, Doc. I'll be offended if you don't."

Smiling, she nodded. "Thank you, Sheldon."

"If you have any problems with Sidney, let me know. As a matter of fact, I think you should press charges against him."

"Nothing happened. I kicked him where it hurts and left. I don't think he'll be bothering me anymore."

"If he calls, don't even talk to him. Just hang up, okay? I'll call you later to check on you."

"Thank you so much, Sheldon. For everything. You've been a good friend."

She failed to notice when he winced from her calling him a friend.

Chapter 20

"Wasn't that Sheldon's Jaguar we just passed?" Audrey asked.

"Probably," Daryl stated nonchalantly as she moved aside to let Margo and Audrey enter. "He just left here."

"Is everything okay?" Audrey wanted to know.

Daryl nodded, not looking at either one of them. "Everything's fine."

Margo motioned toward the package sitting on her coffee table. "Looks like he brought you a gift."

"Yeah, he did. I was trying to decide whether or not I'm going to keep it."

"Girl, keep it," Margo urged.

"I don't know."

"Well at least open it, then decide," Audrey suggested.

Daryl slowly tore off the colorful wrapping to find a beautiful gold box inside. "I can't imagine what this could be."

"Hurry up, Daryl."

"Yeah, Girl. We want to see what Sheldon bought you."

Shaking her head, Daryl put the box down on the coffee table. "Maybe I'll just wait until later."

Margo's green eyes glittered. "Aw, come on. Don't be like that."

"Okay, I'll open it." Laughing, Daryl pulled a beautiful perfume bottle out of the box. Sniffing, she smiled. "It smells wonderful!"

"Looks like he had a scent especially made for you. That's so romantic."

Margo sniffed. "It has kind of a woodsy floral smell."

With her hands wrapped around her waist, Daryl navigated to peer out of her window. She was joined by Margo. "I'm sorry about yesterday."

Daryl frowned. "Yesterday? What are you talking about?"

"Sidney called me and asked me if I'd talked to you. He said the two of you are not seeing each other anymore."

"That's right."

"Sidney said he thought it best since you were still in love with Sheldon."

She turned to face Margo, her arms folded across her heaving bosom. "Oh, did he?"

Margo looked puzzled. "What's wrong? Isn't that what happened?"

"What else did Sidney say?"

Margo shrugged. "Nothing much. Just that he was starting to feel like a third wheel. He said you made it obvious that Sheldon wasn't out of your system—"

"Did he also tell you that he tried to rape me?" Daryl asked as calmly as she could manage.

Margo's mouth dropped open. "WHAT?"

Daryl looked away. "You heard me. The maniac attacked me last night."

Margo leaned on a nearby wing chair for support. "That bastard. I knew he wasn't telling me the entire story."

"That's your nice guy," Daryl said sarcastically.

"Are you blaming me for this?"

Daryl shook her head. "I'm not blaming anyone but myself. I never should have gone to his apartment."

Margo reached over to hug her. "I'm so sorry, Daryl. Wait till I see that lying skunk. I'm gonna cut his—"

"Whoa, girlfriend," Daryl laughed. "Let's just forget about it. I kneed him good, so next time he'll think twice before trying to force himself on someone."

"I'm still gonna curse him from sun up to sun down. And to think I trusted him."

Daryl shivered. "I don't want to think about it anymore, okay?"

"I'm really sorry. God, I feel so bad." Margo's bottom lip trembled. "I guess from now on I'll mind my own damn business."

Audrey walked up. "What's got you two so interested out there? I thought we were going shopping?"

"We are," Daryl announced. Sticking her arm through Margo's, she asked, "Ready, girlfriend?"

For a week, Sheldon called daily to check on Daryl. She was constantly on his mind. Returning from Barry's house, he ran up the steps.

"What in the world . . . ?" Sheldon bent down to retrieve a small, beautifully wrapped present stuck just inside his door. Reading the label, he realized the gift was from Daryl.

Dialing her number, he was surprised when she answered on the first ring. "Merry Christmas, Daryl."

"Same to you, Sheldon. Is this your daily call to check on me?"

Sheldon chuckled. "Yes and no. I found a present outside my door today. The label identified you as the sender."

She laughed. "Well, did you open it?"

"Yes, and I love it. Thank you for being so thoughtful. You always seem to know what I like."

"I spent a lot of time trying to find just the right gift for you. It's not much, but it was my way of saying thank you . . . for everything."

"Doc, you gave me more than you realize. Much more valuable that what I gave you. I've been a jerk—"

"You've been honest with me. I really appreciate it."

"I miss you, Doc."

"How's your mom?"

He knew she was guarding her heart by trying to remain aloof. "She's doing fine. Where are you spending Christmas?"

"I'm leaving tonight for my mother's house. I usually go there every year."

"Oh."

"I heard you and your brother are going to Big Bear for the holidays."

"Yes, we are. Mama's going too. We're going to have a long talk while we're there. We need to clear up some old misunderstandings. Set things right for the future."

"I'm very happy for you."

"Daryl . . ."

"I'm going to have to leave, but thanks again for the Christmas present, Sheldon. I couldn't wait until Christmas to open it. I really like it."

"I know how much you like flowers, so I thought you might like the fragrance. Are you going to Tyrell's New Year's Eve party?"

"I doubt it. I may have to work. What about you? Are you going?"

"We may stay at the cabin until after the New Year."

"Oh. Well, happy holidays."

"Same to you, Daryl."

When she hung up, she felt like crying. Her heart felt vacant without Sheldon in her life. Daryl shook her head in a vain effort to shake those thoughts out of her head. She had to face facts. Sheldon was not the man for her.

Her determination was fierce though. She would not let this get her down. Life goes on. Even as she determined all these things, hot tears slipped from beneath her lids over her breaking heart. It wasn't going to be easy.

Maggie slipped into the living room and tapped Sheldon on the shoulder. He grabbed her by the hand, leading her around the chair to sit next to him. "This was a wonderful Christmas Day, don't you think?"

"Huh? Oh, yeah. Today was nice," he mumbled.

"What are you thinking so hard about, Son?"

"Everything we talked about."

She nodded. "I'm so glad we all had that talk. Maybe now Barry and I can have a better relationship. Where is Barry?"

"He's in his room taking a nap with the kids."

She chuckled. "I guess they all wore each other out." Maggie inclined her head. "I don't think our talk is what's got you preoccupied. I think you're thinking about a certain young lady. I thought that was an interesting present she gave you, don't you think?"

Placing the mug of hot chocolate he'd been sipping on the rustic coffee table, Sheldon looked up at his mother and smiled. "You think you know me so well, don't you?"

Sheldon grew serious as he fingered the gold chain around his neck. On one side was the mascot of the New York Rockets and on the other side, encased in glass, was a tiny mustard seed. "This necklace spoke volumes to me. Daryl believed in me. No matter what others said. She's always been there for me and when I needed space—she gave that to me also. She told me once that all things were possible if I'd only believe. She's a good woman." He glanced over at his mother. "And my best friend."

"Son, I've told you before. I know you better than you know yourself. You're in love with Daryl. It's written all over your face. As plain as day."

In love with Daryl.

He couldn't fight or deny his emotions any longer. When he'd met her, falling in love had been the furthest thing from his mind. Now he found that he wanted nothing more than to be close to her. He lived for the sound of her voice, the way she looked at him; her eyes so full of trust. He craved her touch. Everything about Daryl enchanted him. She'd turned his world inside out and upside down.

Moving to the window, Sheldon studied the star-studded sky. Until now, marriage was a total impossibility, but the sense of yearning that filled him was painful. Had he lost Daryl only to figure out that what he felt for her was love? He had to find out.

Sheldon looked up at the full moon, realizing his decision was made.

Sitting in a chair next to a blazing fire, Daryl watched the dancing flames in colors of red, orange, and yellow. She was still in the same spot two hours later, when Maxine came into the room.

"What's got you so preoccupied, Sweetie?"

Daryl looked up from the fireplace. "Nothing, Mother."

Maxine stretched out on her sofa. "Now why don't I believe that?"

"Mother . . . I really thought . . ."

"I'm so sorry, Daryl."

"It's all right. He's been honest with me. I just can't erase my feelings."

"Are you sure this young man doesn't love you? It's Sheldon Turner, right?"

"Yes, it's Sheldon. I thought he did, but . . ."

"Maybe he's afraid to share his deepest emotions with you. Have you thought of that?"

"I've thought of everything, but the truth. Sheldon is not in love with me. He just wants to be my friend. And he really is a good friend."

Maxine smiled. "I think that's a good start. Maybe he's just not ready to settle down. You've only known him what? A year?"

Returning her gaze to the fire, Daryl sighed heavily. She'd been wrong about Sheldon. He wasn't the one for her.

*   *   *

Sheldon carried the luggage for his mother into her room, dropping the bags on the bed.

"Lord, it's good being back home," Maggie announced as she navigated around Sheldon. "I enjoyed myself, but I sure missed this old house."

"I'm glad to be back myself." Although for very different reasons, he added silently. The brief vacation with his family had been a success. They'd talked about his father, the beatings, and Barry's anger.

Throwing his overnight bag on the floor in his room, Sheldon headed downstairs, where he found Maggie making lunch.

"I'm starving, so I made myself a turkey sandwich. Would you like me to make you one?"

"I'll grab a bite while I'm out. I need to make a run."

"Is it what I'm thinking?"

Sheldon grinned. "Yes. What you said up at the cabin made a lot of sense. I'm going to do it."

Maggie rushed over, hugging him tight. "I'm so glad, Son."

"Let's not get our hopes up too much, Mama. We don't know how things are going to go."

"What does your heart tell you?"

Sheldon smiled.

Chapter 21

"Daryl, you need to get out of the house. Come with us to Tyrell's party."

"I'm not in the party mood. Besides, Sheldon might be there." Her misery was so acute that it was a physical pain. How could she have been so wrong in her beliefs?

"Maybe that's what it'll take to give you a sense of closure."

"I love him, Audrey," she replied in a low, tormented voice. "It's going to take a while to get over him."

"I know. I'm not trying to make light of your feelings. I'm sorry if it came out that way."

"I know you're only trying to help, but you can't. I'm the only person that can work this out."

"Maybe he won't come. I asked Tyrell not to invite him."

"You didn't have to do that, Margo."

"This is New Year's Eve. Let's go out and have a good time. Don't let Sheldon take that away from you."

"I'm not. Margo, you have your husband, and Audrey will be with Tyrell. I don't want to be a third wheel. Or fifth wheel."

"Now, Girl, you know we're all friends. Say you'll go with us," Audrey pleaded.

"All right I'll go, but you all don't have to wait for me. I'll meet you there."

"You're going to drive to L.A. all by yourself?" Margo asked.

"Yeah. I do it everyday."

Audrey sat down on her bed. "We really don't mind waiting for you."

"No, you two go on. I'll be there. I promise."

Margo grinned. "Let's talk about our resolutions. I'll start. Mine is to really start my diet next year."

Daryl laughed. "Yeah right. What's yours, Audrey?"

"Same as last year. Live life to the fullest."

Margo surveyed the walk-in closet. "What about you, Daryl? I couldn't help but notice that you've spread all of your clothes out in the closet. And you're not setting a place for a husband anymore. Does that mean—"

Daryl nodded. "I'm not making anymore resolutions."

Audrey embraced her. "We're so sorry. Even though we teased you—we were both rooting for you."

Daryl nodded sadly. "I know. I guess I was just being silly. Well, those days are over. No more waiting for Mr. Right. He just doesn't exist."

Daryl entered the Precision Club, looking around for Audrey and Margo. Finally, she caught sight of them near the ladies' room. She hurried in their direction, hoping to sneak up on them.

"When are you going to tell Daryl about your engagement?" Margo was asking Audrey.

Daryl drew back, her head pounding. Audrey was engaged. And she never mentioned it? She moved closer to hear Audrey's response.

"Margo, I hate keeping this from her, but you know what she's been through. I'm trying to be sensitive to her feelings right now."

Hurt, Daryl whirled around, wanting to get as far away from her so-called friend as possible. Why would Audrey treat her like this? Someone grabbed her by the hand. Without looking, she knew it was Sheldon.

"Daryl, how are you?"

"I'm fine. I see you made it home in time for the party."

"We came in today. I wanted to hurry back because I needed to see you."

"What for?"

He scanned her face. "What's wrong, Daryl? You look upset."

"It's nothing. Actually, I was just about to leave."

"Daryl—"

"I have to go, Sheldon. Happy New Year." A huge tear slipped down her face, and Daryl started to walk faster. She didn't want to break down into tears in front of Sheldon.

Margo and Rob stood directly in her path. Wiping her face, Daryl quickly hugged her friend. "Margo, have a happy new year. You, too, Rob."

"Are you leaving?" Rob asked.

"Yeah, I can't stay here."

"But it's almost time for the countdown."

"I can't stay here." Daryl turned to leave.

"Where are you going in such a hurry?" Audrey wanted to know. She and Tyrell had just come from dancing. She was slightly out of breath.

"I'm leaving. Happy New Year, Audrey, Tyrell, and congratulations on your engagement."

Audrey gasped in surprise.

Taking a deep breath, she said quietly, "I know why you were trying to keep it a secret, but you really didn't have to. I'm your friend, Audrey. I'm happy for you."

"Daryl . . ."

She waved them away and struggled through the crowd, tears glistening in her eyes.

Just as she neared the door, Daryl heard Sheldon call her name. She turned around to find him on the stage, with microphone in hand.

"Excuse me everyone, but I have a New Year's resolution to make. Daryl, would you join me up here? Please?"

Daryl glanced over at her friends. "What is he doing?"

"Go on up there and find out, girl," Audrey whispered.

The massive crowd parted as she slowly made her way to the stage. Sheldon held out his hand to her as she climbed the steps.

"What are you doing, Sheldon?" she whispered.

"I'm making a resolution of love. Sweetheart, in front of all these witnesses, I promise to always love and accept you as you are; I promise to always be faithful and loving; I promise to always work at making you happy; to be sensitive to your needs and desires." He paused, taking her hand. "I promise to always try to give you the sun, moon, and the stars. Starting now." Sheldon placed around her wrist a gold bracelet with tiny replicas of the sun, moon, and stars dangling. "These things I promise to do, on one condition."

"And what's that?"

"I need you to marry me and make me the luckiest man alive. I love you, Daryl. With all of my being, I love you."

She blinked twice. "D—Did you just ask me to marry you?"

"Yes." He then pulled out a tiny box. Opening it, he took out a pear-shaped diamond ring. "Will you marry me?"

She was afraid to trust her heart, but she couldn't deny the love she felt for Sheldon.

"Sweetheart?"

"Yes, yes . . ." Daryl couldn't talk anymore as tears of joy rolled down her cheeks.

Amidst all the cheering and the applauding, they heard nothing, only each other.

"I thought . . ."

"I know, baby. I'm so sorry. It wasn't until we were apart that it hit me how much I really loved you."

"I love you so much, Sheldon."

"I know. I never meant to hurt you, but I didn't want

to take advantage of the love you gave so generously. I never knew I could feel this way about anybody." The bandleader tapped him on the shoulder. "It's time for the countdown to the new year. I want you in my arms, the same way we brought in this year. I want you in my arms this new year and the many years to come."

Grinning, Daryl said, "A new year and a new beginning. I can't think of any other place I'd rather be."

ABOUT THE AUTHOR

Jacquelin Thomas, a native of Brunswick, Georgia, now lives in Southern California with her family. She is currently at work on her next project. This is her second novel for Arabesque.

Dear Reader,

I hope you have enjoyed Daryl and Sheldon's story. I would like to take this moment to thank the many readers who purchased and read *Hidden Blessings,* my first book for Pinnacle/Arabesque, as well as this novel. I have recently completed a third novel, tentatively titled *Forever Always,* which Pinnacle/Arabesque will release in March 1999.

Please feel free to write me. My address is P.O. Box 7415, La Verne, CA 91750-7415. I would enjoy hearing from each and every one of you. I will try to answer each letter that I receive.

Blessings,

Jacquelin Thomas

COMING IN JANUARY ...

BEYOND DESIRE   (0-7860-0607-2, $4.99/$6.50)
by Gwynne Forster
Amanda Ross is pregnant and single. Certainly not a role model for junior high school students, the board of education may deny her promotion to principal if they learn the truth. What she needs is a husband and music engineer Marcus Hickson agrees to it. His daughter needs surgery and Amanda will pay the huge medical bill. But love creeps in and soon theirs is an affair of the heart.

LOVE SO TRUE   (0-7860-0608-0, $4.99/$6.50)
by Loure Bussey
Janelle Sims defied her attraction to wealthy businessman Aaron Deverreau because he reminded Janelle of her womanizing father. Yet he is the perfect person to back her new fashion boutique and she seeks him out. Now they are partners, friends ... and lovers. But a cunning woman's lies separate them and Janelle must go to him to confirm their love.

ALL THAT GLITTERS   (0-7860-0609-9, $4.99/$6.50)
by Viveca Carlysle
After her sister's death, Leigh Barrington inherited a huge share of Cassiopeia Salons, a chain of exclusive beauty parlors. The business was Leigh's idea in the first place and now she wants to run it her way. To retain control, Leigh marries board member Caesar Montgomery, who is instantly smitten with her. When she may be the next target of her sister's killer, Leigh learns to trust in Caesar's love.

AT LONG LAST LOVE   (0-7860-0610-2, $4.99/$6.50)
by Bettye Griffin
Owner of restaurant chain Soul Food To Go, Kendall Lucas has finally found love with her new neighbor, Spencer Barnes. Until she discovers he owns the new restaurant that is threatening her business. They compromise, but Spencer learns Kendall has launched a secret advertising campaign. Embittered by her own lies, Kendall loses hope in their love. But she underestimates Spencer's devotion and his vow to make her his partner for life.

Available wherever paperbacks are sold, or order direct from the Publisher. Send cover price plus 50¢ per copy for mailing and handling to Kensington Publishing Corp., Consumer Orders, or call (toll free) 888-345-BOOK, to place your order using Mastercard or Visa. Residents of New York and Tennessee must include sales tax. DO NOT SEND CASH.

SPICE UP YOUR LIFE
WITH ARABESQUE ROMANCES

AFTER HOURS, by Anna Larence   (0-7860-0277-8, $4.99/$6.50)
Vice president of a Fort Worth company, Nachelle Oliver was used to things her own way. Until she got a new boss. Steven DuCloux was ruthless—and the most exciting man she had ever known. He knew that she was the perfect VP, and that she would be the perfect wife. She tried to keep things strictly professional, but the passion between them was too strong.

CHOICES, by Maria Corley   (0-7860-0245-X, $4.95/$6.50)
Chaney just ended with Taurique when she met Lawrence. The rising young singer swept her off her feet. After nine years of marriage, with Lawrence away for months on end, Chaney feels lonely and vulnerable. Purely by chance, she meets Taurique again, and has to decide if she wants to risk it all for love.

DECEPTION, by Donna Hill   (0-7860-0287-5, $4.99/$6.50)
An unhappy marriage taught successful owner of a successful New York advertising agency, Terri Powers, never to trust in love again. Then she meets businessman Clinton Steele. She can't fight the attraction between them—or the sensual hunger that fires her deepest passions.

DEVOTED, by Francine Craft   (0-7860-0094-5, $4.99/$6.50)
When Valerie Thomas and Delano Carter were young lovers each knew it wouldn't last. Val, now a photojournalist, meets Del at a high-society wedding. Del takes her to Alaska for the assignment of her career. In the icy wilderness he warms her with a passion too long denied. This time not even Del's desperate secret will keep them from reclaiming their lost love.

FOR THE LOVE OF YOU, by Felicia Mason   (0-7860-0071-6, $4.99/$6.50
Seven years ago, Kendra Edwards found herself pregnant and alone. Now she has a secure life for her twins and a chance to finish her college education. A long unhappy marriage had taught attorney Malcolm Hightower the danger of passion. But Kendra taught him the sensual magic of love. Now they must each give true love a chance.

ALL THE RIGHT REASONS, by Janice Sims   (0-7860-0405-3, $4.99/$6.50)
Public defender, Georgie Shaw, returns to New Orleans and meets reporter Clay Knight. He's determined to uncover secrets between Georgie and her celebrity twin, and protect Georgie from someone who wants both sisters dead. Dangerous secrets are found in a secluded mansion, leaving Georgie with no one to trust but the man who stirs her desires.

Available wherever paperbacks are sold, or order direct from the Publisher. Send cover price plus 50¢ per copy for mailing and handling to Kensington Publishing Corp., Consumer Orders, or call (toll free) 888-345-BOOK, to place your order using Mastercard or Visa. Residents of New York and Tennessee must include sales tax. DO NOT SEND CASH.

WARMHEARTED AFRICAN-AMERICAN ROMANCES
BY *FRANCIS RAY*

FOREVER YOURS   (0-7860-0483-5, \$4.99/\$6.50)
Victoria Chandler must find a husband or her grandparents will call in loans that support her chain of lingerie boutiques. She fixes a mock marriage to ranch owner Kane Taggert. The marriage will only last one year, and her business will be secure. The only problem is that Kane has other plans for Victoria. He'll cast a spell that will make her his forever.

HEART OF THE FALCON   (0-7860-0483-5, \$4.99/\$6.50)
A passionate night with millionaire Daniel Falcon, leaves Madelyn Taggert enamored . . . and heartbroken. She never accepted that the long-time family friend would fulfill her dreams, only to see him walk away without regrets. After his parent's bitter marriage, the last thing Daniel expected was to be consumed by the need to have her for a lifetime.

INCOGNITO   (0-7860-0364-2, \$4.99/\$6.50)
Owner of an advertising firm, Erin Cortland witnessed an awful crime and lived to tell about it. Frightened, she runs into the arms of Jake Hunter, the man sent to protect her. He doesn't want the job. He left the police force after a similar assignment ended in tragedy. But when he learns not only one man is after her and that he is falling in love, he will risk anything to protect her.

ONLY HERS   (07860-0255-7, \$4.99/\$6.50)
St. Louis R.N. Shannon Johnson recently inherited a parcel of Texas land. She sought it as refuge until landowner Matt Taggart challenged her to prove she's got what it takes to work a sprawling ranch. She, on the other hand, soon challenges him to dare to love again.

SILKEN BETRAYAL   (0-7860-0426-6, \$4.99/\$6.50)
The only man executive secretary Lauren Bennett needed was her five-year-old son Joshua. Her only intent was to keep Joshua away from powerful in-laws. Then Jordan Hamilton entered her life. He sought her because of a personal vendetta against her father-in-law. When Jordan develops strong feelings for Lauren and Joshua, he must choose revenge or love.

UNDENIABLE   (07860-0125-9, \$4.99/\$6.50)
Wealthy Texas heiress Rachel Malone defied her powerful father and eloped with Logan Williams. But a trump-up assault charge set the whole town and Rachel against him and he fled Stanton with a heart full of pain. Eight years later, he's back and he wants revenge . . . and Rachel.

Available wherever paperbacks are sold, or order direct from the Publisher. Send cover price plus 50¢ per copy for mailing and handling to Kensington Publishing Corp., Consumer Orders, or call (toll free) 888-345-BOOK, to place your order using Mastercard or Visa. Residents of New York and Tennessee must include sales tax. DO NOT SEND CASH.

LOOK FOR THESE ARABESQUE ROMANCES

AFTER ALL, by Lynn Emery   (0-7860-0325-1, $4.99/$6.50)
News reporter Michelle Toussaint only focused on her dream of becoming an anchorwoman. Then contractor Anthony Hilliard returned. For five years, Michelle had reminsced about the passions they shared. But happiness turned to heartbreak when Anthony's cruel betrayal led to her father's financial ruin. He returned for one reason only: to win Michelle back.

THE ART OF LOVE, by Crystal Wilson-Harris   (0-7860-0418-5, $4.99/$6.50)
Dakota Bennington's heritage is apparent from her African clothing to her sculptures. To her, attorney Pierce Ellis is just another uptight professional stuck in the American mainstream. Pierce worked hard and is proud of his success. An art purchase by his firm has made Dakota a major part of his life. And love bridges their different worlds.

CHANGE OF HEART   (0-7860-0103-8, $4.99/$6.50)
by Adrienne Ellis Reeves
Not one to take risks or stray far from her South Carolina hometown, Emily Brooks, a recently widowed mother, felt it was time for a change. On a business venture she meets author David Walker who is conducting research for his new book. But when he finds undying passion, he wants Emily for keeps. Wary of her newfound passion, all Emily has to do is follow her heart.

ECSTACY, by Gwynne Forster   (0-7860-0416-9, $4.99/$6.50)
Schoolteacher Jeannetta Rollins had a tumor that was about to cost her her eyesight. Her persistence led her to follow Mason Fenwick, the only surgeon talented enough to perform the surgery, on a trip around the world. After getting to know her, Mason wants her whole . . . body and soul. Now he must put behind a tragedy in his career and trust himself and his heart.

KEEPING SECRETS, by Carmen Green   (0-7860-0494-0, $4.99/$6.50)
Jade Houston worked alone. But a dear deceased friend left clues to a two-year-old mystery and Jade had to accept working alongside Marine Captain Nick Crawford. As they enter a relationship that runs deeper than business, each must learn how to trust each other in all aspects.

MOST OF ALL, by Louré Bussey   (0-7860-0456-8, $4.99/$6.50)
After another heartbreak, New York secretary Elandra Lloyd is off to the Bahamas to visit her sister. Her sister is nowhere to be found. Instead she runs into Nassau's richest, self-made millionaire Bradley Davenport. She is lucky to have made the acquaintance with this sexy islander as she searches for her sister and her trust in the opposite sex.

Available wherever paperbacks are sold, or order direct from the Publisher. Send cover price plus 50¢ per copy for mailing and handling to Kensington Publishing Corp., Consumer Orders, or call (toll free) 888-345-BOOK, to place your order using Mastercard or Visa. Residents of New York and Tennessee must include sales tax. DO NOT SEND CASH.